STUART WOODS

and

L.A. TIMES

"**O**ne of the best mystery writers
in the business."

USA Today

"[**W**oods] has a flair and style."

Washington Times

"**H**e's a master of the light-touch action
thriller in which the hero, or in this case
antihero, gets caught up in events beyond
his control. Woods fans will not be
disappointed in *L.A. Times*."

Houston Chronicle

"**A** wild ride and an explosive ending. . . . A
propulsive thriller. . . . Abundant suspense."

Publishers Weekly

"**W**oods reminds us a lot of Robert Parker. He's
so good at narration that he can make just
about any plot work. . . . Woods's smooth,
seamless plotting keeps us turning pages."

Syracuse Post-Standard (NY)

"**W**oods is an engrossing writer."

Seattle Times

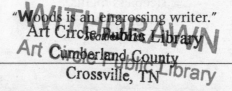

Books by Stuart Woods

STUART WOODS

L.A. TIMES

HARPER

An Imprint of HarperCollinsPublishers

This is a work of fiction. Names, characters, places, and incidents are products of the author's imagination or are used fictitiously and are not to be construed as real. Any resemblance to actual events, locales, organizations, or persons, living or dead, is entirely coincidental.

HARPER

An Imprint of HarperCollins*Publishers*
10 East 53rd Street
New York, New York 10022-5299

Copyright © 1993 by Stuart Woods
ISBN 978-0-06-201754-3

First Harper premium printing: February 2011
First HarperTorch paperback printing: May 2002
First HarperPaperbacks printing: January 1994
First HarperCollins hardcover printing: May 1993

Printed in the United States of America

Visit Harper paperbacks on the World Wide Web at www.harpercollins.com

10 9 8 7 6 5 4 3 2 1

This book is for Steven and Barbara Bochco.

L.A. TIMES

Prologue

Vincente Michaele Callabrese blinked in the midafternoon sunlight as he emerged from the darkness of the York Theater on the Upper West Side after the noon performance of *The Strange One*, a revival starring Ben Gazzara and George Peppard. He sprinted for the subway, and as he rode downtown toward his next movie he was still gripped by the performances of the two young actors who had been among the most promising of their generation.

Woody Allen's movie *Bananas* was next, at the Bleecker Street Cinema, and he would make a seven o'clock double feature of Orson Welles's *The Magnificent Ambersons* and *Othello*. He was short of his record of seven movies in sixteen hours, but that had been made possible by two three-screen houses next door to each other on Third Avenue, so he'd only had to take one subway.

* * *

It was after midnight when Vinnie left the Eighth Street Playhouse and started home; each step he took toward Little Italy was taken with more foreboding. He had cut school again, and he was already a grade behind; his mother would be waiting up for him, and his father, if he were home . . . well, he didn't want to think about that.

Vinnie was fourteen and big for his age. He was already shaving every day, and girls three and four years older were taking him seriously. He didn't have a lot of time for girls, though—when he wasn't in school or at the movies, he was running errands for a loan shark in the neighborhood, which paid for his movie tickets. Since the age of six, when he had belatedly seen his first film, Vinnie Callabrese had been to the movies nearly two thousand times. His friend and benefactor, an older boy named Tommy Provensano, who was very smart, was always telling Vinnie that he should keep his movie-going a secret, because nobody would take him seriously.

He had seen some favorite films four or five times, but *Othello* had been a new experience for Vinnie. He hadn't understood much of the dialogue, but he had been able to follow the story, and the dark drama had riveted him to his seat. He knew guys like Iago on his own block. He admired them; he learned from them.

Vinnie walked up the five flights, his heart pounding from more than the exertion. What if the old man were home? He inserted his key into the lock and turned it as silently as possible, then slipped into the four-room railroad flat. All was quiet; he sagged with relief as he stood still in the kitchen, letting his breathing return to normal. It would be easier if his mother didn't see him until morning, when her anger would have abated a little.

"Bastard!" a voice behind him said.

Vinnie spun around to find his father, Onofrio, sitting in a kitchen chair, leaning against the wall, a pint bottle of cheap whiskey in his hand. Onofrio didn't bother using a glass anymore.

"Bastard from hell!" his father said. "You were never mine; your mother laid down with the mailman, the butcher—somebody."

"Don't you talk about my mother that way," Vinnie said, his voice trembling.

Onofrio stood up and took a long swig from the bottle, then set it on the sink beside him. "You talk back to me?" He unbuckled his wide belt and slipped it from his trousers. "You want this, huh?"

"Don't you talk about my mother that way," Vinnie repeated.

"Your mother is a whore," Onofrio said, almost conversationally. "That's why you are the bastard." He flicked the belt out to its full length.

This time the buckle was not in his hand, but at the swinging end of the belt. This time would be bad, Vinnie thought.

Onofrio swung the buckle at his son. It made a whirring sound as it moved through the air.

Instinctively, Vinnie ducked, and the heavy buckle passed over his head.

"Stand still and take your beating, bastard!" Onofrio shouted.

There was a hammering on a door down the hall, and Vinnie heard his mother's voice faintly pleading with his father. "You beat her again, didn't you?" Vinnie asked.

"She gave me a bastard, didn't she? I beat her good this time."

Without thinking, Vinnie swung a fist at his father's head. The blow caught Onofrio solidly on the jaw, and he staggered back against the wall, dropping the belt.

Vinnie's father stared at him, his eyes wide with anger. "You would raise a hand to your father?"

Vinnie swallowed hard. "I would beat the shit out of my father," he said. Onofrio reached down for the belt, but Vinnie kicked it out of his reach, then straightened him up with an uppercut that would have laid out most men. His father was tough, though; he had been the neighborhood bully in his youth—Vinnie had heard this from his mother, when she had warned him never to resist a beating from his father.

"Now I kill you with my hands," Onofrio said, pushing off the wall and rushing at his son.

Vinnie was as tall as his father, but fifty pounds lighter. On his side he had quickness and, tonight, the fact that his father was drunk. He stepped aside and let Onofrio hit the opposite wall of the tiny kitchen, then stepped in and threw a hard left to the bigger man's right kidney. Onofrio sagged to his knees, groaning, and then Vinnie went to work, choosing his punches and his targets, feeling cartilage and bone break under his fists, hammering his father until the man could only lie on the floor defenseless while his son kicked him into unconsciousness.

Vinnie stopped only because he was tired. He wet a dishcloth and wiped the sweat from his face and neck, and when his breathing had slowed, he went down the hall to his parents' bedroom and unlocked the door. His mother fell into his arms, weeping.

Much later, after he had helped his mother get his bleeding father onto the living room couch, after she had bathed Onofrio's battered face, after sleep had finally come to his parents, Vinnie lay awake and relived the pleasure of what he had done to his father. It was fuller and more complete than any pleasure he would know until he was much more experienced sexually. He felt not the slightest guilt, because Vinnie never felt guilt about anything. He had learned in his short life that other people felt guilt; he understood the emotion, but he did not know it. Now he devoted himself to thinking about the worst possible thing he could do to his father, worse than the beating he had just given him. It did not take long for Vinnie's bright mind to alight on the brown bag.

Onofrio collected numbers money each evening from two dozen locations in Little Italy, then remitted it to Benedetto, a rising soldier in the Carlucci family, the following morning. Onofrio's life was his bond. If he did not take the money to Benedetto, he would die for his greed. Benedetto had a foul temper and a reputation for swift vengeance at any hint of disrespect.

Vinnie got slowly out of bed and tiptoed next door to his parents' bedroom. Silently, he opened the door and crossed the room to the bed, then dropped to his knees beside his sleeping mother. He felt under the bed for the bag, and its handle met his hand. As quietly as he could, he extracted the little satchel, then returned to his own room and switched on the light.

There was nearly three thousand dollars in the bag. Vinnie moved his bed out from the wall and removed the floorboard that covered his secret hiding place. He moved aside the *Playboy* magazines and the condoms and the hundred dollars he had saved and placed the money in the hole; then he replaced the floorboard and the nail that made it look permanently fixed.

He took the brown bag into the kitchen and dropped it out the window into the air shaft, where he knew it would be found; then he returned to his room and stretched out on the bed.

By this time tomorrow, he thought as he drifted off, Onofrio Callabrese would be at the bottom of Sheepshead Bay. Vinnie's sleep was not disturbed by the prospect.

1

Vinnie Callabrese stood on the southeast corner of Second Avenue and St. Mark's Place
in New York City and watched the candy store
across the street. The fat man was due any minute.

Vinnie felt neither guilt nor anxiety about
what he was going to do. In fact, the only emotion he felt at that moment was impatience, because he could see the marquee of the St. Mark's
Theater 80 in the next block, and he knew that
Touch of Evil started in eight minutes. Vinnie
didn't like to be late for a movie.

Vinnie's nose was Roman, his hair and beard
thick and black, his eyes dark. He knew how to
concentrate those eyes on another man and in-
duce fear. Vinnie wasn't the heaviest muscle who
worked for Benedetto, but he stood six-two and
weighed a tightly packed one hundred and ninety
pounds.

The fat man weighed more than three hundred

pounds, but he was soft to the bone. Vinnie wasn't worried, except about the time.

With six minutes left before the movie, the fat man double-parked his Cadillac Sedan De Ville at the opposite corner, struggled out of the big car, and waddled into the candy store. Vinnie gave him long enough to reach his office, then crossed the street. The place was empty, except for the old man who made the egg creams and sold the cigarettes. Vinnie closed the door, worked the latch, and flipped the OPEN sign around. He looked at the old man and gave him a little smile. "You're closed," he said, "for five minutes."

The old man nodded resignedly and picked up the *Daily News*.

Vinnie strode past the magazine racks, his leather heels echoing off the cracked marble floor, and put his hand on the doorknob of the back room. He opened it very gently and peeked into the little office. The fat man sat, his gut resting on the battered desk. With one hand he was flipping quickly through a stack of small bills, and the fingers of his other hand flew over a calculator in a blur. Vinnie was momentarily transfixed. He had never seen anything quite like it; the fat man was a virtuoso on the calculator.

The man looked up and stopped calculating. "Who the fuck are you?" he asked.

Vinnie stepped into the office and closed the door behind him. "I'm a friend of the guy who loaned you five thousand dollars nine weeks ago," he said. His accent was heavy—New York and Little Italy.

The fat man managed a sour grin. "And you've just come to make a polite call, huh?"

Vinnie shook his head slowly. "No. The polite guy was here last week, and the week before that, and the month before that."

"So you're the muscle, huh?" the fat man said, grinning more widely and leaning back in his chair. His right hand remained on the edge of the desk. It was a long reach over his gut, and it didn't look natural. "You ever heard of the law, guinea? You ever heard that what your friend does is against the law? That he has no legal claim on me, not even a piece of paper?"

"You gave my friend your word," Vinnie said slowly. "That was good enough for him. Now you've disappointed him." The fat man's fingers curled over the top of the desk drawer and yanked it open, but Vinnie moved faster. He caught the fat man by the wrist, then turned and drove an elbow into his face. The fat man grunted and made a gurgling sound but didn't let go of the desk drawer. Without a pause, Vinnie lifted a foot and kicked the drawer shut. A cracking sound was heard in the room.

The fat man screamed. He snatched his hand from Vinnie's grasp and held it close to his bleeding face. "You broke my fingers!" he whimpered. He wouldn't be doing any calculating for a while.

Vinnie bent over, grabbed a leg of the chair in which the fat man sat, and yanked. The fat man fell backwards into a quivering heap. Vinnie opened the desk drawer and found a short-barrelled .32 revolver. He lifted his shirt-tail and tucked it into his belt. "This is a dangerous weapon," he said. "You shouldn't have it; you'll end up hurting yourself." Vinnie reached for the stack of bills on the desk and started counting. The fat man watched with an expression of pain that had nothing to do with his bleeding face or his broken fingers. Vinnie stopped counting. "Five hundred," he said, sticking the wad into his pocket and returning a few ones to the desktop. "My friend will apply this to the interest on your loan. On Friday, he'll want all the back interest. A week from Friday, he'll want the five grand."

"I can't raise five thousand by then," the fat man whined.

"Sell the Cadillac," Vinnie suggested.

"I can't; it's got a loan on it."

"Maybe my friend will take the Cadillac in payment," Vinnie said. "I'll ask him. You could go on making the payments."

"Are you nuts? That car is new—it cost me thirty-five thousand."

"Just a suggestion," Vinnie said. "It would be cheaper just to come up with the five grand."

"I can't," the fat man whimpered. "I just can't do it."

"I'll tell my friend you promised," Vinnie said. He left the office and closed the door behind him.

Vinnie was in his seat, eating buttered popcorn, in time to raptly watch Orson Welles's incredibly long, one-take opening shot of Charlton Heston and Janet Leigh crossing the border into Mexico. He'd seen it at least a dozen times, and it never failed to amaze him. So much happening all at once, and yet the shot worked. He loved Welles; he loved the deep rumbling voice. Vinnie could do a very good impression of the Welles voice. He was a talented mimic.

2

Vinnie's beeper went off as he left the movie house. "Shit," he muttered under his breath. "The sonofabitch couldn't wait until tomorrow." He glanced at his watch; he could still make it if he hurried.

He grabbed a cab to Carmine Street in Little Italy. "Wait for me," he said to the cabbie as they pulled up in front of the La Boheme Coffee House.

"C'mon, mister," the cabbie moaned, "it's six bucks. I ain't got time to wait."

Vinnie fixed him with the gaze he used on delinquent debtors. "Stay here," he said, then got out of the cab without waiting for a reply. He hurried into the coffeehouse, past old men at tiny tables, and stopped at a table outside the door of the back room. An enormous man wearing a hat jammed on his head sat there, his gross fingers gripping a tiny espresso cup.

"Hey, Cheech," Vinnie said.

"You din' ansa da beep," Cheech said.

"It was quicker just to come."

Cheech made a motion with his head. "He's in dere."

Vinnie waited for Cheech to press the button, then opened the door. Benedetto sat at a small desk, a calculator before him. Vinnie was reminded of the fat man. Both counted their money every day. Vinnie's old friend Thomas Provensano, now Benedetto's bagman and bookkeeper, sat at a table in a corner, working at a calculator. Tommy Pro winked at Vinnie.

"Vinnie," Benedetto said, not looking up from the tally sheet on the desk. Benedetto was in his late thirties, prematurely graying, a dapper dresser.

"Mr. B.," Vinnie said, "I talked to the fat man."

"Was he nice?"

Vinnie produced the five hundred in cash and placed it on the desk. "He was nice for five hundred after I broke his fingers."

Benedetto held up a hand. "Vinnie, you know it's not good for me to know those things."

Vinnie knew, but he also knew Benedetto loved hearing them. "Just between you and me, Mr. B., I told the fat man all the vig by Friday and the whole five grand in another week."

"Will he do it?"

"He's got a new Cadillac. I told him you'd take that, and he could keep making the payments."

Benedetto laughed. "I like that. You're a smart boy, Vinnie; you could go places, if you could ever stop going to the movies."

This was high praise as well as scorn from Benedetto, and Vinnie nodded gratefully. Benedetto was a capo in the Carlucci family, and rumor was he'd be the new don when the present don's appeals on a triple murder conviction were exhausted. Keeping Benedetto happy was Vinnie's constant worry. The man had the disposition of an unhappy rattlesnake, and there were corpses planted far and wide, men who had once displeased Mr. B., not the least of them Vinnie's father, Onofrio Callabrese.

Benedetto handed the money to Tommy Pro, who quickly counted it, entered the sum into the calculator, then put the money into the safe. Tommy extracted another envelope from the safe and handed it to Benedetto.

"Payday, kid," Benedetto said, handing the envelope to Vinnie.

Vinnie pocketed the envelope quickly. "Thanks, Mr. B.," he said.

"Make sure the fat man keeps his new schedule," Benedetto said. "Come see me after you collect the vig. How's the rest of your list doing?"

Vinnie knew that Benedetto knew the status of every account; he just wanted to hear it aloud.

"Everybody's on schedule this week," Vinnie replied.

"That's what I like to hear," Benedetto replied. "Keep it up."

"Right, Mr. B." Vinnie turned to go.

"And Vinnie . . ."

"Yes, Mr. B.?"

"Next time, bring me the money right away; don't take in a movie first."

"Yes, Mr. B."

"What is it with you and the movies, huh? I never seen anything like it."

"It's kind of a hobby, you know?"

Benedetto nodded. "You're getting too old for hobbies. How old are you now, Vinnie?"

"Twenty-eight, Mr. B."

"Time you was making your bones."

Vinnie didn't speak. Sweat broke out in the small of his back.

"Maybe the fat man don't come through, you can make your bones on him."

"Whatever you say, Mr. B.," Vinnie said.

"Getoutahere."

Vinnie got out. The taxi was waiting, and he gave the cabbie an address in Chelsea, then sat back in the seat, drained. He opened the envelope and counted: three thousand bucks—his best week ever. Working for Benedetto had its advantages, but this thing about making his bones was beginning to weigh on Vinnie. Once he did that, he'd be a "made man," a full member of the family. And once he did that, Benedetto would own him forever. Vinnie didn't like the idea of being owned.

3

Vinnie paid the cabbie, tipped him five, then ran up the steps of the Chelsea brownstone. As far as Benedetto and the rest of the family knew, Vinnie lived in his dead mother's place on Bleecker Street, but he spent fewer and fewer nights there; his real home was three rooms in Chelsea.

He unlocked the mailbox labeled "Michael Vincent." Three years before, he had picked a lawyer out of the phone book, legally changed his name, gotten a Social Security number, a driver's license, a voter registration card and a passport, and opened a bank account. After two years of filing tax returns, listing his occupation as freelance writer, he had obtained credit cards and charge accounts in his new name, signed a lease on the Chelsea apartment, and had even taken out and repaid a bank loan. He made his bank deposits in cash at a different branch each time, he never bounced a check, and he had twelve thousand dollars in a savings account, plus a stash of fifties and hundreds. Michael Vincent was the most respectable of citizens.

"How do you do?" Vinnie said aloud to himself as he climbed the stairs to his second-floor apartment. "I'm very pleased to meet you." After a lot of experimenting, he had settled on the Tyrone Power voice. "One, two, three, four, five, six, seven, eight, nine, ten." Power was the star whose vocal sounds most closely matched Vinnie's own, and the actor's accentless California speech and silken delivery was what Vinnie strived for. He had seen *The Razor's Edge* only the day before, and Vinnie tried to project the serenity of Larry as played by Power into his speech. "I'm extremely pleased to meet you," he said as he unlocked the three locks on the front door of the apartment.

The interior was classic New York Yuppie. Vinnie had exposed the brick on the wall with the fireplace; the furniture was soft and white, with a sprinkling of glass and leather; the art was a few good prints and a lot of original movie posters—*Casablanca, For Whom the Bell Tolls*, and *His Girl Friday* among them. Nearly everything in the place had fallen off the back of a truck, including the posters, which Vinnie had stripped from a broken-down revival movie house before a wiseguy acquaintance of his had torched the place for the strapped owner. There were nearly a thousand videotapes of movies neatly catalogued by title on bookshelves.

He checked his answering machine; there was one message. "Michael, darling," a woman's low voice said. "Dinner's at nine. Don't be late. In fact, try and be early."

Vinnie got out of the black clothes he habitually wore on his collection rounds—his mob outfit, as he thought of it. He took a shower, shampooed his hair, and carefully blow-dried it. He dumped the two gold chains and the flashy wristwatch into a basket on the dresser top and slipped on a steel-and-gold Rolex and a small gold signet ring engraved with a family crest. He had selected a Vincent crest from the files of the genealogical department of the New York Public Library and had taken it to Tiffany's, where he had chosen a ring and had it engraved. The ring was very nearly the only thing Vinnie had ever paid retail for.

He had a small wardrobe of Ralph Lauren suits and jackets that a shoplifter of his acquaintance had systematically acquired for him on order from half a dozen Polo shops, and he selected a plaid tweed jacket and a pair of flannel trousers. Vinnie slipped into a Sea Island cotton shirt and Italian loafers, and he was ready for class. He glanced at the Rolex; he had twenty minutes.

Vinnie arrived at Broadway and Waverly Place with five minutes to spare. He was seated in a classroom of the New York University Film School by the time the professor walked in. The class was on production budgets.

Waring, the professor, held up a sheaf of papers. "Mr. Vincent?" he said.

Vinnie raised his hand.

"Do you really think you can shoot this film for two million six?"

The class of thirty turned as one and looked at Vinnie.

"I believe I can," Vinnie replied in his silky Tyrone Power voice.

"Tell us why, Mr. Vincent," Waring said.

Vinnie sat up. "Well, just because the piece is set in New York doesn't mean it has to be shot in New York. My budget is for an Atlanta shoot with some stock street footage of New York. That's in the budget, by the way."

Across the room a young man with curly red hair slapped his forehead.

"And in what areas did you achieve savings by shooting in Atlanta?" Waring asked.

"In almost every area," Vinnie said. "Cost of housing, transportation, sets. And no Teamsters or craft unions to worry about. I knocked off half a million because of that."

"Can you give me a single example of a film set in New York that was successfully shot in Atlanta?" Waring asked.

"I saw a TV movie, 'The Mayflower Madam,' last week. That was a New York story shot in Atlanta, and it looked good to me."

"Didn't my instructions specify a New York shoot?" Waring asked.

Vinnie pulled out a piece of paper and glanced at it. "Where?" he asked. "You may have implied a New York shoot, but you didn't specify it."

"You're right, Mr. Vincent," Waring said, "and

you were the only one in the class who figured that out. That's why you came in eight hundred thousand dollars under anybody else's budget. Congratulations, it was a good, workable budget, and you saved your investors a lot of money."

"Thank you," Vinnie said, feeling very proud of himself.

After class the redheaded young man approached Vinnie. He was wearing jeans, an army field jacket with an outline where sergeant's stripes had been, and wire-rimmed glasses. He needed a haircut. "I'm Chuck Parish," he said, sticking out his hand.

"How do you do?" Vinnie replied. "I'm very pleased to meet you."

"You're Michael Vincent, right?"

"That's right."

"Can I buy you a cup of coffee? There's something I'd like to talk to you about."

Vinnie glanced at the Rolex. "I've got twenty minutes," he said, "before I'm due somewhere."

The waitress put the coffee on the table. Chuck Parish paid her, and when she had gone he pulled a script from a canvas briefcase. "I'd like you to read this and cost it for me. I'm going to shoot it in New York, and I need a production manager."

Vinnie flipped through the pages, one hundred and nineteen of them.

"It's a caper movie, about some Mafia guys who steal two million dollars of their godfather's money and nearly get away with it."

"Who's financing?" Vinnie asked.

"I can raise three hundred thousand," Parish said. "Family connections."

"You think that's enough?"

"That's what I want you to tell me. My girlfriend's doing the female lead, and there are enough people in her acting classes to cast from. There's one guy I think looks good for the male lead."

"Do you have a distributor?"

"No."

Vinnie nodded. "I'll read it and call you."

"My number's on the back of the script."

They shook hands and parted.

Fifteen minutes later a cab dropped Vinnie at a prewar apartment building on Fifth Avenue near the Metropolitan Museum of Art.

"Good evening, Mr. Vincent," the doorman said, opening the door for him.

"Good evening, John," Vinnie said smoothly. He took the elevator to the top floor, emerged into a marbled vestibule, and opened a door with his key.

"In here, darling," she called.

Vinnie walked down the long hall past twenty million dollars' worth of art and turned into the huge master bedroom. She was in bed; a rosy-tipped breast peeked out from under the sheet. She had wonderful breasts for a woman of forty-one, Vinnie thought.

"We have half an hour before our guests arrive," she said, smiling. "Don't muss my makeup."

4

Vinnie had met Barbara Mannering at a benefit for the NYU Film School eight months before. He had been waiting in line for a drink when she appeared at his elbow.

"Shit," she said.

He turned and looked at her. A blonde of five-seven or eight, expensively coiffed and dressed, discreet but very real diamonds. "I beg your pardon?" he said.

"I am unaccustomed to standing in lines," she replied. "Would you be a prince and get me a double scotch on the rocks?"

"Of course," Vinnie had replied.

"Are you a budding movie director?"

"A budding producer," he said.

"You look a little old for NYU."

Vinnie knew he looked thirty-five. "I'm not a full-time student."

"What do you do full-time?"

"I'm a writer."

"Of what?"

"Books, magazine pieces, speeches sometimes."

"Anything I would have read?"

"Of course."

"Such as?"

"I have a rather peculiar specialty; I'm a ghost-writer."

"And whom do you ghost for?"

"If I told you, I'd no longer be a ghost. Business people, the odd politician."

"How do you find your clients?"

"They seem to find me—a sort of grapevine, I guess."

"You must do very well."

"Not all that well. I didn't write the Trump book or the Chuck Yeager book. My clients are more modest."

"So that's why you want to be a film producer, to do better?"

"I want to produce because I love film. I think I love it enough to do very well at it."

"I'm inclined to believe you will," she said. "Do you know, you sound just like Tyrone Power?"

Vinnie smiled more broadly than he had intended. "Do I?"

He took her home, and they began making love while still in the elevator. They had been making love ever since, once or twice a week. She gave a dinner party regularly, twice a month; Vinnie was invited about every other time. He had met a couple of ex-mayors, some writers, and a great many other interesting people.

*   *   *

Vinnie kissed a breast, unstuck his body from hers and headed for the shower. When he came out of the bathroom she was leafing through Chuck Parish's script.

"What's this?"

"A guy in my budgeting class asked me to cost it for him. He's scraped up some money and wants to shoot it."

"Is it any good?"

"I haven't had a chance to read it yet, but he has a reputation at NYU as a kind of genius. I've seen a couple of short films he's done, and they were extremely good. My impression is that he doesn't have much business sense." He went to the closet that held the wardrobe Barbara had chosen for him and selected a dinner jacket and a silk shirt. Both had been made by a London tailor who visited New York quarterly, and Barbara had picked up the bill. The clothes were the only thing he'd ever taken from her, although the first time he had seen the twelve-room Fifth Avenue apartment and its art and furnishings, his first impulse had been to tell Benedetto about it and get the place cleaned out some weekend when she was out of town. He'd liked her, though, and he'd thought she might be more useful to him as a friend. He'd been right. "Who's coming to dinner?" he asked.

"Senator Harvey and his wife; Dick and Shirley Clurman—Dick's retired from Time and Life—he was chief of correspondents—and he's got a wonderful new book out about the Time-

Warner merger; Shirley's a producer at ABC; Leo and Amanda Goldman. We're just eight to-night."

"Leo Goldman of Centurion Pictures?"

"I thought you'd like that. Quite apart from running the studio of the moment, he's an interesting man. Very bright."

Vinnie pulled his bow tie into a perfect knot, exactly the way Cary Grant had in *Indiscreet*. "I'll be interested to meet him," he said.

Everybody arrived almost at once. Vinnie shook Goldman's hand but made a point of not talking to him before dinner. Instead, he listened quietly to a conversation between the senator and Dick Clurman that was practically an interview. Clurman was quick and asked very direct questions, and he got very direct answers from the senator. Vinnie learned a lot.

At dinner he was seated between Shirley Clurman and Amanda Goldman; Leo Goldman was one place away, but still Vinnie did not press conversation with him. He was charming to Mrs. Clurman and devoted a lot of attention to Amanda Goldman, a beautiful blonde in her early forties, but not so much attention as to irritate her husband.

It was not until after dinner, when they were having brandy in the library, that Vinnie said more than two words to Goldman, and luckily, Goldman initiated the exchange.

"I hear you're at NYU Film School," he said.

He was a balding, superbly built man in his mid-forties, obviously the product of a strenuous daily workout.

"Part-time," Vinnie replied.

"What's your interest in film?"

"Production."

"Not the glamour stuff—writing or directing?"

"No."

"What draws you to production?"

Vinnie took a deep breath. "It's where the control is."

Goldman laughed. "Most people would say the director has control."

"Producers hire and fire directors."

Goldman nodded. "You're a smart guy, Michael," he said. "You think you have any sense of what makes a good movie?"

"Yes."

Goldman fished a card from his pocket. "When you've got something you think is good, call me. That's the private number."

Vinnie accepted the card. He smiled. "I'll call you when you least expect it."

Vinnie spent an hour in bed with Barbara, and when he had finally exhausted her, he slipped into the shower again, got into a robe, and took the Parish script into the library. He read it in an hour, then got a legal pad from the desk and started breaking it down into scenes and locations. By daylight he had a rough production schedule and budget. He didn't need a calculator to add up the figures. Vinnie had always had a facility for numbers and an outstanding memory.

He got an hour's sleep before Barbara woke him for breakfast.

"What were you doing all night?" she asked over eggs and bacon.

"Reading Chuck Parish's script and working up a production budget."

"Was it any good?"

He turned and looked at her. "Barbara, it is very, very good. It's a caper film, but it's funny. It moves like a freight train, and if it's properly produced it can make money."

"What do you need to produce it?"

"I can bring it in for six hundred and fifty thousand," Vinnie replied. "Parish has already got three hundred thousand."

"Sounds like a low budget to me," she said.

"It is. Leo Goldman wouldn't believe it."

"Are you going to take it to Goldman?"

"No. If Parish is game, I'm going to make it before anybody sees it."

"Risky."

"Not as risky as you think. You haven't read the script."

"Why don't I invest?"

"I don't want your money, Barbara." He smiled. "Just your body." He knew that she was heir to a very large construction fortune.

"The project interests me," she said. "I'll put up two hundred thousand; you come up with the rest."

"I'll think about it," Vinnie said.

He had already thought about it.

As he was leaving she said, "You know what Leo Goldman said about you last night?"

Vinnie looked at her questioningly; he didn't want to ask.

"He said, 'Your friend Michael is a hustler, but he doesn't come on like a hustler. I like that.'"

Vinnie smiled and kissed her good-bye. He was going to have to be very careful with Leo Goldman.

5

Vinnie worked on the production budget for two days, between collecting debts for Benedetto. He sat at his computer in the Chelsea apartment and constructed beautiful schedules and documents. He was impressed with his own work.

When he was ready, he went to see Tommy Pro. Vinnie had known Thomas O. Provensano since childhood. Tommy was two years older, but they had formed a friendship early. Vinnie thought Tommy was, in some ways, the smartest guy he had ever known. He had gotten an accounting degree from CUNY, passed the CPA exam, then gone to NYU Law School. Tommy knew as much about Benedetto's business as Benedetto did—maybe more.

The office was behind an unmarked door upstairs over the coffeehouse that was Benedetto's headquarters. Tommy had two rooms—one for an assistant, a fiftyish Italian widow—and one for himself and his computers. Tommy had three computers, and it seemed to Vinnie that all three of them were going full blast all the time. The furniture was spartan—a steel desk and filing cabinets that had come from a restaurant Benedetto had bankrupted some years back, and a very large safe. Tommy had told him once how all the real records were kept on computer disks, and how the safe was wired to destroy them—from a remote location, if necessary. Tommy left work each evening with a duplicate set of disks in a substantial briefcase, and *nobody* knew where he kept that.

Tommy wheeled his considerable bulk from computer to computer in a large executive chair, his only concession to comfort or luxury. "What's happening, kid?" he asked when Vinnie had been admitted to the inner sanctum.

"I'm going to make a movie, Tommy," Vinnie said, sitting down and opening his briefcase.

Tommy Pro spread his hands and grinned. "It was only a matter of time," he said. "Can I help?"

"I want to show you what I got here, and see what you think." Vinnie spread out his schedules and budgets and explained the whole thing to Tommy, who was the only person Vinnie trusted even a little. When he had finished, he sat back. "So, how'm I doing?"

Tommy smiled broadly. "It works for me," he said. "Except you gotta come up with a hundred and fifty grand, clean. How you gonna do that?"

"Between you and me, I've got nearly seventy," Vinnie replied. He had never told anybody about his stash.

"If I know you, you'll find the other eighty."

"Believe it," Vinnie said.

"This stuff amounts to a real good business plan," Tommy said, leafing through the budget. "What do you need from us?"

"From you," Vinnie said. "Not Benedetto. I've got this thing trimmed to the bone to make it work, and if Mr. B. gets wind of it he'll want a rake-off." He allowed himself a small smile. "You," he said, "I can owe."

Tommy Pro laughed. "Okay, so what are you going to owe me for?"

"Logistical help, mostly. I want to shoot in the neighborhood, and I don't want any flak from anybody."

"I can do that."

"I'm shooting this strictly nonunion, and I don't want any pickets."

"A phone call," Tommy said.

"And I want you to draw all the contracts," Vinnie said.

"Well, I haven't done a lot of entertainment work, but I've got a lot of boilerplate in the computer. You'll want to incorporate, of course."

"Of course," Vinnie said. He hadn't thought of that.

The two young men spent three hours listing contracts to be drawn and looking for holes in Vinnie's business plan. There weren't many.

When Vinnie was about to leave, Tommy Pro said, "I know a pretty good actress who's available."

"Sure; I'll find something for her. Who is she?"

"Remember Carol Geraldi?"

"Sure, *Widow's Walk*, four or five years ago. I haven't seen anything of her for a while."

"Neither has anybody else; she's on the skids—a junkie."

"Too bad."

"I think she could still work, and she's still got a name."

"How do you know about this?"

"I've got a couple pushers on the street; one of 'em's supplying her. She owes me eight grand. If you want her, pick up her tab, and I'll make you a gift of her."

"I'll think about that, Tommy, and thanks."

Vinnie was as nervous as he ever got. Chuck Parish was on his way over to the Chelsea apartment, and Vinnie made sure everything was neat and that his papers were laid out. He jumped when the doorbell rang.

Chuck was accompanied by one of the most beautiful girls Vinnie had ever seen.

"This is Vanessa Parks," Chuck said. "She's my girl and my leading lady."

"Great," Vinnie said, shaking the girl's hand. She was tall and willowy, with lovely light brown hair. Her skin was without blemish, her breasts were full and high, and her mouth was wide and lush, with excellent teeth. Vinnie wanted her immediately.

He put them on the sofa, got them a drink, then sat opposite them.

"Nice place," Vanessa said, looking around.

"Thank you, Vanessa," Vinnie said. He had found it effective to address women by their names often early in a relationship.

"So," Chuck said, "what've you got for me?"

Vinnie placed the screenplay on the coffee table. "First of all," he said, "I want to tell you that I think your screenplay is extremely good. You're a very fine writer."

Chuck glowed a little. "Thanks," he said, "but let's get down to it. What's it going to cost to produce?"

"There are three ways you can make this picture," Vinnie said. "Actually, there are dozens of ways, but only three make sense."

Chuck leaned forward. "What are they?"

Vinnie held up a finger. "One," he said, "you can make this film as a project. You can take your three hundred thousand dollars, hire some students as cast and crew, and make a nice little movie that will probably win you the NYU Film School award for best picture and best screenplay. It will be unreleasable in that form, but you can take it to the studios and use it to get a shot at writing and directing a feature, or you might get a contract to do a TV movie."

"Sounds good to me," Chuck said.

"But—and you should think seriously about this—it will be the most expensive master's thesis in history, and you'll no longer have your three hundred thousand."

"I could live with that if it helped me launch a career," Chuck said.

"It's your own money, then."

Chuck nodded. "An inheritance."

"Chuck, it's my view that a man ought to be paid for his work. If you do this, you won't be paid, and you'll squander your inheritance as well."

"I see your point," Chuck replied. "What are the other two ways?"

"You can get an agent—I've got some contacts—and sell your screenplay to a studio. It's good enough that you might get two, three hundred thousand for it."

"I like the sound of that," Chuck said, grinning.

"But they'll never let you direct it."

"Oh."

"You'll have to rewrite it half a dozen times for the studio, then, when they're happy, you'll have to rewrite it for the director, and when he's happy, you'll have to rewrite it for the star. That's the way it's done, and I don't think what you'd end up with would much resemble what you started out with."

"I see your point," Chuck said. He was looking discouraged. "What's the third option?"

"The third option," Vinnie said, "is to make a releasable film and then take it to the studios. Hire professionals for all but the menial work; cast good people who will work for scale."

"Can I do it for three hundred grand?"

"No. You'll need six hundred and fifty grand."

"I can't raise the rest," Chuck said.

"I can," Vinnie replied.

"You'd invest in my movie?" Chuck asked, astonished.

"If I produce it," Vinnie replied.

Chuck sat back on the sofa and sipped his drink. "I want to write, produce and direct my own stuff."

Vinnie sat back, too. "If that's what you want, then that's what you should do."

Chuck looked at him cautiously. "But you won't bring your investors in if I do."

Vinnie shook his head. "I couldn't do that, and I'll tell you why. You're an intelligent man, a good writer, and, from what I've seen at the film school, a good director. You ought to concentrate on what you're good at, and my guess is you're not a very good businessman. I am. I can organize this project, run the business side, and leave you free to do what you do best. That's what you need, Chuck, whether it's me or somebody else. You need a producer."

"What have you produced?"

"Nothing," Vinnie said. "But let me take you through the business plan I've worked out and show you how I'd do it." He went to his desk, picked up copies, and handed them to Chuck and Vanessa. "Page one," he said, "are overall costs, broken down by category."

When he had finished, Vinnie got up and fixed himself a drink, his first. Chuck and Vanessa whispered back and forth while he was gone. When he returned, Vanessa smiled at him, and he knew he was home free.

"I like this," Chuck said.

"It's not going to be a piece of cake," Vinnie

replied. "You and I are going to have to defer compensation. It's a twenty-three-day schedule, and you're going to have to be very well prepared to bring that off. You're going to have to shoot with Mitchell cameras instead of Panavision; you'll have to edit on a Movieola, not a Steenbeck—in fact, it would be best if you could edit at school, use their stuff—even if you have to do it in the middle of the night."

"I don't need much sleep," Chuck said. He flipped through the pages quickly. "I don't see a Steadicam in here," he said. "I specified a Steadicam for three scenes."

"You can't have a Steadicam," Vinnie said. "You can have a rented wheelchair, if we can't steal one, and all the sheets of plywood you can borrow, for track."

"How much time for preproduction and casting?" Chuck asked.

"A month. That's ample, I think. I've already found all the locations."

"All of them?" Chuck asked incredulously.

"I've put the addresses by each scene."

"What about interiors?"

"We'll borrow them. You can use this place for the girl's apartment. We won't be renting any soundstages."

"That's gotta mean a lot of looping, then."

"It's in the budget," Vinnie replied.

"Holy shit," Chuck said, wiping his brow. "This is really possible, isn't it?"

"It is."

"How do you know we can sell it to a studio when it's finished?"

"I have contacts. I believe it's doable, or I wouldn't bring my investors into it. You're going to have to depend on my business judgment, though, when we do the deal."

Vanessa put a hand on Chuck's. "I think you should do it Michael's way," she said.

Chuck looked at her, then turned back to Vinnie and stuck out a hand. "You've got a deal," he said. "When do we start?"

Vinnie took the hand in both of his. "We start tomorrow at a meeting with our lawyer. You can bring your own lawyer, of course. You should do that."

"I don't have a lawyer," Chuck said.

Vinnie smiled reassuringly. "Don't worry about it," he said.

6

Vinnie loved the work. He tried to get his collection business done in the mornings, then devoted his afternoons and evenings to mounting the production. He wheeled and dealt, offered cash for discounts, rounded up equipment, hired crew, attended casting sessions. He was a *producer*.

There was one thorn in his flesh: the fat man. He had come up with the vigorish on schedule and had made two payments. Then, when Vinnie stopped by the candy store to collect the next payment, he walked in and saw a cop. The man was loitering near the office door, reading a magazine from the rack; he was in plainclothes, but Vinnie made him in a second. The old man behind the counter raised an eyebrow and glanced at the cop. Vinnie left before he was made.

The sonofabitch, he thought as he walked on to his next customer. Benedetto would definitely lose patience now. The fat man had called the cops! Was he insane?

* * *

Benedetto was pissed off. "Why should this man treat me this way?" he asked Vinnie plaintively.

"You're right, Mr. B.," Vinnie said. "He needs a real shock to the system."

"He needs getting dead," Benedetto said flatly.

"Give me one more shot at him," Vinnie said. "After all, he won't pay you if he's dead. I'll have him on schedule by next collection day."

"All right, Vinnie, I'll leave it in your hands."

"Right, Mr. B. I'll take care of it right away." He turned to go.

"And Vinnie?"

Vinnie stopped. "Yeah, Mr. B.?"

"I'm holding you responsible."

Vinnie didn't like the sound of that. He got out fast.

Later in the day Vinnie sat in on a casting session in a basement room at NYU and watched actors read for the three principal male roles. Vanessa Parks was reading with them, and Vinnie didn't like what he heard. He thought she had the makings of an actress, but she was too young for the part, too inexperienced for the role. A week of rehearsals started in a few days. Time was short.

He got up and went to a pay phone.

"Yeah?" Tommy Pro said.

"Tommy, it's Vinnie. I need some personnel," Vinnie said.

"What kind?"

"Somebody with some medical training and a

knowledge of drugs. A little muscle wouldn't hurt."

"I think I know what's in your mind, Vinnie," Tommy said. Vinnie could hear him grinning. "When?"

"Over the weekend." Vinnie could hear pages turning.

"Roxanne," Tommy said. "She's an R.N. Them that knows her well calls her Roxy Graziano."

"Perfect," Vinnie said.

At 3:00 A.M. Vinnie turned into an upper-middle-class street in Queens and cruised slowly down the block, checking each window in each house. Not a light was on. He spotted the Cadillac, parked in a driveway; the house number was right. Vinnie drove to the end of the block, made a U-turn, and came slowly back, his headlights off. He parked and got out.

The device was a quart bottle of gasoline and a detonator with a two-minute fuse. Looking carefully up and down the street, he approached the Cadillac, set the device on the ground under the gas tank, and activated it. He walked quickly back to his car and drove away, not hurrying.

At the end of the block, he turned the corner, then stopped. He could still see the Cadillac. There was a "whomp" sound as the detonator lit the gasoline, then, after a short delay, a big fireball of an explosion. Vinnie smiled to himself and drove back toward Manhattan. The sonofabitch would pay on time now.

* * *

The following afternoon Vinnie dressed in his blue pinstriped suit and met Roxanne in a delicatessen on West Eighth Street. "It's a short walk," he said.

"Suits me."

Roxanne was a good six feet tall and weighed about a hundred and sixty, Vinnie guessed. She listened to him as they walked, nodding occasionally.

"I can handle that," she said.

"Did you bring the stuff?"

She patted her large handbag.

They came to a handsome brownstone on West 10th Street, on the elegant block between Fifth and Sixth Avenues. Michael rang the bell and waited.

She looked like hell when she came to the door. She was dressed in clean jeans and a work shirt, but her hair was dirty, and she looked older than her thirty-four years. "Yes?" she said.

"Miss Geraldi," Vinnie said, "my name is Michael Vincent. I'm a film producer. There's a script I hope you'll read—a wonderful part—and I wanted to deliver it myself." He handed her a brown envelope.

"Oh," she said, surprised and pleased. "Thank you. I'll read it over the weekend."

"This is one of my production assistants, Roxanne," he said, gesturing toward the large woman. "I wonder if we could come in for just a moment? I'd like to tell you about the project."

"Well, the place is a mess," she said. "But . . ."

"Thank you," Vinnie said, brushing past her.

She had been right; the place was a mess. Vinnie moved a pizza box from a sofa and sat down.

Carol Geraldi sat opposite him, and Roxanne stood quietly in the doorway.

Vinnie told Geraldi about the film, about her part. "There are only four scenes," he said, "but it's the only female part of any consequence, and the quality of the writing, I think you'll agree when you read it, is extraordinary. I don't want to oversell it, but I think there's an opportunity for an Academy Award nomination in this part."

"Well," Geraldi said, taking the script from the envelope. "*Downtown Nights*. It's an interesting title."

"Why don't you read the scenes now?" Vinnie suggested. "The pages are flagged."

She glanced at her watch. "I'm sorry, but I don't have time right now; I'm expecting someone."

"Take the time," Vinnie said. "You certainly won't be sorry."

"Mr. . . . . Vincent, is it?" she said, an edge in her voice. "I really am expecting someone, and I'm in no mood to read this at the moment."

"I'm afraid the man you're expecting isn't coming, Miss Geraldi."

She looked alarmed. "I beg your pardon?"

"The man with the drugs is not coming."

She was trembling now. "I don't know what you're talking about. Who are you, anyway?"

"I'm a film producer, as I told you a moment ago. I assure you, this is a genuine offer."

"Offer? You haven't made an offer. You'll have to call my agent," she said, rising.

"I'm afraid you don't have an agent anymore, Miss Geraldi. You haven't had one for some time."

She sat down again. "What is this, exactly?"

"I won't waste your time," he said. "I'll be direct with you."

"I'd appreciate that." She was twitching now.

"I have bought your debt from your pusher. Eight thousand dollars—that's a lot of drugs, Miss Geraldi. You're up to two grams of cocaine a week now, plus whatever else you can get your hands on."

"I'm going into rehab next week," she said.

"Not just yet," Vinnie replied. "You have a part to do first."

"Look, I don't know if this film is real or not, but I'm in no shape to deliver any kind of performance right now. And I really am expecting someone."

"He was about to cut you off anyway. Look at me as a rescuing angel."

"You're going to supply me with drugs?" she asked incredulously.

"That's right, Miss Geraldi, and Roxanne here is going to administer them. Roxanne is going to see that you feel just fine right through a week's rehearsals and ten days of shooting. I'm arranging to shoot your scenes almost back to back, so that we won't take any more of your time than absolutely necessary. And as soon as you've finished shooting, we'll get you into rehab, I promise."

Geraldi looked at Roxanne. "Can you give me something now?" she asked.

"Of course she can," Vinnie said, rising. "I'm just about finished. But I want to be sure you understand me clearly. Roxanne is moving in with you from this moment. She's going to maintain you through the weekend, the rehearsals, and the shoot, and I don't want you to give her the slightest difficulty. Is that clear?"

Geraldi nodded dumbly.

"You must understand that I'm giving you a great opportunity, and I expect your full cooperation. If you don't cooperate with me, the director, and Roxanne at all times, I'm going to drop you right back into the frying pan; I'm going to sell your debt to a man who's not nearly as nice as I am and who deals in a different kind of movie than I do—then you'll have to work your debt off, and it will take a long, long time. Do you understand me, Carol?"

"I understand," Geraldi said weakly. She turned to Roxanne. "Now, please?" she whimpered.

"Help her, Roxanne," Vinnie said. "Carol, your first reading will be at one o'clock on Monday afternoon. Be sure you know your lines." He smiled. "Roxanne will read with you."

7

Vinnie sat in the rehearsal hall at Central Plaza on Second Avenue and watched Chuck Parish rehearse his cast. They spent the morning running through the four scenes between Vanessa Parks and the three male leads. Chuck moved quickly, only occasionally stopping to make a suggestion. Vinnie was impressed with the way he handled the actors, never criticizing, always encouraging.

At noon, lunch was delivered from a delicatessen, and Vinnie took the opportunity to call Chuck aside. When they were alone in the stairwell Vinnie spoke quietly. "Chuck, at the risk of insulting you, I'm going to tell you something you already know."

"What's that?" Chuck asked warily.

"Vanessa is wrong for the part. Wrong for the movie, in fact."

"What the hell are you talking about?" Chuck demanded defensively. "I've cast her, and that's it."

"Come here," Vinnie said, leading him over to the door to the rehearsal hall. They looked in at the group of actors eating lunch. "Look at that group and tell me this: who's out of place?"

Chuck looked at his cast—most of them Italian, all of them ethnic-looking in some way.

"Look at them," Vinnie repeated. "We've got Italians, Jews, Puerto Ricans, a couple of blacks. It's a gritty group." He paused. "And then there's Vanessa."

Chuck said nothing, but continued to stare at the group.

"She's a promising actress, I'll give you that, but she's too WASPy, she's too delicate, she's too young, she's too green. We need an older, more experienced actress, someone who can bring some personal weight to the part."

"If I tell her that she'll walk right out on me," Chuck said.

"If she loves you she won't," Vinnie said smoothly. "She'll understand you're doing it for the production."

"I just can't do it," Chuck said. "Will you tell her?"

"If she hears it from me she'll never forgive you."

Chuck turned away from the door. "But we're too far along now. How can we recast the part in the time we've got? You're always bitching at me about schedule."

"I understand that Carol Geraldi is available," Vinnie said.

Chuck looked at him. "You think we could get her?"

"I do."

"Can we afford her?"

"Yes."

"Where has she been the past couple of years? I haven't seen her in anything since she won the Oscar for *Widow's Walk*."

"She took some time off."

Chuck walked back to the door and looked at Vanessa. "She's so goddamned beautiful," he said. "I always wanted somebody as beautiful as that."

"Your career is at stake here, Chuck. She can't carry the part, and nobody will blame her; they'll blame you for casting her."

Chuck leaned against the wall and wiped his brow with his sleeve. "I guess I just have to be ruthless, huh?"

"It won't be the last time, Chuck; it's a tough business. I think maybe Vanessa understands that better than you. When she's had time to think about it, she'll see that you're doing it as much for her career as yours. Everybody who'd see the film would know she was out of her depth."

"You're right," Chuck said. "I can't let her do that to herself."

Vinnie put a hand on Chuck's shoulder. "You're a good man. Best to tell her now."

Chuck nodded. "Just give me a minute, okay?"

"Sure," Vinnie said. "I'll have Carol Geraldi here at one o'clock."

Chuck nodded and looked at his feet.

Vinnie walked downstairs and out onto the street, breathing more easily. He looked up to see Carol Geraldi and Roxanne getting out of a taxi. He walked over to them. "You look terrific," he said to Geraldi, taking her hand.

"I had a good weekend," she said.

"Good, good. Now, you're a few minutes early, so you and Roxanne go across the street and get a cup of coffee. At one, go up to Studio A and introduce yourself to the director, Chuck Parish."

"Won't you be there?" she asked nervously.

"I have to do something else for a couple of hours, but Chuck is expecting you, and he's very excited about working with an actress of your caliber."

She smiled. "That's nice."

"Now go get your coffee." He watched the two women cross the street, then went and stood inside the door to the building, waiting. Five minutes later he heard a door slam, then the ring of high heels on the steel stairs, then Vanessa Parks nearly fell into his arms. She was weeping and nearly hysterical.

"Vanessa, honey, take it easy," he said, holding her at arm's length and looking at her closely.

"The bastard!" she said. "The bastard fired me!"

"Are you all right?" he asked.

"Of course I'm not all right! My boyfriend just fired me off his picture! Don't you understand?"

"Come on," Vinnie said, putting an arm around her. "Let's get out of here." Outside, he hailed a cab and bundled her into it. He gave the driver the address of the Chelsea apartment, then turned to Vanessa, who was trembling with fury, tears streaming down her face. "Take it easy now. We'll talk this whole thing out and see what we can do about it." He pulled her head to his shoulder and let her do her sobbing there.

In the Chelsea apartment he mixed her a strong Scotch. She wolfed down half of it. "The bastard," she kept saying.

Vinnie pulled her onto the sofa and stroked her hair. "Listen, it's just a job," he said. "You're going to have better parts than that, I promise you."

"You think so?" she asked, wiping her nose with a tissue.

"Vanessa, look at me," he said, cupping her face in his hands.

She looked up at him, doe-eyed, snuffling.

"You have something very special, something the camera can see, something an audience can identify with."

"I do?" she whimpered.

"More than being very beautiful, you have a rare talent that, properly developed, is going to propel you to a high place in the film business."

"Do you really think so?" she asked. She had stopped crying.

"Absolutely. Chuck is going to do okay, I'm going to do okay, but you are going to be a very great star. I promise you that."

"Oh, Michael," she said, placing a hand on his cheek. "You always believed in me from the start, didn't you? I knew you did, I could tell. Chuck just wanted to fuck me."

"Listen, Chuck thinks you're great, but let me tell you, as good as you would have been in that part, the part wouldn't have been good for you."

"Why?"

"Because the character isn't anywhere near as young and beautiful as you are. I'm going to find you parts, create parts for you that will send you to the top of this business."

"You'd do that for me?" she asked.

"I'll do it for you, I'll do it for myself. I want to see you on top, and I want to be the one who puts you there."

She kissed him.

He kissed her back, but he held himself away. Her mouth was incredible and he wanted more of it, but he wanted her to be the aggressor.

She did not disappoint him. She pushed him back on the sofa, got his zipper undone, and in a moment she had him in her mouth.

If he thought her mouth had been incredible on his lips, then where it was now was right next to heaven, he thought. He looked at the top of her head, ran his hand through her thick hair, played his fingers at the corner of her mouth, felt himself swelling, swelling, then exploding. She kept sucking until he pulled her head away, got an arm around her waist and swept her into the bedroom, both of them shedding clothes along the way.

* * *

Vinnie made it back to the rehearsal hall before the reading broke for the day. "How did it go?" he asked Chuck.

"Geraldi is absolutely wonderful," Chuck replied. "She walked in here, and in five minutes, she *was* the part, and everybody in the cast knew it. She was inspired casting, Michael."

"I'm glad you're happy."

"I'm delirious. Did you see Vanessa when she left?"

"No, I had to go uptown and fix a hassle with the lighting. It's okay now."

"I dread seeing her when I get home," Chuck said. "I feel just terrible about this."

"You'll get over it, and so will she," Vinnie replied. "She'll probably throw herself into your arms the moment you walk in."

An hour later, the phone rang in the Chelsea apartment.

"Hello," Vinnie said.

"Michael," Chuck Parish sobbed, "she's gone!"

"Take it easy now," Vinnie replied soothingly.

"All her stuff is gone; she's vanished. None of her friends know where she is."

"It's how it had to be, Chuck," Vinnie said. "Let her go. Get your head back into the film. Don't think about anything else."

Chuck heaved a deep sigh. "You're right," he said. "The film is the important thing. I don't know why I let the cunt upset me so much."

"Get a good night's sleep. I'll see you in the morning."

"Sure, Michael. Thanks." He hung up.

Vinnie hung up and looked toward the kitchen, where Vanessa, dressed only in a shirt, was making pasta.

"You like a lot of garlic?" she asked, smiling at him.

8

Vinnie sat straight up in bed. Something had awakened him, some noise, but it was gone. Vanessa was stretched out beside him, sleeping quietly. He looked at the bedside clock: just after 3:00 A.M. The noise came again, and this time he knew what it was: his beeper, sending muffled signals from his trousers pocket.

He got out of bed, switched off the beeper, and went to the living room phone. He didn't like this; Benedetto had never once called him in the middle of the night. The fat man's collection day was tomorrow—that must be what it was about. He dialed the number.

"Yeah?" the voice of Cheech, the bodyguard, said.

"It's me. What the fuck?"

"Now," Cheech said.

"Right now?" He tried to keep his voice down so as not to wake Vanessa. "Does he have any idea what the fuck time it is?"

"Gee, I dunno," Cheech said. "You want I should ask him?"

"I'll be there in twenty minutes," Vinnie said, exasperated.

"Make it ten," Cheech said.

"Tell him I'm not at home, and I have to find a cab."

"Yeah," Cheech said, then hung up.

Vinnie got into the clothes he had taken off at bedtime. He hated wearing clothes twice, but he couldn't afford to waste time. He didn't like being on the streets of New York at this time of night, either; he opened a drawer and found the fat man's gun, then left the building. A miracle; it took him only five minutes to find a cab going south on Seventh Avenue.

They were two thirds through shooting the film, and Vinnie had already shaved a day off the schedule. He was proud of himself, but he was nervous, too. He was right on budget, but most of Chuck's and Barbara's investment was gone, and soon he was going to have to come up with his hundred and fifty thousand. He had seventy, which he hated to think of using, but he needed another eighty at least.

The cab driver was on his way home to Brooklyn and refused to go any farther south than Houston Street. Vinnie jogged the rest of the way.

The streets of Little Italy were deserted, and his soft Italian loafers made little sound as he ran along. He was swept back to his childhood, when running had meant that somebody was chasing him, usually for stealing. As he approached the

La Boheme Coffee House, he slowed to a walk, willing his heart to slow down. He stood outside the door and panted for a moment. Suddenly the glass behind him rattled. Vinnie spun around, his heart racing again, to find Cheech standing there, his bulk filling the doorway.

"Christ, Cheech, you scared the shit out of me," he panted.

"You better get in there," Cheech said, indicating the back room with a thumb. "He's pissed off."

Vinnie walked quickly through the dark coffeehouse, aiming at the light under the door of the back room. His shirt was sticking to him, and he didn't have his breathing under control yet. He hated not being perfectly in control of himself, hated it that Benedetto was going to see him this way. He knocked, then opened the door.

Benedetto was sitting in his usual place, and there were stacks of money on the table. The door to the big safe was ajar. Cheech went and sat at the desk where Tommy Pro often worked.

"Evening, Mr. B.," Vinnie said, trying to calm his breathing.

"Evening, my ass," Benedetto said, becoming red in the face.

"What's up? How can I help?" Vinnie asked.

"This is your problem, not mine," Benedetto replied. "You can fucking fix it."

"What's the problem, Mr. B.?" He had a sickening feeling that he knew what the problem was.

"You see the late news tonight?"

"No."

"The fat man was the star of it. Oh, they had a goddamned coat over his head, but it was him getting into the car."

"The fat man's been busted?" Vinnie asked, mystified.

"Not exactly," Benedetto replied snidely. "The fat man is trying to get *me* busted. He's been to the DA, who has a hair up his ass about loan-sharking, and who now has a warrant out for me. I couldn't even get into my office until an hour ago. There's been cops all over."

Vinnie was stunned. The fat man didn't know his name, but he could certainly give the cops a good description. "I don't believe it," he said. "The man can't be that crazy."

"Well, he is that crazy," Benedetto said, "and it was your job on his car that pushed him over the edge."

"He'd never testify against you, Mr. B.," Vinnie said. "He'd know what that'd mean. He's not *that* crazy."

"They got him sequestered," Benedetto said.

"Oh, shit."

"Exactly, except I found out where. Cost me ten big ones."

"You know where they got him?"

"Fortunately, yeah. Otherwise Cheech would right now be breaking your head like a walnut."

Vinnie looked at Cheech, who seemed disappointed that he was not breaking Vinnie's head. "Mr. B.," he said, "just tell me what you want me to do."

Benedetto took a slip of paper from his pocket and pushed it across the table. "That's where he is," the capo said. "It's a place in Oyster Bay, on the North Shore. You go do it."

"Do what, Mr. B.?"

"Make him dead. Cheech'll give you a gun." He turned and looked at his bodyguard. "Give Vinnie something heavy to make his bones with. I don't want no surprise recovery."

Vinnie's mind went into a kind of crazy fast-forward. He would try to get to the fat man, and the cops would kill him. He would never see his film released, never make love to Vanessa again, never go to another dinner party at Barbara Mannering's to meet the rich and powerful.

But then again, maybe not. Maybe he would pull it off and get the credit for saving Benedetto's ass. He would make his bones and be one of the boys. And Benedetto would have him by the balls for the rest of his life, tell him what and what not to do, rule his life, *own* him.

Benedetto was turning back toward him; Cheech had a .45 automatic by the barrel, wiping it with an oily cloth.

Decide! Decide! He decided. His hand went to the waist of his trousers and grasped the fat man's revolver. He was moving too slowly, he knew; Cheech was big, but he was quick as a cat. Vinnie started up with the gun, saw the surprise in Benedetto's face. Vinnie shot him in his surprise.

The bullet went in under the left eye, and Benedetto spilled backward from his chair. Vinnie knew he might not be dead, but Cheech was doing something with his hands. Vinnie turned, crouched, and fired twice. The first one got Cheech in the left shoulder, the second hit him in the neck. He still had the .45 in his hand, clasped in the oily cloth. He was having trouble getting a finger on the trigger through the cloth.

Vinnie quickly walked toward him, stopped three feet away. He put one into Cheech's head, saw some skull come away and blood splash the desk. He fired one more into the forehead.

There was a noise behind him. Benedetto was on his hands and knees struggling toward him. His face was contorted with pain and rage. He reached up and got hold of Vinnie's trouser leg. Vinnie backhanded him with the pistol; he didn't want blood all over him. Benedetto reeled, but recovered and started toward him again, blood pouring from his face. Vinnie shot him twice more in the top of the head, and the pistol was empty.

Vinnie turned back to Cheech, terrified that the giant might still be able to fire the heavy pistol at him, but Cheech was on his back, bleeding into the floorboards. He wheeled back to Benedetto, but Mr. B. was very dead, too.

Vinnie stood, frozen, in the middle of the room, the gun in his hand, taking deep breaths, trying to stop his heart from flying from his chest. Then a deep voice behind him shook him to his roots.

"Well, Vinnie," Tommy Pro said, "you've really made a mess, haven't you?"

Vinnie whipped around, the pistol out in front

of him, to find Tommy standing in the doorway, a sawed-off shotgun in his hands.

"Your piece looks empty," Tommy said.

"Empty," Vinnie said, recovering. "Yeah, it's empty."

"Is it yours?"

"No, I got it from a guy."

"It's clean, then?"

"Yeah, I guess so."

Tommy reached out and took the pistol from Vinnie's hand and pocketed it. "I was upstairs working late; an all-nighter. I'm glad it was you." He looked at Vinnie closely. "Thank Christ you were empty, I think."

"Yeah," Vinnie said. "I probably would have kept shooting. You scared me bad." He was feeling numb now, tired to the bone. "You gonna give me to the Don, Tommy?" he asked weakly.

"Are you insane?" Tommy Pro asked. "Look around here, don't you see what I see?"

"I see Benedetto dead," Vinnie said.

"You don't see any money on the table, Vinnie? You don't see the safe open?" Tommy chuckled. "Even *I* don't have the combination to that safe."

Vinnie began to recover; the numbness was leaving him. "You and me, Tommy? We take everything?"

"Not exactly, Vinnie," Tommy Pro said. "You take half the money. I take everything else."

"What else?" Vinnie asked, looking around the nearly empty room. Then he understood.

Tommy went to the safe and opened it wide.

He took two bank bags from a shelf and began to stuff money into both of them. When he had finished, he stood up and began bagging the money on the table. Finally, he held out both bags to Vinnie. "No time for counting. I divided it up; you got dibs."

Vinnie took one of the bags.

"You remember how we used to run across the roofs?" Tommy asked.

"Yeah," Vinnie replied.

"You go out the back way, go up the fire escape, across the roofs to your mother's place. Hide the money somewhere *good*. Stay at your mother's until you hear from me. People are going to want to talk to you. I'll handle things here."

"I've got another place, in Chelsea," Vinnie said.

"Can anybody put you there tonight?"

"Yeah, there's a girl."

"Wait'll morning, when there's people on the street. Go back to Chelsea and call me around ten. Act surprised on the phone."

Vinnie nodded. Without speaking again, he left through the back door. A moment later he was flying across the roofs, a child again with Tommy Pro, running from somebody.

9

Vinnie lay on his dead mother's bed and tried to think. For an airtight alibi, he needed to get back to Chelsea before Vanessa woke up. Thank God, he thought, she sleeps like a rock. But how would he do that? He'd never get a cab at this time of night, and he might be noticed at this hour on the subway. He certainly didn't want to be walking the streets in the middle of the night with a lot of money in a bag. Then he remembered something.

He got off the bed and went to the chest of drawers where his old clothes were. He got into some athletic shorts, a sweatshirt, and sneakers, then picked up the money and left the apartment. As silently as he could, he tiptoed down the stairs. There it was, at the bottom. A bicycle, with a helmet dangling from the handlebars. The kid who lived downstairs worked for a messenger service. Vinnie stuffed the money into a saddlebag, donned the helmet, and very quietly got the bike out of the building. The gears were a little crazy, but he soon got the hang of it. He pedaled through the silent streets, past the groceries and coffeehouses he had known since boyhood, and soon he was headed uptown.

At Sixth Avenue and Twelfth Street a police car gave him a bad moment when it pulled up next to him. He gave them a smile and a wave and kept pedaling.

He left the bicycle leaning against a bus stop shelter on Seventh Avenue and jogged the rest of the way home.

Back in the apartment, he got a knife and cut through the plastic bonding material that held four bricks in place. He stuffed the moneybag into the hole and replaced the bricks, carefully filling the cracks again. A little soot from the fireplace and the filling matched the cement holding the other bricks together. It was near dawn when he gratefully crawled into bed next to the sleeping Vanessa.

She was up first; she had a modeling job that morning. "Where were you last night?" she asked. "I got up and went to the bathroom, and you were gone."

He knew what kind of sleeper she was. "Sweetheart, you had a dream. I never budged at all last night."

"Oh," she said, then kissed him and went on her way.

When she had gone, he resisted the temptation to count the money. Instead, he called Tommy Pro. "Just checking in," he said.

"Bad news," Tommy said. "Benedetto got hit last night. Cheech, too."

Vinnie always assumed the line was tapped. "No shit," he said, sounding as astonished as he could. "Who did it?"

"We're working on it, and so are the cops, but no leads so far. They cleaned out the safe, too. Wasn't much in it, just the proceeds from the coffeehouse for a couple days."

"Anything I can do?"

"I'll let you know," Tommy replied, then hung up.

The phone rang.

"Hello?"

"It's Barbara. How about tonight?"

"Dinner party?"

"Just you and me, babe."

He didn't have to think long. "I'll look forward to it."

He stayed away from the shoot that day, since they were still in Little Italy and he didn't want to be seen there, even though there was no reason for the cops to question him. They were only a couple of weeks away from a rough cut of the picture, and he had to think about the next stage.

Finally he was unable to resist the temptation; he took out the bricks and had a look at the money. It was in bills of all sizes, and it came to a little over a hundred and ninety thousand. He could finish the picture now, even if he went over budget, but he was determined not to do that. He hid the money again.

Barbara Mannering ran a long fingernail down Vinnie's chest to his pubic hair. "Again, lover?" she asked sweetly.

Vinnie still hadn't caught his breath from the first time. "Barbara, you are insatiable, you know that?"

She chuckled. "I know that. I'll give you a minute."

"Thanks."

"How's your movie coming?"

"We wrap next week."

"When can I see it?"

"I want it finished before you see it—scored, the titles and the opticals in."

"Oh, all right, I'll be patient."

"You know anybody at the New York Film Festival?"

"Sure. A girl I knew at Bennington is the executive director."

"Can you get her to look at the picture?"

"I expect so. The festival's next month, though. She'll need to see it very soon if she's to schedule it. In fact, it might be too late already."

"Tell her I'll have a rough cut in ten days. I'll book a screening room at the film school."

"I'll see what I can do. You all rested now?"

He turned back to her. "I'm all rested."

Since there were no titles yet, the film just stopped.

"I love it," the woman said. "I just love it. But we've booked the whole festival."

"Surely you can squeeze us in somewhere," Vinnie said. "Look, this is a homegrown New York product, with a score by a student at Juilliard and a director from the NYU Film School who's going to be very hot. A couple of months from now you'll look very smart to have had this in the festival."

"Can you finish it in time?" she asked.

"We can," Vinnie replied. He hoped that was true.

"Tell you what. We've only got a single feature scheduled for the second night—a new film from England. I'll run yours first."

"Run it second," Vinnie said. "Everybody will show up for the English film. We'll be dessert."

She stuck out a hand. "You're on."

Vinnie held his breath and dialed the number. "Mr. Goldman's office," a businesslike female voice said.

"Hello, this is Michael Vincent. May I speak to Leo, please?"

"Does he know you, Mr. Vincent?"

"How else would I have this number?" Michael said, laughing.

"Just a moment."

There was a very long wait, but finally the voice was male. "Leo Goldman," he said briskly.

"This is Michael Vincent; how are you?" God, is he going to remember?

"Barbara's friend. What can I do for you?"

"Will you be in New York for the film festival?"

"I'm there for the opening, then I have to go on to London."

"I've got a film showing the second night."

"Bring it to our screening room—the Centurion Building, on Fifth Avenue. Let's see . . ."

Vinnie could hear pages turning.

"Three o'clock on opening day."

"That's good."

"See you then." Goldman hung up.

Vinnie replaced the receiver and held his breath for a moment. Then he exploded in laughter. "A screening with Leo Goldman!" he shouted to the empty room.

10

Vinnie sat in a taxicab and sweated. He had less than ten minutes before his appointment with Leo Goldman and he was still forty blocks away. The film lab had been late finishing the print, and he was nearly crazy. He had meant to have the film delivered to the Centurion offices, but now he had to hump the cans up there himself. He found a handkerchief and patted his face; he breathed deeply, settled himself into a kind of mild trance. There was nothing he could do about this; he would go with the flow.

He was ten minutes late for his appointment, and when he reached Goldman's office, his secretary said he was waiting in the screening room. He took the elevator down, handed all the film cans to a waiting projectionist, straightened his tie, and entered the screening room.

Leo Goldman sat hunched in a chair, cigar smoke rising from him. He nodded at Vinnie, then pressed a button, and said, "Let's go, Jerry."

Vinnie took a seat as the film began to run.

They were thirty seconds into the titles when a phone rang.

Goldman picked it up and started to talk rapidly, alternately puffing on the cigar.

Vinnie reached over and pressed the intercom button. "Jerry, please stop the film and back it up to the beginning."

Goldman stopped talking and placed a hand over the receiver. "I was watching," he said.

"Leo," Vinnie said calmly, "all I want is ten minutes of your undivided attention. If you'd like to take calls after that, feel free."

Goldman looked at him oddly for a moment, then spoke into the phone again. "I'll get back to you." He hung up and pressed the intercom. "Let's go, Jerry."

The film started again, and Vinnie made every effort not to look at Goldman. This was easy for him, for he had not seen the finished film himself, and he was entranced.

Ten minutes into the film Goldman glanced at his watch, then picked up the telephone.

Oh, shit, Vinnie thought, *I blew this one.*

"Bernice," Goldman said into the telephone, "hold my calls."

Vinnie sank back into the big chair and started to enjoy the film again.

Goldman had gone through two more cigars during the film, but he had not shifted in his seat. He waited until the final credit had rolled before he spoke. "Who owns this movie?" he asked.

"The Downtown Nights Company, Incorporated," Vinnie replied.

"And who owns the corporation?"

"I do."

"A hundred percent of the stock?"

"That's correct."

"What about your investors?"

"They invested in the film, not the corporation."

"So you're free to deal, without encumbrance?"

"I am."

"Who else has seen this film?"

"Nobody but you; not even the director has seen this print, and it's one of only two prints. The other is for the festival."

"What do you want for the negative?"

"Make me an offer."

"I'll give you two million dollars for it, lock, stock, and barrel."

"No."

"Are you crazy?"

"Leo, tomorrow night the film is going to be shown at the New York Film Festival. The reviews will appear in the *Times* the following morning. It won't be a secret anymore."

"All right, two and a quarter million."

Vinnie shook his head slowly. He was waiting to be asked again what he wanted.

Leo stood up. "See you around, kid," he said, and strode up the aisle of the little theater.

Keep functioning, Vinnie said to himself. He

pressed the button on the intercom. "Jerry, please rewind the reels."

Goldman walked through the swinging doors.

Vinnie sat and waited for the projectionist to finish rewinding. He willed himself not to run after Goldman. *Never mind*, he was thinking, *they'll all see it tomorrow night.*

Goldman came back through the swinging doors, strode down the aisle, and sat down next to Vinnie. "All right, let's see how smart you are," he said. "Tell me what you want. Be reasonable, be realistic. If you do that, I'll buy it."

"I want three million dollars cash," Vinnie said. "I want ten gross points—that's me, personally, not the corporation—a separate contract; I want a guarantee of a minimum of eight million dollars spent on advertising and promotion; I want a guarantee that it will open on not less than one thousand screens; I want a guarantee that nobody will touch one frame of it."

"I don't do gross points," Goldman said.

"Leo, you're going to have a terrific finished film in the theaters for a third of what it would cost you to produce it yourself."

"It may have to be edited for television."

"You can dub language, you can't edit."

"I want you to come to work in development for me. I'll give you six hundred grand a year and a good expense account, five-year contract."

"I don't want to develop, Leo, I want to produce. I want a production deal."

"What kind of a deal?"

"Three-quarters of a million a year, the expense account, and overhead of three hundred thousand; a million a year in development money; three-year contract."

"Three years and an option for two more; any budget over a negative cost of twenty million, you fund elsewhere."

"All right, but you get thirty days to green-light; after that, I can take it anywhere I want, but shoot at Centurion. If you pick up my option, I get a million and a half a year."

"Six weeks to green-light."

"Done," Vinnie said.

Goldman picked up a phone and punched in a number. "Murray, I want a negative buyout contract right now; the price is three million; the film is called *Downtown Nights*, we're buying from Downtown Nights Company, Incorporated. I said *now*. Further, I want a separate contract giving ten gross points personally to one Michael Vincent. Further, I want a producer's contract drawn." He dictated the terms exactly as he and Vinnie had agreed. "One more thing," he said. "Cut me a check for three million dollars to the corporation and another one for a hundred thousand to Vincent. I want everything in my office in half an hour." He hung up.

"You can generate those contracts in half an hour?" Vinnie asked incredulously.

Goldman waved a hand. "It's all boilerplate; he'll insert the numbers and spew the whole thing out of a word processor. It'll take him forty-five minutes." He got up. "Where's the negative?"

"In your screening room," Vinnie replied.

"I like the way you do business, Michael. Come on."

Vinnie followed Goldman at a near-trot to his office. It was a square room, about thirty feet on a side, and the walls were hung with a mixture of abstract paintings and impressionists.

"A beautiful collection," Vinnie said.

"You should see the stuff at my house," Goldman replied. He riffled through his calendar. "Let's see, I'm back from London on Saturday. You show up on the lot on Monday morning; come to dinner on Tuesday. Want me to arrange a girl?"

"I've got one of those."

"Married?"

"No."

"Smart."

The contracts arrived. Vinnie went through them carefully, taking his time, while Goldman caught up on his phone messages. He complained about some clauses, quibbled about others. Goldman was reasonable. By seven in the evening the contracts had been revised, and Goldman and Vinnie signed.

Goldman handed him two checks. "There's your buyout. Here's another for a hundred grand, the first payment on your contract."

Vinnie stood up and shook Goldman's hand. "Thank you, Leo."

"Let me ask you something, Michael: what did it cost you for the negative?"

"Six hundred and thirty thousand dollars," Vinnie replied.

Goldman roared with laughter. "I love it!" he shouted. "I figured a million eight! I paid you more than you wanted! Of course, you're screwing your investors, taking the ten points directly to you."

"I only have two investors, and they'll make out like bandits. You got a good deal, too; you don't make bad deals."

"It's always like this, kid; two guys make a deal, they both always know something the other doesn't. It works out in the end."

Vinnie looked at Goldman sharply. "Leo, what do you know that I don't know?"

Goldman permitted himself a small smile. "Carol Geraldi checked out this morning. An overdose. That's going to guarantee ten million dollars worth of free publicity for this movie, and I'm going to get her a posthumous Academy Award. You wait and see."

Vinnie sat back in the cab and looked at his two checks. If he had known about Geraldi's death, he could have gotten at least another million, he thought. Never mind, he reasoned, he'd make out just fine with his gross points.

11

Vinnie had three meetings on the morning of the showing of *Downtown Nights* at the New York Film Festival. First, he met Chuck at the coffeeshop where they had first talked about making *Downtown Nights*.

"Where have you been?" Chuck asked. "I ran the film last night, and it looks great. You haven't even seen it."

"I saw it yesterday afternoon with Leo Goldman of Centurion Pictures."

"How did you get to Goldman?"

"I told you I had some connections."

"What did he think?"

"He loved it. He paid me three million dollars for it."

Chuck's mouth fell open; he seemed unable to speak.

"Is that all right with you, Chuck?" Vinnie asked.

"Well . . . I don't know. Is that a good deal? You never checked with me."

"It's a very good deal, Chuck, and our contract stipulates that I conduct all negotiations and have the final say."

"Well, if that's what it says. When do I see some money?"

Vinnie produced an envelope. "Here's your first payment," he said.

Chuck ripped open the envelope. "A hundred and fifty grand, all at once!"

"That's your fee for writing and directing." Vinnie produced another check.

Chuck's hands were trembling as he opened the envelope. "Five hundred ninety-seven thousand, four hundred and twenty-five dollars," he said weakly.

"That's your investment of three hundred thousand, plus the earnings."

"That's . . . that's . . ." Chuck was looking at the ceiling, concentrating.

"That's a total of seven hundred forty-seven thousand dollars and change," Vinnie said. "Let me tell you how it breaks down. We spent six hundred and fifty thousand shooting the film. We got three million for it, leaving two million, three hundred and fifty thousand. Out of that, your fee for directing and writing was a hundred and fifty thousand; my fee for producing was two hundred and fifty thousand . . ."

"How come you get more than me?" Chuck demanded. "It was my film."

"For two reasons," Vinnie said calmly. "First, I'm picking up the legal work, which is going to be expensive. Second, none of this would have happened without me; you wouldn't have three quarters of a million dollars in your hand, and your film wouldn't be showing at the New York Film Festival tonight."

"You're right, Michael," Chuck said sheepishly. "I didn't mean to be ungrateful."

"To continue: that leaves a million nine hundred and fifty thousand dollars profit. Taxes are something over six hundred and fifty thousand, leaving a net of a little under a million three to distribute to investors. Your share is forty-six percent. It's all right here," he said handing Chuck a document. "Believe me, if a studio had done the film they'd have raked off most of the profits."

Chuck was looking at the checks and nodding. *"Yes!"* he shouted.

Vinnie's second meeting took place later that morning. He and Tommy Pro sat in the little office at the back of La Boheme and drank espresso.

"Is this place clean?" Vinnie asked, looking around the room. There was a constant fear of electronic bugs in the place.

"It was swept this morning," Tommy replied. "You hear from the cops?"

"Not a word."

"I know you didn't hear from our people; I kept you out of it."

"Thanks, Tommy."

"So, how's your movie coming along?"

"It's finished. It's being shown at the New York Film Festival tonight."

"Fantastic! So maybe a studio will pick it up?"

"A studio picked it up yesterday."

"Wonderful, Vinnie; how'd you do?"

"I did okay." Vinnie shoved a briefcase across the table. "Your legal fees," he said.

Tommy Pro lifted the lid of the case and peeked inside, then closed the case and shoved it back across the table. "Completely unnecessary," he said.

"Tommy, you did the legal work, and you . . . made it possible for me to make the movie."

"I did all right, too, remember?"

"I remember, but it's not enough."

"I got a lot more than you did out of all this."

"How do you mean?"

Tommy shrugged. "Look around you. Where are we sitting?"

"You're the new . . . ?"

"I am. And if I say so myself, the family couldn't have done better."

"You're right, they couldn't do better."

"So what's next for you, Vinnie? Another movie?"

"A lot of movies," Vinnie replied. "I got a production deal at Centurion Pictures. I leave the day after tomorrow for L.A."

"So I'm going to know somebody in Hollywood? I get starlets when I come out?"

"You get whatever you want, and it'll always be on me."

"I'm looking forward," Tommy said.

"By the way, from now on I'm known as Michael Vincent. Think you can handle that?"

Tommy Pro stood up, grabbed Vinnie, and hugged him. "Michael," he said.

"I still owe you," Vinnie replied.

Vinnie's third meeting took place at Le Cirque, at lunch. Barbara, who was a regular, had booked the table. When the champagne had arrived he handed her the check.

"Just over a hundred percent profit in less than three months," she said, tucking it into her purse.

"Here's a statement of where all the money went," he said, handing her a sheet of paper.

She tore it up and put the pieces in the ashtray. "Honey, I've made a profit, and that's all I want. I don't care how much you skimmed off the top."

"Barbara, I assure you . . ."

She put a hand over his mouth. "I know you would never cheat me. I'm happy as a clam." She sipped her champagne. "But," she said, "I have the feeling I'm not going to be seeing as much of you."

He told her about his production deal with Centurion. "And it was all because you introduced me to Leo Goldman. I won't forget that."

She kissed a finger and placed it on his lips. "As long as you don't forget me," she said.

That afternoon, he picked up Vanessa from a modeling job and took her to the Palm Court of the Plaza for tea. When they had been served he handed her a slim book.

"What is it?" she asked, leafing through it.

"It's a little-known nineteen-twenties novel called *Pacific Afternoons*," he said. "It's a wonderful book, and it's going to be your first starring vehicle."

Vanessa jumped up and down and made little squealing noises.

Vinnie took a sheaf of papers from his briefcase and handed it to her with a pen. "You'll be under contract to me, personally, for five years, starting at five thousand dollars a week, with raises each year."

She took the pen and signed the contract.

"I think you should have your lawyer read it before you sign it," Vinnie said.

"I don't need a lawyer," she said. "I've got you."

Vinnie took a thick envelope from his briefcase. "Here's your first month's salary," he said. "Why don't you go shopping this afternoon? Save something for Rodeo Drive, though."

Her eyes widened. "Are we going to California?"

"The day after tomorrow, first class," he replied.

Vanessa got up from her chair, walked around the table, sat in his lap and began kissing him.

That night, *Downtown Nights* got a standing ovation at the film festival, and at a cocktail party afterward, Vinnie and Chuck received the congratulations of hundreds. The evening was marred only by Chuck's first sight of Vinnie with Vanessa.

* * *

The morning following the screening, Vinnie and Vanessa boarded an MGM Grand flight to Los Angeles. They settled into the luxurious seats and ordered champagne. Vinnie had a cashier's check in his pocket for six hundred and sixty thousand dollars, representing his profits thus far from *Downtown Nights,* and in a carry-on bag in the overhead compartment was two hundred and sixty thousand dollars in cash, representing his savings and the proceeds from the murder of Benedetto. He was not quite a millionaire.

As the airplane left Kennedy Airport and turned west, Vinnie looked down at lower Manhattan and raised his glass. "Good-bye Vinnie Callabrese," he whispered, "and hello Michael Vincent!"

12

Michael opened his eyes and listened hard. There was a noise, a sound he was unaccustomed to. The room was dark, and he wasn't sure where he was; then he recognized the sound.

He got out of bed and stumbled across the room, groping for the curtain pull. He swept open the drapes and blinked in the morning sunlight. A limb of a giant tree spanned the length of the windows, and on it sat two fat birds, singing loudly. Birds singing, Michael thought to himself. California!

Vanessa slept soundly, a mask over her eyes. Michael went to his luggage and dug out a small box, then went into the bathroom and regarded his image in the mirror. Vinnie Callabrese stared back at him. He opened the box and installed the batteries in the electric clippers. It took two minutes to dispose of Vinnie. He whipped up some lather and shaved off the remaining stubble. *There,* he said to himself, *finally*. Michael Vincent smiled back at him.

"Jesus," Vanessa said from behind him.

He turned and looked at her. "I thought you were sound asleep."

"The birds woke me up," she said. "You are gorgeous—you look so much better without the beard. All you need now is a haircut."

"It's Sunday; the barbershops are closed."

She dragged a stool over to the mirror and dug into her makeup kit, coming up with a shiny pair of scissors. "How do you think I made my living before I got a modeling job?"

"Are you any good?"

"Trust me," she smiled. "Now sit down and shut up. I know exactly how you should look."

Michael sat down nervously. "Not too much off," he said.

"I told you to shut up," she said, running her fingers through his thick hair, snipping away.

When she had finished, he stood up and looked closely at his reflection while she held a mirror behind his head. "It's a lot shorter," he said.

"It's a lot *better*," she replied. "Now you look like a businessman instead of a film student."

She ordered breakfast sent to the suite, and he went through the real estate section of the *Los Angeles Times*, occasionally marking something.

"What are you doing?" she asked.

"Looking for a place for us to live," he replied, marking another apartment.

"We'd better rent a car," she said, "if we're going househunting."

"That won't be necessary," he said. "I've arranged something."

At 10:00, Michael left the suite. "Meet me out front in fifteen minutes," he said to Vanessa, picking up his briefcase and the newspaper.

"Okay. How shall I dress?"

"Like a Californian out for a Sunday drive." He closed the door and stepped out onto a shaded walkway. He loved the Bel-Air Hotel, he thought as he walked through the densely planted gardens. He walked through the lobby and out the front entrance, then over a bridge. Below him, swans paddled up and down a little stream.

As he came to the parking lot an attendant approached. "Good morning, Mr. Vincent," the young man said. "There's a gentleman waiting for you just over there." He indicated the other side of the lot, where a man waited in the shade of a tree, leaning against a car.

Michael walked over to him, looking the car over closely.

"Mr. Vincent?" the man said, sticking out his hand. "My name's Torio. What do you think of the car?"

Michael walked slowly around the machine, a new Porsche Cabriolet, painted metallic black, with a black leather interior. "Have you got the title?" he asked.

The man opened a briefcase and handed him a

sheet of paper. "It's the real thing," he said. "All registered in your name."

"How do you do this?" Michael asked, looking at the title. "This looks genuine."

"It *is* genuine," the man replied, sounding hurt. "You think I'd palm off bad paper on a friend of Tommy Pro's?"

"I suppose not," Michael said.

"We got our own man at motor vehicle registrations," the man said, looking around him to make sure no one was listening. "When we yank a car we already got the numbers from a vehicle that's already trashed. This car has got less than a hundred miles real miles on it, but it's registered as last year's model. We turned up the speedometer to show three thousand miles. Our guy registers the car, and your title is absolutely clean, I guarantee it. You want to drive the car? It's perfect, I promise."

"That won't be necessary; I'll take your word for it." Michael opened his briefcase, took out a thick envelope, and handed it to the man. "Twenty-five thousand cash, as agreed."

He accepted the envelope. "I won't need to count it," he said, sticking out his hand again. "Give Tommy my best when you see him."

"I'll do that," Michael replied, shaking the man's hand.

"Oh," the man said, producing a business card. "If it ever comes up, you bought the car from this dealership out in the Valley, okay?"

"Okay," Michael replied and watched the man climb into a waiting car and be driven away. He got into the Porsche, started the engine, and drove up to the portico just as Vanessa appeared.

"Wow!" she said, running a hand over the car.

"Hop in, Ms. Parks," Michael replied, grinning. "Let's go find a place to live."

Late in the afternoon, after looking at half a dozen houses and apartments, Michael and Vanessa stood in the living room of a large penthouse in Century City.

"It's available for a year," the agent was saying. "The owner is making two films in Europe and will be based in London."

"We'll take it," Michael said.

"Well," the woman said, "I'm afraid there are three more people to see the place, then we'll pick the best-qualified tenant. There will be some formalities to go through."

"I don't think we need worry about formalities," Michael said.

"I beg your pardon?"

"I'll pay the year's rent in advance," he said, opening his briefcase, "in cash. Right now."

"In *cash*?"

"That's what I said. Now I'm sure you have a standard lease form in your briefcase, and if we can wrap this up *right now* there's a two-thousand-dollar bonus in it for you. In cash. And I don't think we'll find it necessary to mention this to your broker."

The woman licked her lips. "You say you're at Centurion?"

"Starting tomorrow. Leo Goldman's office will confirm."

"Well," she said, "I don't see why we can't forget the formalities."

When she had gone and the keys were in Michael's pocket, he and Vanessa stood on the terrace and looked out over the city. "Right out there," he said, pointing.

"Where?"

"Follow my finger; see the gate and the big sign?"

"Centurion Pictures," she said.

"I like being able to see it from here," he said.

"Michael, what'll we do when the year's lease is up?"

"Don't you worry, babe," he said, giving her a hug. "We'll find something a *lot* nicer."

When they had moved their things into the new apartment, Michael drove them out to Malibu, and they found a restaurant and a table overlooking the Pacific. As the sun went down, they raised their glasses. "To Hollywood," Michael said. "It's going to be ours."

13

Michael approached the gates of Centurion Pictures slowly. He had seen photographs and film of this famous entrance all his life, and he wanted to savor the moment.

He stopped at the little guardhouse, and for a moment he felt as though he were an intruder.

A uniformed guard stepped out. "May I help you?"

"My name is Michael Vincent," he said. "I . . ."

"Oh, yes, Mr. Vincent," the guard said, smiling. "Just a moment." He disappeared into the guardhouse and came back with a plastic sticker, which he affixed to the Porsche's windshield. "That'll get you in any time and without delay," he said. "The Executive Building is at the other end of the grounds. Take your first right and follow your nose. My name is Bill, if I can ever be of any service."

"Thank you, Bill," Michael said, smiling at the man. "I'll remember that." He drove slowly past a row of neatly painted bungalows; each had a sign out front with the occupant's name painted on it. He recognized the names of directors and writers. Then he turned right and found himself on a New York City street.

Downtown, he thought. Not Little Italy—the Village, maybe. Rows of neat brownstones ran down the block, with small shops interspersed. On an impulse he stopped the car and ran up the front steps of a house, peering through the glass of the front door. As he had expected, there was nothing beyond but a weeded lot and the back of another row of façades. The whole street was propped up with timbers.

He continued to the Executive Building and drove slowly around the parking lot, looking for a place. To his surprise, he found one marked by a freshly painted sign reading MR. VINCENT. He paused. Could there be another Vincent at Centurion? Then he decided the paint was so fresh, it must be his. He parked the Porsche, noting the distance from his parking place to the front entrance of the building. Not too far, he noted—at least, not as far as some.

The Executive Building was a substantial structure with a stone façade and a row of columns. There was an air of permanence about it. Michael trotted up the front steps and entered the building. A large desk straddled the broad hallway, occupied by two very busy telephone operators and a receptionist. She smiled coolly at him. "Good morning," she said. "May I help you?"

"My name is Michael Vincent," he said. "I'm . . ."

"Oh, yes, Mr. Vincent," she interrupted. "Just a moment, I'll ring Mr. Goldman's secretary for you. Won't you have a seat?"

Instead of sitting, Michael wandered up and down the entrance hall, inspecting the original posters that hung there—posters for movies that were like a history of his life, movies he'd seen at dozens of New York movie houses from his earliest years. There were many Academy Award-winners among them.

Shortly, a small, plump woman in a business suit appeared. "Mr. Vincent? I'm Helen Gordon, Mr. Goldman's secretary. Mr. Goldman isn't in yet—still recovering from jet lag, I believe. He's asked me to take care of you."

"How do you do?" Michael said, taking the woman's hand and turning on a businesslike charm. "I'm sure I'll be in good hands."

"Mr. Goldman thought one of two offices might be to your liking," she said. "Please follow me, and I'll show them to you."

Michael followed her up the broad staircase behind the reception desk, past a set of heavily varnished mahogany doors, then down a hallway that ran the length of the building. At the very end, she showed him a large office with a reception room of its own.

"It's very nice," Michael said noncommittally. He wanted to know what the second one was like before he chose.

"The other office is really a little building of its own," she said, leading him back down the hallway and out of the building. "It's only a short walk." She led him down a broad sidewalk that ran between two rows of huge, hangarlike sound-stages. At the end, she turned a corner, and they approached a small adobe building, one end of which was half a story higher than the other. Producing a key, she led him inside.

"This is very interesting," Michael said, looking around the empty reception area.

She opened the doors of two good-sized offices, then led him toward a large pair of double doors. "In the old days they used to shoot screen tests in this room," she said, opening the doors and stepping back for him to enter.

The room was large, with a very high ceiling. This was the extra half-story he had noticed from outside. Sunlight poured in through high windows at one end.

"By shooting tests here, they didn't take up time on the big stages," she said. "I think it's rather nice, don't you?"

"I do," he replied, turning to her. "May I ask your advice? Which should I take?"

Helen Gordon nearly blushed. "Well," she said haltingly, "there is a body of opinion which holds that it is not wise to work too close to Mr. Goldman's office. He does rather have a tendency to look over one's shoulder."

"I see." Michael laughed. "Well, I think I'll be very happy in this building. I'm going to need some space for one or two other people anyway."

"Good," she said. "Now, let's see about getting you some furnishings. Follow me." She led him out of the building and down the street. At a small door in what he assumed was a soundstage, she pressed a bell and waited. "I'll introduce you to George Hathaway," she said.

"The art director?" Michael asked. "I'd assumed he was dead."

"He's very much alive, I assure you, though he's sort of retired. He manages props and costumes now. Mr. Goldman has kept a number of the old-timers on retainer. They seem to prefer it to a pension."

The door opened and a tall, slender, elderly man with a clipboard in his hand waved them in. "Good morning, Helen," he said.

"Good morning, Mr. Hathaway. I'd like you to meet Michael Vincent, who's going to be producing on the lot."

"I'm an admirer of your work," Michael said to the man, shaking his hand. "I've always been particularly impressed with your designs for *Fair Weather* and *Border Village*."

Hathaway beamed. "How very nice of you to say so." He seemed to have a slight English accent.

"George," Helen Gordon said, "Mr. Vincent has decided to use the old screen test building. Do you think you could put together some furnishings for him? Mr. Goldman says he's to have whatever he wants."

"Why, of course, Helen," Hathaway replied. "I'd be delighted. I'm always happy to have a new producer for a client."

"Mr. Vincent," Helen said, "I'll leave you in George's capable hands. When you've finished here, come on back to the Executive Building;

Mr. Goldman should be in by that time, and he'll want to greet you himself."

"Thank you, Helen," Michael replied.

She left the building, and George Hathaway beckoned for Michael to follow. He led the way to another door and opened it.

Michael stepped through the door and stared. What he had thought was a soundstage was a vast warehouse of furniture and other objects, stacked high on steel shelving. The central aisle seemed nearly to vanish into the distance. "It's like something out of *Citizen Kane*, Mr. Hathaway," he said wonderingly.

George Hathaway laughed. "Yes, I suppose it is. And please, you must call me George."

"And I'm Michael."

"Let's have a wander around, and if you see a desk or a sofa or anything else that catches your eye, you just let me know."

Michael followed the old man slowly through the building, gazing at the collection of seventy years of movie making—furniture, paintings, objets d'art, hat racks, spittoons, bars from English pubs and Western saloons. At the end of a row, Michael spotted something familiar. Leaning against the outside wall was an eight-foot-wide stretch of oak panelling surrounding a stone fireplace. "George, isn't that the fireplace from Randolph's study in *The Great Randolph*?"

"It is," George beamed, "and how nice it is to find someone with the eye to recognize it."

"I always loved that room," Michael said.

"When I was about twelve, I had this fantasy of living in it."

"Tell me," George said, scratching his chin, "were you thinking of using the tall room for your office?"

"Yes, I was."

"Well, you know, that whole study is here in this warehouse—the desk, furniture, books— everything, and I think it might fit the tall room, with an adjustment or two. How would you like it if I reassembled it for you?"

"You could do that?"

"Of course. Mr. Goldman says you're to have whatever you want."

"That would be absolutely wonderful, George. I'll feel like Randolph himself."

"Consider it done. Will you want the other rooms furnished?"

"Yes, I'll be hiring a few people soon."

"Well, if you'll leave it to me, I'll choose some things for them."

"Thank you very much."

George picked up a phone against the wall and punched in a number. "I'll get a crew on it right away," he said. "We're not too busy at the moment, so I should be ready for you tomorrow."

"Tomorrow? As soon as that?"

"Well, Michael," George Hathaway said, "this is Hollywood, after all."

Michael left the warehouse and started back toward the Executive Building walking on air, headed for his first meeting with Leo Goldman. He passed a small bungalow, and through the open windows came the sounds of a string quartet, playing something Michael didn't know. He thought it must be recorded, but when he stopped and looked inside, he saw three elderly men and a woman playing their instruments, lost in the music. He continued on toward the Executive Building. This was indeed Hollywood, he thought.

14

Michael entered the Executive Building again and found Helen Gordon waiting for him.

"Oh, good," she said. "Mr. Goldman has just come in. Let's go up to his office."

At the top of the stairs she opened one of the large, gleaming mahogany doors he had noticed before and led him through an elegant waiting room where two young women were typing furiously on word processors. Helen rapped on an inner door, then opened it and showed Michael into Leo Goldman's office. The room was large enough to contain a huge desk, a pair of leather sofas in front of a fireplace, a grand piano, and a conference table with seating for twelve. One wall was a floor-to-ceiling bookcase with a ladder on rails. Leo Goldman sat in a large leather chair, his feet on his desk, talking into a telephone headset that was plugged into one ear. He waved Michael to one of the sofas and continued talking rapidly.

Michael sat down and regarded the room's furnishings. Every object seemed to be the best of its kind, carefully chosen to make the enormous room comfortable and beautiful.

Leo tossed the headset onto his desk, walked the twenty feet to where Michael sat, shook his hand, and sprawled on the opposite sofa. "Well, did you have a good flight?"

"Yes, just fine, Leo."

"Your rooms at the Bel-Air all right?"

"Perfect. We enjoyed it, but we've already found an apartment in Century City."

"Good; fast work. Who's *we*?"

"My lady friend, Vanessa Parks."

Goldman nodded. "Have you moved in yet?"

"Vanessa is moving us today."

"Will we meet her tomorrow night at dinner?"

"You will."

"Good; Amanda will be delighted. By the way, is there anybody special you'd like to meet?"

"At dinner?" Michael asked, a little nonplussed.

"Sure. Anybody in town you'd like me to ask?"

"I don't know a soul here."

Leo shook his head. "I mean, is there *anybody* you'd like to meet?"

Jesus, Michael thought, can he just summon anybody he wants? "Well, there are lots of people I'd like to meet."

"Name somebody."

Michael thought. "Yes. I'd like to meet Mark

Adair." He had read in the *Times* that the novelist was in town.

"I'll see what I can do," Leo said.

"And I'd like to meet Robert Hart."

"Well, at least you want to meet movie stars, just like everybody else," Leo said, laughing. "Bob Hart is just back from a month at Betty Ford's," he said. "Booze, not drugs. He hasn't worked in over a year."

"If you don't think it's a good idea . . ."

"No, it's fine; I like Bob, and I've always loved his work. His wife can be a little hard to take." He picked up a phone on the coffee table between the sofas, pressed a button, and spoke. "Helen, invite Bob and Sue Hart to dinner tomorrow night; you've got the number. And call the Beverly Hills and see if Mark Adair is there; ask him, too. Let me know." He hung up. "If they're not in town, think of somebody else."

"This is very kind of you, Leo," Michael said, meaning it.

"Not at all." Leo leaned back on the sofa and threw a leg onto the cushions. "Now. Let me tell you about Centurion. You may already have heard some of it, but I'll tell you again."

"Fine."

"Centurion was founded in 1937 by Sol Weinman, who had run an important unit at MGM for Irving Thalberg. When Thalberg died, Sol couldn't stomach being directly under L. B. Mayer, so he got out. Sol was a rich man—inherited—and he got some other rich men together and started Centurion. They bought a broken-down Poverty

Row studio that had some good real estate, built four soundstages, and started to make pictures. It was tough at first, because they had to borrow talent from the majors and that was expensive, but they had a string of hit pictures, and by the time the war was over Sol had bought out his partners and had a profitable studio. He ran his own show, the way Sam Goldwyn did, and his pictures were at least as good. When TV came along, he didn't get hurt quite as badly as MGM and the other big studios; his overhead was lower, and he kept on making good pictures until he died twenty years ago.

"The studio floundered around for a while, had some hits and some flops, but it was going downhill pretty fast. Fifteen years ago, I borrowed a lot of money and put together a deal with some investors to buy the studio from Sol's widow. I kept control. I moved in here, sold the back lot to some developers, paid off most of the debt with the proceeds, and Centurion was back in business. I expect you know our output pretty well since then."

"Yes, I do, and I admire it."

"Thanks, you ought to; we do good work here. I keep the overhead low; we rent a lot of space to people whose work I like—you've seen the signs outside the buildings."

"Yes."

"I hung onto props and costumes, mostly out of sentiment, I guess, and we rent to everybody; just about breaks even. We've still got the four soundstages Sol built, plus two more, and we keep 'em busy. We make a dozen or so pictures a year, and a lot more get made on the lot by independents." Leo leaned forward and rested his elbows on his knees.

"What I want from you is a new picture next year, while you're getting your feet on the ground, and then two pictures a year after that. I want good work on tight budgets, commercial enough to make money. We've had a blockbuster or two around here, but that's not what pays the rent. We do it with good material, intelligently made, year in and year out. Once in a while I like a beautiful little picture, something a little arty that doesn't lose too much money. It's good for the studio, and you can get expensive talent to work cheap in a project like that. You cop an occasional Oscar that way, too.

"I have broad tastes; I like cop movies, comedies, heavy drama, classy horror, medical stories, westerns, biographies, musicals—God, I *love* musicals, but you can't make 'em any more without losing your ass. I'm *very* leery of blockbuster-type material, unless there's an absolutely *superb* script before another dime is spent. I tell you the truth, if Arnold Schwarzenegger came to me today with just an *idea* for something like that, I'd say, 'Thank you very much, Arnold, but fuck off until you've got a script that puts my blood pressure dangerously up.' I swear to God. What makes a blockbuster a blockbuster changes so quickly that it scares me to death. My idea of a nightmare is a movie—any kind of movie—that goes into production without a perfected script. I know, I know, *Casablanca* started without a finished script, but that's a very wild exception. Don't ever come to me, Michael, with a script you know is half-baked and ask me to make it. Don't ever commit me to a star without a finished script. You'll end up making a hash of it, trying to get it written while the star is still available, and you'll hurt us both. If you've got a *good* script, there's *always* a star available, believe me.

"We've got a television production company on the lot that does very nicely. If you come across something you don't want to make, but that you think would make a good TV movie, mini-series, or series, send it to me. You'll make friends on the lot that way. Speaking of making friends, you're going to have a hard time doing that. Studio executives are envious of guys with production deals, and my people are no exception. They make a lot of money for what they do, but they know that you have the *potential* of making a hell of a lot more, and that drives 'em crazy, so if you want to get along with the people in this building, work at it. Do them favors, compliment their work, kiss their asses when you can stomach it, and if somebody gets in your way, go around him, not through him.

"I know you're smart, Michael, and I don't have to tell you this, but I'm going to anyway. You're a young guy, good-looking, in a glamorous business with money to throw around. Be careful. Don't get into debt—in fact, pay cash for everything you possibly can. Don't use drugs. I've seen fifty bright young guys go right down the tubes on that stuff. Don't let your dick get in the way of your business. I'm glad to hear you've got a girl, because there are ten thousand women in this town who will suck your cock for a walk-on as a hatcheck girl in a bad movie, and a thousand who can do it so well they'll make you forget your business and do the wrong thing."

Leo sat back and took a deep breath. "That's all I can think of at the moment."

"Thank you, Leo," Michael said. "It's all good advice, and I'll try to follow it."

"Now," Leo said. "About *Downtown Nights*. I'm going to open it on a total of nine screens in New York and L.A. the week before Thanksgiving."

Michael's face fell, and he started to speak.

Leo held up a hand. "Wait a minute," he said, "let me finish. I'm going to run it for two weeks, then pull it until after the New Year. Between Thanksgiving and Christmas I'm going to screen the shit out of it on the lot, and we're going to get some good word-of-mouth going. Then, in mid-January, when a lot of big Christmas releases are starting to drop out of sight, I'm going to open it on twelve hundred screens and spend eight million dollars on advertising and promotion. It's good timing for the Academy Awards, and believe me, Carol Geraldi is going to be nominated. We'll do thirty, forty million, and with what we've got invested, that'll be a solid hit for us."

"Sounds wonderful," Michael said.

"Damn right," Leo said, looking at his watch. "I've got a lunch," he said. "I wanted to take you somewhere, but this can't be postponed. You take the rest of the day off; your office won't be ready until tomorrow anyway, and you need to get moved into your new place. Come over to the house early tomorrow night—say, six o'clock—that'll give us an hour to talk before the others get there. I want to hear about what you want to do next."

"Fine, I'll look forward to it."

Leo walked to his desk, retrieved a sheet of paper, then walked Michael to the door. "Here," he said, handing him the paper. "I had Helen put this together for you, stuff you'll need. Doctor, dentist, bank, barber, maid service, florist, caterer, whatever I could think of. There's a list of good restaurants. I've had Helen call them and tell them who you are, so don't worry about getting in. My address and home phone are there, too. See you tomorrow at six."

Five minutes later, Michael stood in the parking lot and watched Leo Goldman being driven off in an enormous Mercedes. Through the back window, he could see the phone at Leo's ear.

He got into the Porsche and just sat for a moment, remembering everything Leo had said. Michael had a superb memory. He could have recited it all verbatim.

15

Michael had a prearranged appointment downtown at 2:30, and there was time to stop along the way and shop for a car phone. He bought a handheld portable, too, and left the car for the phone installation. He took a shopping bag from the trunk and walked to his meeting a few blocks away.

He checked the directory in the lobby of a gleaming skyscraper and took the elevator to the top floor, to the offices of a discreet private bank. The Kensington Trust, the lettering on the glass doors told him, was based in London and had branches in New York, Los Angeles, Bermuda, Hong Kong, and the Cayman Islands.

At the reception desk he gave his name as Vincente Callabrese and asked for Derek Winfield. He was shown immediately to a panelled office with a spectacular view of the L.A. smog.

Winfield, a tall, thin man in his fifties wearing a Savile Row suit, rose to meet him. "Good afternoon, Mr. Callabrese," he said, extending a soft and beautifully manicured hand, "I've been expecting you." He offered Michael a chair.

"How do you do, Mr. Winfield?" Michael replied. "I expect you've been told of my banking needs."

"Yes, yes, our mutual friend in New York called a week ago. We're always happy to do business with friends of his. Have you known each other long?"

"Mr. Winfield," Michael said, ignoring the question, "I would like to open an investment account with you."

"Of course," Winfield replied. "I understood from Mr. Provensano that you also had something in mind."

"That's correct," Michael said, taking an envelope from his pocket. "Here is a cashier's check on my New York bank for six hundred and sixty thousand dollars." He placed the shopping bag on Winfield's desk. "There is a further one hundred thousand dollars cash in this bag." He endorsed the cashier's check. "I want to invest the entire amount on the street."

"I see," Winfield said. "What sort of a return were you anticipating on your investment?"

"Our friend said I could expect three percent a week; that's good enough for me."

"I think we can manage that," Winfield replied. "How would you like to collect the interest?"

"I'd like to roll it into the principal each week. From time to time I may withdraw some capital, but I expect this to be an investment of at least a year, perhaps much longer." Michael knew that if he took the interest each week, the annual income on his investment would be in excess of a million dollars, but if he let the interest ride, compounding weekly, his income would be much, much more, and it would be tax-free. The loan sharks would be lending his money at ten percent a week, so everybody would make money.

"Will you require facilities for, ah, movement of funds?" Winfield asked.

"Perhaps; I'm not certain at the moment."

"There would, of course, be a charge for that service."

"Of course. In such a case, how would the money be returned to me?"

"We could arrange for you to collect fees as a consultant to one of a number of corporations," Winfield explained. "You would have to pay taxes on the proceeds, of course, since the relevant corporation would be filing Form 1099 with the Internal Revenue Service. We could also move the funds through our Cayman branch, but in order to have safe access to them in this country you would have to travel there and return with cash. One must be careful with large sums of cash these days."

"I understand."

"If you will wait a moment, I'll get you a receipt. Oh, how shall I list the name and address of the account?"

"My name, but no address; just keep my statements on file here, and I'll pick them up when it's necessary."

Winfield smiled. "Of course," he said, then left the room.

Michael wandered around the office, inspecting paintings and looking out at the view. A few minutes later, Winfield returned.

"Here is your receipt," the banker said.

Winfield saw him to the elevator. "You may call me at any time for a confirmation of your current balance," he said.

"Thank you," Michael replied. He boarded the elevator, pressed the button for the lobby, and rode down feeling very rich.

That night, Michael and Vanessa dined at Granita, Wolfgang Puck's new restaurant in Malibu. The headwaiter had been solicitous when Michael had called at the last minute. Leo Goldman's name worked wonders.

They sipped champagne while Michael touched on the highlights of his day. "What did you do?" Michael asked.

"Oh, I moved our luggage into the apartment and got the phone working, then I did a little shopping on Rodeo Drive."

"How much did you spend?"

"Does it matter?" she asked kittenishly.

"Not at all," he laughed. "It comes out of your pay. But then, you're very well paid, aren't you?"

"I'd like a car, Michael. Do you think that would be all right?"

"Of course; what would you like?"

"One of those new Mercedes convertibles, I think. Silver."

"I think you can afford that," he said.

"When do I start to earn my keep?" she asked.

"You mean, when do you become a movie star?"

"That's exactly what I mean," she said.

"You begin tomorrow night," Michael said, touching his glass to hers. "All you have to do is relax and be your charming self."

16

Michael arrived at his offices the following morning and was not surprised to find workmen in the place. A pair of men were hammering in one of the small offices off the reception room. Hollywood or not, he thought, nobody could put all this together in a day.

The doors to his office had been replaced by a heavy, dark-stained oaken set; he passed through and stopped, staring. He was standing in the study from *The Great Randolph*, complete in every detail. One entire wall, floor to ceiling, was covered with bookcases, and they were filled with leatherbound books in matched sets. The opposite wall was panelled and covered in paintings that looked English—portraits of men in uniform and women in ball gowns, landscapes and still lifes, and one or two that appeared to be old masters. In that wall was a huge fireplace, and over the mantel hung a full-length portrait of Randolph himself, replete in white tie and tails, looking sternly toward Michael.

"A very impressive fellow, isn't he?" a voice behind him said.

Michael turned to find George Hathaway standing there.

"Sir Henry Algood as Randolph," Hathaway said. "I knew him well, before the war. Mind you, the portrait adds about a head in height to the old boy, that's why he loved it so much. He tried a dozen times to buy it, but he and Sol Weinman had some sort of falling out, and it gave Mr. Weinman the greatest pleasure to deny him the picture."

"George, I'm overwhelmed by the room," Michael said.

"Let me show you a few modifications," Hathaway said. "The width was perfect, but the room was about eight inches too long for the set. We made a false wall, then made good around the windows." He opened a cupboard to reveal a gas bottle. "This runs the fireplace. Don't ask how we did the flue, and don't, for Christ's sake, ever try to burn anything but gas in it." He walked across the room and behind the massive desk facing the fireplace, then pulled out a couple of large drawers. "We managed to conceal a couple of filing cabinets in here, but if you run out of space we'll have to add some cabinets to the reception room. Incidentally, we've found some panelling for that area that matches this pretty well, and there's a good desk for out there, too. Not a single one of the books is anything but a spine," he said, hooking a fingernail over one and pulling away a whole row of them to reveal a small wet bar. He opened another spine-concealed door and showed Michael a small refrigerator with an icemaker.

"It's astonishing," Michael said, meaning it. "This really is Hollywood, isn't it?"

"As real as it gets," Hathaway said.

Michael set his briefcase on the desk and took out a copy of *Pacific Afternoons*. "George," he said, handing him the book, "have you ever read this?"

"No," Hathaway replied, "but I know a little about it."

"I'd appreciate it if you'd read it. I'd like to get your advice on how it might be designed for a film."

"Of course, Michael, glad to."

There was a knock at the door, and Helen Gordon appeared, followed by a tall, handsome woman who appeared to be in her early forties, wearing a well-designed business suit.

"I'd better get going," Hathaway said. "I'll read this tonight." He left the room and Michael was alone with the two women.

"Mr. Vincent," Helen said, "I'd like you to meet Margot Gladstone."

"How do you do?" the woman said.

Michael shook the woman's hand, admiring her poise and the low, mellifluous voice that accompanied it. "I'm very glad to meet you, Ms. Gladstone."

Helen spoke again. "Mr. Goldman has suggested that Margot serve as your secretary. She's been with the studio for quite some time, and he thought she might help you find your feet."

"That was very kind of him," Michael said. "Perhaps Ms. Gladstone and I could have a talk?"

"Of course," Helen said. "Call me if there's anything you need." She took her leave.

"Will you have a seat, Ms. Gladstone?" Michael asked, showing her to one of the leather Chesterfield sofas before the fireplace.

"Thank you," she replied, sitting down and crossing her long legs. "And please do call me Margot."

"Thank you, Margot." Michael caught her accent. "I didn't realize at first that you were British."

"I was, a very long time ago," she replied. "I've been in this country since I was nineteen."

"It hasn't harmed your accent a bit," he said.

She smiled broadly, revealing beautiful teeth. "Thank you. I learned early on that Hollywood loves an English accent, so I made a point of hanging on to it."

Michael sat down opposite her and regarded her quizzically. "Certainly I can use someone who is at home in the studio," he said, "but I'm puzzled about something."

"Perhaps I can clear it up for you?"

"Perhaps you can, and I hope you'll be frank with me."

"Of course."

"Why am I, the new boy on the lot, being rewarded with such an elegant and, no doubt, accomplished assistant? Surely there are top studio executives ahead of me in line who would be very pleased to have you working for them."

She regarded him coolly. "You're very direct, Mr. Vincent."

"It saves time."

"Very well," she said. "I don't see why you shouldn't know what everybody else on the lot already knows."

"And what is that?"

"Let me begin at the beginning. I was born in a village called Cowes, on the Isle of Wight, daughter of a butcher. I exhibited some talent for drama at school, and afterwards I sought a career on the London stage. I got a small part in a Noël Coward play almost immediately, and almost immediately after that, Sol Weinman saw the play and came backstage to see me. He offered me a studio contract, and within a month I was on the Centurion lot, the perfect little English starlet.

"I played small parts and an occasional second lead for a few years, and then the studio system came crashing down around me. Being of a practical bent, I went to Mr. Weinman and asked him for a secretarial job. He put me to work as one of half a dozen girls in his office, and then, a couple of years later, he died.

"When Leo Goldman took over the studio I remained in the office and, eventually, became his secretary. We had an affair; it ended when he married. It became awkward having me around, so Leo passed me on to the studio's head of production, Martin Bell, and I became his secretary. We had an affair.

"This continued until quite recently, when, in short order, his marriage ended, and he married a girl in her twenties." She spread her hands. "So, you see, I'm awkward again, and nobody else in the Executive Building wants me in his office. Everyone is afraid I'll report back to either Martin or Leo. I'm regarded as something of a political bombshell."

"I see," Michael said. "Apart from your personal relationships with Leo and Bell, are you very good at your work?"

"I am very good indeed," she replied evenly.

"Didn't it occur to you to seek work at another studio? Surely with your background you would be a good candidate for secretary to some top executive."

"I am fifty-one years old," she replied. "I have twenty-three years vested in the studio pension plan, not to mention profit sharing and my Screen Actors Guild pension. All that matures in two years; then I can take my pensions and my profits and my savings and do as I please."

"Well, Margot," Michael said, "I think I would be very lucky to have you spend those two years with me."

"Thank you," she replied, "I think I would like that, as well."

"I must tell you: I'm new at this, and I'm going to need all the help I can get. You might make it your most important duty to keep me from making an ass of myself."

Margot laughed. "I am so glad you are intelligent enough to know that. I think we'll get along."

"I think we will, too," he replied. And, he thought to himself, you are not only going to keep me out of trouble, you are going to tell me, in very short order, where the bodies are buried in this studio—and who buried them. "Let's get to work."

She stood up. "Fine. Why don't we start with these?" She walked over to a table against the wall and picked up a stack of half a dozen packages.

"What are those?"

"These are scripts."

"From where?"

"From all over the place. Your deal with Centurion was reported in the trade press on Friday. You'll get more scripts tomorrow; it's best if we deal with them directly. You'll get a reputation around town as somebody who doesn't waste time."

"When am I going to have time to read them?"

"You won't have time; I'll screen them first." She began looking at the return addresses on the packages. "This one's been around for years," she said, tossing it back onto the table. "This writer's an unreliable drunk; this one's from an agent who doesn't represent anybody worth reading; this one's from a New York playwright who hasn't had anything produced since the mid-eighties—still, it might be worth reading; I'll look it over for you."

"What's next?" he asked.

"I'll order you some studio stationery and some business cards and get you subscriptions to the trades; leave restaurant bookings and screening invitations to me; I'll handle your expense reports; if you need a house, a haircut, or a whore, let me know, and I'll arrange it. I'll tell you what I know about the people you'll be working with."

That, he thought, *is what I want to know.*

"There's something you could do for me right away," he said.

"Of course."

"I want you to call every used bookstore in the Yellow Pages and buy every copy you can find of a novel called *Pacific Afternoons*. Please send a messenger to pick them up; I'd like them by four o'clock."

She smiled. "Not taking any chances, are you?"

Michael smiled back. "I never do."

17

Michael and Vanessa found the Bel-Air house of Leo and Amanda Goldman on Stone Canyon, up the street from the Bel-Air Hotel. Michael pulled the Porsche into the driveway at precisely 6:00, and he thought he had never seen anything so beautiful.

There was no imposing edifice, just a comfortable-looking exterior that only hinted at what must be a large place. Michael had not yet become accustomed to the profusion of plant life that could exist in a desert when it was well watered; the landscaping looked as if it had always been there.

Leo answered the door himself, clad in a plaid sport jacket over an open-neck shirt. "Come in, come in," he said, giving Vanessa a huge smile.

"Leo," Michael said, "this is Vanessa Parks."

"She certainly is," Leo said, clasping her hand in both of his. "Welcome to Los Angeles and welcome to our home."

Amanda Goldman appeared, wearing a floral-printed silk dress and a knockout hairdo. "Michael," she said, pecking his cheek rather close to the corner of his mouth, "how nice to see you again." She turned to the younger woman. "And you must be Vanessa."

"Hello," Vanessa said shyly.

"You come with me," Amanda said to her. "I know Michael and Leo have some talking to do, so I'll show you the garden."

The two women departed together, and Leo led Michael into a small study lined with books and pictures.

"Let me get you a drink," Leo said.

"Just some mineral water. I'll have some wine with dinner."

Leo went to a butler's tray that held drinks and poured Michael a Perrier and himself a large Scotch. They sat down in comfortable chairs before the fireplace and raised their glasses to each other.

"So," Leo said. "How are you settling in?"

"Very well, thanks. We're comfortable in the new apartment, and amazingly, George Hathaway has managed to put my office together in little more than a single day."

"I heard about the *Randolph* set." Leo chuckled. "It's all over the lot already. Expect people to drop in to see you just to see that room."

"I hope I haven't overdone it," Michael said.

"Don't worry about it. A little flamboyance is good for business in this business. What do you think of Margot?"

"I'm very impressed with her; thank you for sending her to me."

"She's a smart girl," Leo said, nodding in agreement with himself. "We were an item a few years back. She's a few years older than I am, but it never seemed to matter." He raised a warning finger. "Never mention her name in Amanda's presence."

Michael nodded.

"Treat her well, and she'll help you more than you can believe."

"I'll remember that; she's easy to treat well."

"What's this about you cornering the market on some book?"

"You heard about that?" Michael asked, surprised.

"Of course. My girl, Helen, doesn't miss anything on the lot." He raised a hand. "I swear, I'm not getting stuff on you from Margot."

"The book is the next project I want to do," Michael said.

"What is it? Helen didn't pick up on the title."

"*Pacific Afternoons*. It was written in the twenties by a woman named Mildred Parsons; the only thing she ever wrote."

"I read it at Stanford," Leo said. He got up and walked along a bookcase for a moment, then plucked out a slim, leatherbound volume and handed it to Michael.

"You had it bound?"

"I liked it that much," Leo said. "How the hell did you ever come across it?"

"A girl I knew in New York passed it on to me. I was enchanted."

"You think a movie could make money?"

"I do," Michael replied. "If it's a quality production, using the right people."

Leo sat up straight. "Wait a minute," he said. "Now I know why you wanted Mark Adair and Bob Hart here tonight."

Michael nodded.

Leo pondered this for a moment. "They're both perfect," he said, "but Hart will never do it."

"Why not? He's not in all that much demand these days, is he?"

"Nope. He made two expensive flops—I mean flops with the best people—and then he hit the bottle hard."

"Does he look like staying sober?"

"So I hear."

"So what's the problem?"

"His wife. Susan will never let him do it."

"Does he listen to her about these things?"

"He relies on her completely. She's the one you'd have to sell, and she'll never buy it. Bob is fifty-four or -five, but Susan sees him the way he was ten years ago, still making big-time thrillers, playing cops and cowboys."

"He was at the Actors Studio, wasn't he?"

"He was, and he was outstanding there. Then he came out here and went for the big bucks, and although he helped support the Studio for years with the money he made, Lee Strasberg would barely speak to him."

"Maybe he's ready for a change of pace, then."

Leo gave a short laugh. "Sure he is, but Susan isn't. She handled his money well and he's a rich man, so he doesn't *have* to make movies."

"He's an actor, isn't he? How many actors have you known who'd turn down a really good part like this one?"

"Not many. Brando; that's about it. Sure, Bob's an actor, but never underestimate an actor's vanity. If Susan tells him it's wrong for his image, that's it, he won't do it."

"I would *really* like him for the part."

"You brought some books?"

"Yes, they're in the car."

"We're going to screen *Downtown Nights* after dinner. My advice is, give both Bob and Susan the book, then get her alone and try to tell her before they leave. For Christ's sake, don't tell her what the book is about during dinner; she'll have already made up her mind before you can talk to her."

"All right, I'll do that."

"Adair's a different sell. I think you must know that he's mainly a novelist; everything he's done as a screenplay is a small, beautiful, and vaguely important film."

"Yes, that describes it well."

"Try and challenge him in some way; don't just offer him a job."

"All right."

"Who do you want for the girl? You'll need somebody hot to make the picture noticed."

"You met her a few minutes ago."

Leo's eyebrows went up. "Your girl? Vanessa?"

Michael nodded. "Vanessa Parks."

Leo gazed into his drink. "Michael, didn't you hear anything I said to you yesterday? She's gorgeous, I'll grant you that, but you're following your cock around."

"No," Michael said, "I'm not. She's going to be startlingly good in this picture, Leo. In some ways, Vanessa *is* the girl in the book. It will come naturally to her, and she has it in her to be a very good actress. All she needs is some confidence, and this picture will give it to her."

Leo shook his head. "I don't know."

"Leo," Michael said, leaning forward, "I've got a budget together on this. I can shoot it in northern California for eight million dollars, *if* I can keep salaries in line. If I cast an established star, her money is going to put everybody else's money up. Which would you rather have, a twenty-five-million-dollar movie with a star in that role, or an eight-million-dollar movie with a girl who will be a star as soon as it's released?"

"I like your economics," Leo said. "You feel that strongly about Vanessa in the role?"

"Yes, I do."

"Well, I'm paying you for your judgment," he said. "Just be sure you give me my money's worth."

Michael stood up. "I promise you, I will."

"By the way," Leo said, "I suppose you've optioned the book."

Michael shook his head and smiled. "The copyright expires in three weeks."

"Absolutely not," Leo said.

"What?"

"Option the book *tomorrow*. You should be able to lowball the heirs, but I'm not going to have articles in the trades saying how Centurion waited for expiration, then pounced."

"All right, I'll option it tomorrow."

"Who were you thinking about for a director?"

"George Cukor, if I could raise him from the dead. I want someone like him, who's good with women."

"How about the guy who directed *Downtown Nights* for you? He did a good job."

"He's wrong for this; believe me, I know him. I'll use him again, but not for this." Michael knew he was in a position to reap good publicity for his first film, and that if Chuck Parish directed his second film, the industry would think of them as partners, and he would be sharing the glory. He wanted somebody else.

"Let me know who you want."

The doorbell rang.

"Let's go meet the others," Leo said.

The two men rose and started for the door.

"By the way," Leo said, "Bob Hart is shorter than you think; don't look surprised."

18

Robert Hart was indeed shorter than Michael had thought. Even in the cowboy boots he was wearing, he came only up to Michael's chin. He had lost weight and become grayer than in his last film, too, and Michael immediately saw him as Doctor Madden in *Pacific Afternoons*.

His wife, Susan, was very small and pretty, with graying blonde hair pulled back in a bun, but in the firmness of her handshake and the directness of her gaze, Michael saw the kind of strength that her husband lacked.

Hart was cordial, but reserved; he was obviously accustomed to homage from others, and he accepted it in a charming, almost princely way. Susan was talkative and down-to-earth. They seemed a compatible pair.

"What are you doing next?" Leo asked Hart when they had settled in the living room for drinks.

Susan Hart spoke before her husband could.

"We're looking at a couple of offers," she said. "Everybody's after Bob."

The doorbell rang again, and a moment later Amanda brought Mark Adair into the room. Adair was expansive and witty from the moment he arrived, Michael thought. He was sixty-ish, white-haired, and conveyed a sort of rumpled elegance—just the right image for an eminent novelist.

When they were seated, Leo again asked the mandatory question: "What are you up to, Mark? What brings you to the Coast?"

"Turning down awful ideas, mostly," he said cheerfully. "Paramount got me out here on the pretext of doing something significant, but it was junk. Half a dozen Hollywood hacks could do it better than I. Why the hell do you think they would even consider me for that sort of stuff?"

"They want the weight of your name to give some substance to their project," Leo said smoothly.

"You're so full of horseshit, Leo," Adair said, but he basked in the compliment nevertheless.

A man in a white jacket entered the room and announced dinner.

They dined in a glassed-in room with tile floors and many plants. Since Adair had come alone, the usual man-woman alternation had not worked at Amanda Goldman's table, and Michael was seated between Amanda and Mark Adair.

"I've greatly enjoyed your work over the years," Michael said to Adair when he had a chance. "I particularly enjoyed *Halls of Ice*." It was the only book of Adair's he had read.

"Thank you," Adair said, beaming as if he had never received a compliment. "Leo tells me you've produced an outstanding film, and that we're seeing it after dinner."

"I just learned that myself," Michael said, "and when you see it, I hope you won't think that my interests are confined to that genre."

"I'll try to keep an open mind," Adair replied.

"In fact, I'm putting something together right now, and it occurs to me that you might be the only writer I know who could do it justice."

"Michael," Adair said, "you may be new out here, but you've certainly copped on to the Hollywood horseshit in a hurry."

Michael laughed. "When you know more about the project you may think I was only speaking the truth."

"Tell me about it," Adair said.

Michael looked around to be sure everyone else was absorbed in their own conversations. "Do you remember a novel called *Pacific Afternoons*?"

Adair nodded. "I read it as a teenager, did a high school book report on it, in fact, but for the life of me the only thing I can remember about it is a scene where the middle-aged doctor sings to the young girl."

"It was Mildred Parsons's only novel; she committed suicide a year or so later, before the book had achieved a wide readership."

"I remember something about that."

"I think she would have had a brilliant career," Michael said, "and I think it's a great pity that the book isn't better known than it is."

"Well, that's a nice ambition for a dead author. I hope when I'm gone somebody will think as kindly of me. Now, why do you think I'm so uniquely qualified to adapt this book?"

"Because you're the sort of novelist that Mildred Parsons was; your sensibilities are not those of a Hollywood hack, as you put it earlier, but those of a genuine writer. The novel is highly adaptable for film, but I want it preserved as Parsons wrote it, both in structure and intent. The dialogue in the book is brilliant—you may not have considered it so as a teenager, but when you read it again, you'll see what I mean."

Michael took a deep breath. "Look, this is the main reason I'd like you to do it: Writers have egos like everyone else, of course, but a Hollywood screenwriter would take this book and, in adapting it, rewrite it to make himself look good. What I want is for Mildred Parsons to look good, for her book to be seen almost as it is read, and it will take a very fine novelist to do that. The success of the book rests entirely on the feeling that she put into it—it was almost certainly autobiographical—and I want someone to get inside her head and put that very real emotion and sentiment on the screen."

Adair looked thoughtful. "Sentiment is a good word for that book," he said. "I recall it as conveying sentiment without sentimentality."

"Then you already know what I want," Michael said. "All that remains is for you to read the book again."

"I'll be glad to."

"You'll have a copy before the evening is over," Michael said.

When the screening was over and Michael had accepted the praise of those present, Leo leaned close to him and said, "I'll tackle Bob Hart; you take on Susan."

Michael found her in the hallway on her way back from the ladies' room. "Susan," he said, taking her arm, "Leo is in there offering Bob a part. I'd like to talk with you about it for a moment, if I may."

"All right," she said.

He steered her through some French doors into the garden and found a bench for them to occupy. The California night air was heavy with the scent of tropical blossoms. Michael looked her in the eye. "I wanted to talk with you because I think I can say some things to you that I can't say to Bob."

"That happens all the time," she said. "Shoot."

He handed her a copy of the book. "Leo is giving Bob a copy; I wanted you both to have one. Bob has had a wonderful career; he's done some very fine work here and there, but I think that the sort of roles that have been available to him in the past have shown only a small part of what he is capable of."

Susan Hart looked thoughtful. "I think I can agree with that," she said.

"There is a role in this book that will give him an opportunity to make his audience aware of a whole new dimension of his talent, which I consider to be a very large talent." He took a deep breath. "This part will take courage. Bob will have to bare himself in a way that has never been asked of him. There are no bad guys to conquer in this story; there are no drug busts or shootouts on Main Street; there is no action that takes place outside of a summer house overlooking the Pacific Ocean. But this book is full of meaning and real emotion, and the part I'd like Bob to play— Doctor Madden—is the best role in the book. He'll be playing opposite a new actress—a very talented girl, but he'll have to carry her at times. He'll speak in the idiom of a cultivated set of people in the nineteen-twenties. It is a courtly language, and there is very fine dialogue for him to speak. I've asked Mark Adair to do the screenplay.

"I wanted to talk to you about this because it will be a departure for Bob, and he may need your help to make that departure. But this role is something else: *Pacific Afternoons* will open up his career and make it possible for him to play virtually anything he wants; it will release his talent from the confinement of genre films and show the industry what hidden reserves have lurked in this man for so long. And I'll tell you this—I would never say this to Bob—it would make Lee Strasberg proud of him if he were alive to see Bob in the role."

Susan Hart regarded him with a look of surprise. "Well, Michael, I don't know whether I'll like this book or not, or whether Bob will want the part, but I'll tell you one thing: That's the greatest line I've ever heard from a producer."

Michael laughed out loud. "You have a great surprise coming, Susan," he said.

"It's been a long time since I've been surprised, Michael."

"The surprise is, when you've read the book, you'll know that everything I've said to you is understatement."

Michael and Vanessa were the last to leave. Amanda pecked them both on the cheek, and Leo walked them to their car.

"Well, how did it go?" he asked.

"I had a chance to make my pitch to both Mark and Susan. I think they'll read the book; let's hope they like it."

"If these two guys come on board," Leo said, "I won't hold you to your eight-million-dollar budget; I'll go to twenty million. I want this to be a first-class production, and Susan's not going to let Bob do it on the cheap."

"Thanks, Leo," Michael said, "but I don't think the extra budget will be necessary. I think Bob will be on board before the end of the week, and I'll be willing to bet that Mark Adair will be on the phone before lunch tomorrow."

"What on earth did you say to Mark that makes you believe that?" Leo asked incredulously. "He's a tough sale, you know; tougher than Bob Hart."

"Well, for a start," Michael said, "I gave him your beautiful leatherbound copy of the book."

Leo looked at Michael blankly for a moment, then burst out laughing. "You son of a bitch!" he crowed.

"See you tomorrow, Leo," Michael said. He put the Porsche in gear and drove away down Stone Canyon.

"Well," Vanessa said, resting her head on Michael's shoulder, "am I going to be a movie star?"

"It's in the bag, sweetheart," Michael replied. "Don't worry about a thing."

19

Michael arrived in his office to find his secretary standing at her desk, holding her hand over the phone receiver. "There's somebody on the phone who will only identify himself as 'Tommy,'" Margot said, exasperated.

"It's okay," Michael replied, hurrying into his office. "You can always put him through if I'm alone." He picked up the phone. "Tommy?"

"So, how's it in Hollywood, kid? How's the big-time producer?"

"You wouldn't believe how good," Michael said, laughing. "When you coming to see me?"

"How about Saturday?"

"You serious?"

"I'm serious, kid; where should I stay?"

"The Bel-Air, and I'll take care of it. How long you gonna be here?"

"Just until Monday. I got a little business to do over the weekend. We'll have dinner Saturday, though, okay?"

"Sure, okay."

"Get me a girl?"

"Sure, no problem."

"I get in about four."

"We'll meet you in the bar at the Bel-Air at seven."

"Look forward to it," Tommy said. "See ya." He hung up.

Michael stood holding the phone and staring at the ceiling. Where the hell was he going to get a girl? He didn't know anybody in L.A.

"That was very strange."

Michael looked and saw Margot standing in the doorway. "What?"

"You were speaking in a thick New York accent. I've never heard you speak that way before."

Michael managed a laugh. "It was an old friend from New York. We talk that way to each other as a kind of joke."

"Oh."

Michael remembered something. "Margot, he's coming in on Saturday. Do you think you could find him a girl for the evening?"

"Of course. Anything in particular?"

"Somebody beautiful. And it wouldn't hurt if she's in the business in some way; he'll like that. And make it somebody discreet; he's a married man."

"Consider it done. Anything else?"

"Yes, get him a suite at the Bel-Air for Saturday and Sunday nights—something nice; tell them to send the bill to me."

"Would you like some flowers and a bottle of champagne in the room?"

"Yes, please."

"By the way, you had a call from Mark Adair ten minutes ago. He's at the Beverly Hills; want me to get him for you?"

"Please." Michael sat down at his desk and waited for the call to go through. Please, God, he muttered under his breath. Adair was the key to everything. The phone buzzed; he picked it up. "Mark?"

"Yes, Michael."

"Good morning; did you sleep well?"

"Hardly at all. I stayed up most of the night reading your goddamned book and making notes."

Making notes; that sounded good. "What do you think?"

"I think it'll make a brilliant film—*if* you can get Bob Hart to play the doctor. Get him, and I'm yours."

"That sounds wonderful, Mark." He sensed he had an advantage at this moment. "Mark, I have to tell you, Leo's got me on a very tight budget for this film."

There was a brief silence. "How tight?"

"Have your agent call me."

"Come on, Michael, what're you offering?"

"Mark, I know you're used to more money, but the best I can do is a hundred thousand."

"Jesus Christ, Michael! Do you really expect me to fall for that tight budget crap?"

"Mark, I'm being honest with you. This picture comes in under eight million, or Centurion won't fund. That's it, I'm afraid."

"I want a quarter of a million. I usually get four hundred thousand."

"Mark, I'll make it a hundred and fifty, but fifty is going to have to come out of my producer's fee. That's how much I want you to do this picture."

"Oh, shit, all right. Two drafts and a polish, and not a word more."

"Done. If you can't write this in two drafts and a polish, it can't be written."

"You're the worst kind of flatterer. I'll have a first draft in six weeks; send me fifty grand and a contract—*after* you get a commitment from Bob Hart." He slammed the phone down.

Michael did a little dance around the room, while Margot watched from the door. He saw her and froze; that was twice she'd caught him out this morning.

"George Hathaway called. He'd like a meeting at three."

"A meeting? George?"

She looked secretive. "I told him you were free for half an hour."

"Oh, all right. I guess I owe him some time for putting together these offices so fast."

"Susan Hart called, too; I wouldn't keep her waiting, if I were you."

Michael's heart nearly stopped. "Get her." He sat down and took some deep breaths; he didn't want to sound anxious. The phone buzzed. He took one more breath and picked it up. "Susan? I'm sorry to be so long; I was on the phone with Mark Adair."

"Is he going to do it?"

"He certainly is; he was up all night reading it."

"So were Bob and I. It was smart of you to give us each a copy."

"What did you think?"

"I think it's interesting. Bob's doing a thriller for Fox; he'll consider it for next fall."

"Susan, we start shooting April first. We have to get the spring season on film."

"Out of the question," she said. "The Fox project is a fifty-million-dollar production with a major female star, not an art film with a nobody. You *need* Bob for this one, Michael; postpone until October and set the film in autumn."

"It can't be done without screwing up the story, Susan; it's a spring story, and that can't change."

"Michael, if you want Bob, schedule for October. He'll want two million."

Michael thought fast. Leo had said he'd up the budget for Hart. "Susan, can you hold for a minute? I've got Paul Newman incoming on the other line." He punched the hold button before she could speak. Christ, he thought, staring at the flashing light. Have I pushed her too far? He glanced at his watch; he'd have to leave her on hold for at least a minute, or she'd know he was lying. After a minute and fifteen seconds he picked up the phone.

"Susan, I'm so sorry, but I had to take that call."

"How *dare* you put me on hold!" she sputtered.

"I'm truly sorry, I really am, but I want you to know I understand Bob's position on the Fox project, and if that's what he wants to do, I'll just have to live with it. It wouldn't have worked, anyway; I'm stuck with an eight-million-dollar budget, and I could only have offered Bob half a million for the part."

"You expected Bob to work for half a million?" she asked incredulously.

"Sweetheart, Centurion won't let me do this unless I bring it in for eight million, and anyway, the picture is going to shoot in forty-one days, and Bob would've only had to work twenty-two."

"How could the lead work only twenty-two days on a forty-one-day shoot? That's crazy."

"I juggled the schedule for Bob, but to tell you the truth, I'm relieved I don't have to do that now. I'd rather shoot in sequence, to tell you the truth. Anyway, the girl has more scenes; Bob just has the *best* scenes."

"When do you plan to start shooting?"

"April one, in Carmel, if we can nail down the locations."

"How much time in Carmel?"

"Three weeks; the rest is interiors we can do on the lot."

"God, I haven't been to Carmel in years."

"It's gorgeous up there, isn't it?" Michael had never been to Carmel, but that was where the book was set. "I'm so looking forward to it."

"What kind of accommodations?" Susan asked.

"The best available, of course. I can do that on my budget."

"We'd want a suite at the Inn."

"You mean you're considering this, Susan?"

"I'd better not find out you're lying about Mark Adair writing it."

"Susan."

"And Bob will want a million."

"Susan, there isn't a million in the budget. At half a million, Bob would be the highest-paid cast member. I'm only taking a hundred thousand for a fee."

"I want a copy of the budget," she said, "by noon today." She hung up.

"Margot!" he shouted.

She appeared in the doorway. "Yes?"

"Print out a copy of the budget for *Pacific Afternoons*! I've got three quarters of a million in for the male lead and three hundred thousand for script; change those figures to half a million and a hundred and fifty thousand, then spread the money over the other categories. Can you do that in an hour?"

"Sure."

"Get me legal."

When the phone buzzed Michael picked it up. "Who's this?"

"This is Mervyn White, head of the legal department," a voice said, sounding annoyed.

"Mervyn, this is Michael Vincent. I need a contract drawn immediately, for a picture called *Pacific Afternoons*."

"Nothing like that on the schedule," White said.

Michael could hear him shuffling papers. "I

don't care if it's on the schedule," he said firmly. "Draw the contract for Robert Hart at half a million dollars, working from April first of next year to May first, deluxe accommodations, travel on the Centurion jet, deluxe motor home for dressing. He can have one assistant for ten thousand bucks."

"I'll have to clear this with Mr. Goldman," White said stiffly. "Especially the part about the airplane."

"Mervyn," Michael said slowly, "when Leo sees that he's getting Bob Hart for half a million, he'll fly the airplane himself. I want that contract drawn and on my desk in . . ." he glanced at his watch, ". . . ninety minutes, and if it's not here, I'll come over there and set your desk on fire, do you hear me?"

"Oh, all right," White said petulantly.

"Good." Michael hung up the phone. He had Mark Adair and Robert Hart on board for four hundred thousand less than he'd budgeted for. He was in Hollywood heaven.

Then a niggling doubt pricked at his brain. There was something else. Oh, yes, he didn't own the film rights to the book.

"Margot," he called, "when that contract arrives, send it with the budget to Susan Hart. And by the way, find out who owns the copyright to *Pacific Afternoons*."

20

Michael sat in the lawyer's office and stared at the man. He was in his mid-seventies, Michael reckoned, and a little worse for the wear. A bottle of single-malt Scotch whiskey stood on his desk, a crystal glass beside it. Michael had already refused a drink.

What was it with this guy? The whole city of L.A. *existed* on the telephone, people walked around with the phone plugged into their heads, and this guy had insisted on a face-to-face meeting.

"You're sure you won't have a taste?" Daniel J. Moriarty asked.

"Quite sure," Michael replied. "Now, can we get down to business, Mr. Moriarty?"

"Of course, of course," the lawyer replied. "What can I do for you?"

"You do remember our brief phone conversation of an hour ago?" Michael asked. He was steamed.

"I do, I do. It was film rights you wanted to meet about?"

"*I* did not want to meet, Mr. Moriarty; I am here only at your insistence. I am interested in acquiring the film rights to the novel *Pacific Afternoons* by Mildred Parsons. I understand that in some way you control those rights?"

"Indeed I do, Mr. Vincent, indeed I do. You see, Mildred's younger brother, Montague—Monty, we all called him—was my closest friend. Monty and I went to law school together. Very close, we were."

"And Montague Parsons controls the rights?"

"Monty, alas, passed on last year. I am his executor."

"Were there no other relatives surviving?"

"None. The rights to all of Mildred Parsons's works passed to Monty on her death; those rights rest in his estate. The income from those rights passes as a bequest to Carlyle Junior College. And, as I mentioned before, I am the executor."

"As executor, are you empowered to act for the estate?" Michael hoped the hell he was; he didn't want to have to deal with the trustees of some college.

"I am so empowered."

"You don't have to have the permission of anyone at Carlyle Junior College?"

Moriarty chuckled. "I do not. Carlyle gets the income, but as long as I'm executor, I make all the decisions."

"Good. I would like to purchase the film rights to *Pacific Afternoons*. I am in a position to offer you five thousand dollars for a one-year option, renewable for an additional year at the same rate. On exercising the option, I will pay a further twenty thousand dollars."

"And just who are you, Mr. Vincent? I mean, do you represent a major studio?"

"I am an independent producer," Michael said.

"Ah, an independent," Moriarty said, sipping his Scotch. "This town is full of them. Tell me, Mr. Vincent, do you actually *have* five thousand dollars?"

Michael checked his temper. "Mr. Moriarty, I am an independent producer with a production deal at Centurion Pictures, and as such, I have the full backing of that studio. If you like, I will have Mr. Leo Goldman call you and confirm my position there."

Moriarty held up a hand. "Please don't take offense, Mr. Vincent; it's just that this town is full of people who style themselves independent producers. Centurion is a reputable studio, and I accept that you represent them."

"Thank you. Do you accept my offer?"

"What offer was that?"

Michael tried not to grind his teeth. He repeated his offer.

"Alas, no," Moriarty said. "I cannot accept such an offer."

"What sort of price did you have in mind?" Michael asked.

"Oh, I didn't have anything in particular in mind," Moriarty said, replenishing his drink.

"All right, Mr. Moriarty, I will offer you ten thousand against twenty-five, but that is the best I can do."

"Is it, Mr. Vincent; is it, indeed?" Moriarty swivelled slightly in his chair and gazed out the window.

Michael stared at the man, fuming. What was his game? What kind of negotiation is this?

"Mr. Moriarty, you are wasting my time. What do you want for the rights?"

Moriarty jumped, as if startled from a reverie. "Mmm? Oh, the rights, the rights, yes."

"Yes," Michael said.

"Yes."

Michael wanted to strangle the man. "Mr. Moriarty, you must be aware that the copyright on *Pacific Afternoons* expires in three weeks, and, if I wish, I can simply wait and have the rights for nothing. So if you expect to earn anything for your college, put down that glass and start doing business."

"Ha-ha!" Moriarty cried. "So you were operating on the premise of the life plus fifty years copyright law! Well, my fine fellow, that doesn't apply here! The copyright to Miss Parsons's novel runs on the old copyright law—the one that was in effect when she died. So if you wish to threaten me with expiration of copyright, you'll have to wait another twenty-four years! Ha-ha!"

This is some sort of nightmare, Michael

thought. It's a bad dream, and I'll wake up in a moment and it will be all right.

"Is there anything else you wish to say, Mr. Vincent?"

"Frankly, Mr. Moriarty, I'm speechless. Do you wish to sell these rights?"

"As a matter of fact, I would love to sell the rights, but I can't."

"What?"

"I promised Monty Parsons when I became his executor that I would never, ever sell the film rights to Mildred's little novel. He hated the films, you see; thought they were common and vulgar. He would never allow his sister's only work to be corrupted in such a fashion." Moriarty tossed down the remaining Scotch in his glass and emitted a low chuckle. "Did you think you were the first, Mr. Vincent? I've had a regular parade of 'independent producers' in here over the years wanting to film that book. I've always thought it would make a fine little film myself, but I had to say no to all of them."

Michael was stunned. "Then why, may I ask, did you drag me down here for this ridiculous meeting?"

Moriarty spread his hands. "Well, it gets lonesome in this office, you know, the Parsons estate being my last client. It passes the time to bandy a bit with a producer. I'm afraid, Mr. Vincent, that you'll have to wait until I've passed on. Then you can go to the trustees of Carlyle Junior College and make a deal with them. *They* didn't make any promises to Monty Parsons."

Michael stood up. "Good day, Mr. Moriarty."

Moriarty waved his glass. "Good day to you, Mr. Vincent. And thank you for your visit. Come back any time!"

21

Michael drove back to the studio in a fury, whipping around corners, passing other cars, twice nearly running down pedestrians. There were two cars ahead of him at the gate, and he waited, taking deep breaths and trying to regain control of his anger. By the time he was let through he was able to smile and wave back at the guard.

He parked in his reserved spot and walked the few yards to his building, his mind still racing. He didn't have the rights to *Pacific Afternoons*. How could he make the picture? He had a top star and a top writer ready to work, and he didn't have the rights to the property!

He walked through the waiting room and Margot thrust a handful of pink message slips at him.

"We've got a request from the PR department for an interview and photographs with one of the trades," she said, following him into his office.

"It's a real coup, getting that kind of space. When do you want to do it?"

"Set it up for next week," he said. "A morning."

"Fine." She wrinkled her brow. "Michael? Are you all right?"

"I'm fine," he said, sitting down at Randolph's huge desk. "I'm just thinking about something."

The phone rang and she picked it up at his desk. "Mr. Vincent's office. Oh, yes, Leo, he's right here." She punched the hold button. "It's Leo on one."

"Tell him I'll get back to him."

"I can't do that," she said, alarmed. "I've already told him you're here. Leo hates being put off; you'll have to answer."

Michael picked up the phone and forced a smile into his voice. "Leo, how are you?"

"Great, kid. I just had Sue Hart on the phone; she told me the news. Congratulations!"

"Thanks, Leo."

"And you got Mark for the screenplay, too! That's a tour de force performance, Michael. I'm proud of you."

"It's going to be a good production," Michael said lamely.

"How you coming on the rights to the book?"

Michael gulped. "It's in the works; I don't anticipate any problems."

"Good, good. I'm glad everything is going so smoothly. Catch you later, kid." Leo hung up.

Michael hung up and found that he was sweating heavily.

Margot stuck her head into the office. "George Hathaway is here; he seems pretty excited."

"Sure, sure," Michael said, struggling to put the rights problem out of his mind and concentrate on the business at hand.

George Hathaway came into the room, a thick roll of heavy paper under his arm. "Michael," he beamed, placing the roll on the desk, "I read the book, and I loved it! I was up all night thinking about it and making sketches." He unrolled the papers to reveal a sketch of a cottage.

Michael stared at the sketch. It was as if George had reached into his mind and extracted his image of the northern California house of the protagonist of *Pacific Afternoons*.

"What do you think?"

"It's perfect, George; it *is* the cottage. How did you do it?"

"Well, I used to be an art director, my boy, not just in charge of the props department." He flipped through his sketches: it was all there—the cottage, the music room, her bedroom, the doctor's study—every important scene in the book had been rendered.

"I'm overwhelmed," Michael said. "How did you do all this so quickly?"

"I've always been a fast study," George said. "Would you believe I drew this set—" he waved a hand at *The Great Randolph*'s study "—in half an hour?"

Michael sat back in his chair. "George, will you do this film with me?" he asked.

George turned pink and beamed. "My boy, I'd

be honored." He blinked rapidly, and his voice became husky. "It's been a long time since somebody offered me something important."

"And it is important," Michael said, standing and clapping the designer on a frail shoulder. "Mark Adair is doing the screenplay, and Robert Hart has agreed to play the doctor."

"Why, that's fabulous," George said. "Who for costumes?"

"Who would you recommend?"

"Edith Head, but she's dead, like just about everyone else I know."

"Think about it."

"There is somebody," George said. "She lives in the group of apartments where I live, and she's been trying to get work. Young, but she's very talented, I think."

"Ask her to do some sketches for me, and to call Margot for an appointment. What's her name?"

"Jennifer Fox—Jenny. I'll tell her, and I'll work with her myself on the sketches." George smiled. "You know which scene I loved best in the book?"

"Which one?"

"The one where the doctor sings to the young woman. *'Dein ist mein ganzes Herz'*—'My Whole Heart is Yours.'"

"Yes, that is a wonderful scene. We'll have to cut it from the film, though. I doubt if Bob Hart could carry it off."

"Why not? He doesn't have to sing—you could dub it—he's actor enough to bring it off."

"I think the scene might be too much in conflict with his previous image in films."

"Too bad, I love Lehár."

"Who?"

"Lehár, Franz Lehár."

Michael searched his mind for the reference. "Opera?" he hazarded.

"Operetta," George said. "He wrote *'Dein ist mein ganzes Herz.'* "

"Ah," Michael said. He didn't have a clue.

"Have you never heard it?"

"Not for a long time," Michael lied.

"Will you give me just ten minutes more of your time?"

"Of course, George." What the hell was the old man running on about?

George ran from the room, picked up Margot's phone, and made a call. Five minutes later, two workmen appeared pushing a grand piano on a dolly and set it up at one end of Randolph's study, then two elderly men walked in. One of them was carrying a sheaf of music.

"Please," George said, waving Michael to a sofa, "sit."

Michael sat down.

"Mr. Vincent," George said formally, "may I present Anton Gruber and Hermann Hecht?"

"How do you do," Michael said. Then the Gruber name struck home. The man had written scores for dozens of films in the thirties and forties. Michael had never heard of Hecht.

Anton Gruber sat at the piano and played a

soft introduction, then Hermann Hecht, assuming a concert position, his hands folded before him, began to sing.

Michael had never heard the music before. It was old-fashioned, certainly, but the melody was wonderful. The old man sang it in a slightly cracked baritone, but with such feeling that when he had finished and the piano was quiet, Michael had a lump in his throat. He stood up and clapped loudly. "Gentlemen, that was wonderful. I've never heard it done better!"

"I thought you'd like it," George said. "Now you can see why it's so important in the story, the doctor finally expressing himself to the young woman in a song, in *German* yet, when before he couldn't tell her of his feelings."

"You're right, George," Michael said. "It could be the emotional high point of the film. It could be perfectly wonderful, if I can get Bob Hart to do it."

"He's an actor, isn't he?" George asked. "All actors are hams. He'd never pass up a scene like that, even if he can't sing. Hermann here could dub it for him."

"It might work," Michael said. It damned well would work, he thought; it could bring the audience close to tears, as it had him.

It was a wonderful scene that could be played by a huge star in a film that he could not make unless he owned the rights to the novel. He could hear Daniel J. Moriarty laughing at him.

22

Michael drove the Porsche slowly up Sunset Boulevard toward the Bel-Air Hotel. Vanessa sat beside him, checking her makeup in the mirror on the back of the sun visor.

"Tell me who this guy is again," she said.

"His name is Tommy Provensano," Michael said. "I knew him as a kid in New York, growing up."

"Oh, right."

"Don't be surprised if he calls me Vinnie sometimes. It's kind of a nickname."

"Okay. Is he bringing anybody?"

"Her name is Mimi; that's all I know about her. It may be their first date."

"How old a guy is Tommy?"

"A couple of years older than I am."

"If he's boring, do I still have to be nice to him?"

"Vanessa, in Hollywood, you have to be nice to *everybody*. You never know who you're talking to."

"That's a good policy, I guess."

"Believe me, it is."

Tommy opened the door and grabbed Michael in a bear hug. "Hey, *paisan*," he roared. "It's the big-time Hollywood producer!" He had slimmed down some and was wearing an expensive Italian-cut suit.

"Hello, Tommy," Michael said. "I'd like you to meet Vanessa Parks."

Tommy suddenly became the gentleman. "How do you do, Vanessa," he said. "I'd like you both to meet Mimi."

A small, dark-haired girl stood up from the sofa and shook both their hands. She was demurely dressed and very beautiful. Michael thought Margot had done her job well.

Tommy popped a bottle of champagne for them. Dom Perignon, Michael noted, remembering that he was paying for it. Tommy poured, and when their glasses were full he addressed the little group.

"This guy," he said, taking Michael's shoulder and shaking him like a rag doll, "and I were greasy kids on the street together. We stole fruit from the pushcarts, we rolled drunks, we did all the terrible things young kids on the street do, and we went home every night to our mothers."

"Tommy," Michael said reprovingly, "you know very well that we never stole any fruit." He turned to the others. "Tommy has a romantic view of our youth."

"And listen to him talk," Tommy said, pinching Michael's cheek. "He used to talk like me!"

Michael bore his gaze into Tommy, and he seemed to take the hint.

"That was a long time ago, of course," he said, glancing apologetically at Michael. "Now, where are we eating?"

"I thought you might enjoy Spago," Michael said dryly. "The pizza's great."

"I get it, I get it," Tommy said. "I'll behave."

"No," said Michael, "you'll really like the pizzas. They're different from what you're used to."

Their table overlooked Sunset and the big movie billboards. Tommy couldn't get enough of the place.

"I can't believe I'm sitting in the same restaurant as Burt Reynolds," he whispered hoarsely to Michael.

"I'm sorry there aren't more stars here," Michael replied. "There usually are." It was the first time he had been to the restaurant, but the headwaiter had been ready for him.

Vanessa stood up. "I'm for the little girls' room," she said. "Join me, Mimi?" The women left Michael and Tommy alone.

Tommy was suddenly quiet and serious. "So, tell me how it's really going, Vinnie. No bullshit, now."

"Tommy, it is difficult for me to explain coherently to you just how well it is going. *Downtown*

Nights opens later in the fall, and I've already got Robert Hart starring in my next picture."

"Robert Hart the movie star?" Tommy asked, amazed.

"Movie stars are who star in pictures, Tommy. And a great novelist named Mark Adair is writing the screenplay."

"I heard of him. My wife read one of his books one time."

"How is Maria?"

"She's okay. She likes being a capo's wife, I can tell you. She's getting a lot of new respect from her friends."

"And how do you like being a capo?"

"My first taste of real power," Tommy said. "It's like fine wine; you can't get enough."

"Come on, you've had a lot of juice for a long time."

Tommy shook his head. "It's not the same as manipulating Benedetto to get what I want. Now, I want something, I say so, and I get it." He looked around the restaurant. "I really like this place. You don't think it's bugged, do you?"

Michael laughed. "Certainly not. You have nothing to worry about."

"Listen, you always have to worry about taps these days—that and guys wearing wires. Seems like the FBI is everywhere." He leaned closer across the table. "Just between you and me, looks like the Don is going to take a fall."

Michael became Vinnie for a moment. "No shit?"

"A big fall. He's going to be inside by Christmas, the way things are going. Frankie Bigboy's blabbing his head off on the stand; he's all lined up for the witness protection program, and nobody's been able to get a shot at him."

"I never thought Frankie was the type to testify—especially against the Don. He's a dead man."

"I doubt it. A minute after the jury says 'guilty,' he'll be running a bowling alley in Peoria or someplace. We won't see him again."

Michael looked at Tommy closely. "You don't seem all broken up about the Don going away."

Tommy smiled slyly. "It's an ill wind that don't blow somebody some good."

"Is there going to be trouble about who succeeds?"

Tommy glanced around the room. "I'm out here to be out of it," he said. "I got word that somebody's going to get whacked this weekend. I don't want to be around."

"Am I an alibi?" Michael asked anxiously.

"Don't worry, it won't come to that. A couple stewardesses could make me on the plane, and there's always the hotel."

"If you need it, say the word," Michael said, relieved that he wouldn't be involved. "Say, Tommy, thanks for the car and the help with the banker. You wouldn't believe what a sweet deal that bank is. My dough's on the street already."

Tommy put his hand on Michael's. "Anytime, you need anything, kid, anytime. I'm connected pretty good out here."

"That you are," Michael said. "By the way," he

took a deep breath, "I got a little legal problem, maybe you could help me with."

"Speak to me," Tommy said.

"I'm having a little trouble getting the rights to this book that I want to make into a film."

"Who's giving you a hard time?"

Michael took a cocktail napkin and wrote down the name of Daniel J. Moriarty and the address of his law office, then he told Tommy about his conversation with the lawyer.

"I'll look into it," Tommy said, pocketing the napkin. "Call you when I know something." He looked up to see the women returning. "Say," he said, "that's some broad you got me. Is she gonna get mad if I want to fuck her?"

"She's yours for whatever you want," Michael said.

Tommy slapped him on the shoulder. "That's it, kid, you take care of me, I take care of you."

23

Michael jerked awake to the sound of the telephone. He glanced at the bedside clock; just past 6:00 A.M. on Monday morning. He picked it up. "Hello?" he croaked. Some goddamned wrong number, he knew it.

"Rise and shine, kid," Tommy's voice said.

"Jesus, Tommy, you know what time it is? You never got up this early in your life. Where are you?"

"In New York; where else? I just want you to know I'm taking care of that little problem of yours."

"Thanks, Tommy. I owe you."

"Forget it. You know where the corner of Sunset and Camden is?"

"Sure, in Beverly Hills."

"Park your car there at eight o'clock sharp this morning, southeast corner; a guy will pick you up. He's kind of a consultant on these things."

"What's his name?"

"You don't need to know; he won't know yours, either."

"Right."

"Listen, I left kind of a mess at the hotel; I'm sorry about that."

"Don't worry about it; they're used to it."

"Yeah? Well, you got class, kid, and I thank you for the night on the town."

"Thanks for your help, too, Tommy. Keep in touch."

"Don't worry about that. *Ciao.*" Tommy hung up.

Michael rolled out of bed and put his face in his hands. Jesus, what did they drink last night? He glanced at Vanessa. Sawing away, just like always; nothing could wake the girl until she was ready.

He got out of bed, showered, and fixed himself some breakfast, feeling relieved. He didn't know how Tommy was going to fix the rights thing, but he had complete faith in him. If Tommy said it was fixed, it was fixed.

He got dressed, took the elevator down to the garage, and drove to Sunset and Camden, arriving ten minutes early. He sat idly just off Sunset, listening to a drive-time disc jockey, drumming his fingers on the wheel in time with the music.

A large Cadillac pulled up next to him and the electric window on his side rolled down. A man in his early twenties, unshaven, with greasy hair, looked at him.

"You and me got a mutual friend?"

"Yeah," Michael replied.

"Get in."

Michael got out of his car and into the Cadillac. Traffic on Sunset was full-bore rush hour now. "Where we going?"

The driver had turned down Camden and was now making a left turn.

"This guy Moriarty," he said.

"Yeah?"

"I gotta know what he looks like, right?"

"Okay, but where we going?"

The driver held up a page torn from a phone book; the lawyer's name was circled. "To have a look at him."

"Oh."

The Cadillac swung into Bedford Drive and stopped.

"Now what?" Michael asked.

"Look," said the driver, exasperated, "let me handle this, okay?"

"Okay, sorry."

"That's his house right there," the driver said. "We'll wait."

Michael switched on the radio and found some music. They sat there for better than half an hour, then he looked up and saw Daniel J. Moriarty leaving his home, a briefcase in his hand. "That's him," Michael said. "Get a good look." The way Moriarty was swinging the case, Michael could tell it was empty, except maybe for a bottle of Scotch. Why did the old guy bother going to the office, anyway?

The driver started the Cadillac and moved slowly away from the curb, checking his rearview mirrors. Momentarily there was no traffic. Moriarty stepped off the curb and walked around an elderly Volvo station wagon, digging for his keys. As he put the key into the door lock, the driver gunned the Cadillac.

"What the hell . . ." Michael yelled, bracing a hand against the dashboard. "What are you—"

The Cadillac scraped the side of the Volvo, then struck Moriarty, sending him up into the air. Michael heard him hit the top of the Cadillac, then saw the door of the Volvo spinning off in another direction. The Cadillac screeched to a stop, throwing Michael against the dashboard.

"Are you out of your fucking mind?" Michael screamed.

The driver was looking back over his shoulder. "Shit!" he said through his teeth. "Wait here." He got out of the Cadillac and started walking back toward Moriarty, who was not only alive but was, unaccountably, trying to pull his battered body across the street with his elbows.

Michael started to hip his way across the seat to the wheel and drive away; then he saw there were no keys in the ignition—indeed, there was no ignition. He looked across the street to where a man in a Mercedes had been pulling out of his driveway. He had stopped and was looking, first at Moriarty, then at Michael. Michael looked to his right and saw a middle-aged woman in a bathrobe and curlers holding a newspaper, looking straight at him. He turned and looked out the rear window of the car.

The driver was walking the hundred yards

that separated the Cadillac from Moriarty; purposefully, but not fast. A knife was in his hand. He covered the last few yards to the struggling Moriarty, kicked him over onto his back, plunged the knife into his chest, twisted it once, then walked back toward the Cadillac, leaving the knife in the now-dead body of Daniel J. Moriarty.

Michael looked again at the man in the Mercedes and the woman with the newspaper. They were watching the driver walk back to the car and following his progress to the Cadillac, where Michael still sat.

The young man got into the car, reached under the dash, did something with some wires, and the engine came to life. He put the car in gear and drove away, turning right at the next corner. "You'd think the car would do it to an old guy like that, right? I mean, Christ, a Cadillac!"

Michael was speechless with rage and fear. He scrunched down in the seat; why hadn't he done that before? A couple of minutes later, he was left standing at his car. He got in, started the engine, drove to the corner, then turned onto Sunset, blending in with the traffic, terrified of everybody around him. He could hear police cars in the distance.

They had seen him, those two people. The man in the Mercedes, he could be in the business, somebody he might have to deal with someday. The woman could be married to somebody at Centurion; how did he know? They had bored

their curious eyes into him, memorized his fea-
tures; he was sure of it. He put on his dark glasses
and turned toward Sacramento on the freeway.
He would turn back toward the studio in a few
minutes; right now, he had to swallow his heart,
get his pulse back under two hundred. Driving
would do it.

24

Driving didn't do it. When he got to the studio an hour later, Michael's heart was still pounding. He slammed the car door and walked into his office.

"Morning," Margot said, handing him his messages.

Michael said nothing, but went into his office and sat down heavily at his desk.

Margot followed him in. "There's a problem."

"Huh?" He hadn't been listening.

"At the Bel-Air."

"What are you talking about?"

"Your friend, he beat up the girl I arranged."

"*What*?"

"Put her in the hospital. I'm afraid that I am in trouble with her madam, and you are in trouble with the Bel-Air."

"Tommy beat her up?"

"Michael, try and listen to me. Your friend made such a mess of that girl that she may never look the same again. Her madam is up in arms, the hotel is up in arms—I persuaded them not to call the police—and you are going to find this very expensive."

"What do you mean?"

"The girl wants twenty-five thousand dollars before noon today, or she says she'll go to the police."

"Tell her okay."

"The madam is probably raking some of that off. I can try to get it down some."

"Tell her it's okay, I'll pay the money." He flipped through his address book, found the number, and dialed. The banker came on the line. He waved Margot out of the office. "This is Callabrese."

"Yes, Mr. Callabrese; what can I do for you?"

"I want twenty-five thousand in cash left at your reception desk immediately. A woman will ask for it; don't ask for I.D., just give it to her."

"As you wish."

Michael hung up the phone and went to the door. "Margot, please go to this address and pick up an envelope; there'll be money inside; pay the madam and do what you can to see that she keeps her mouth shut." He handed her a slip of paper.

Margot grabbed her handbag and headed for the door. "You'll have to cover your own phones."

Michael picked up the phone and called home.

"What?" a sleepy Vanessa said.

"Vanessa, wake up and listen to me carefully."

"Huh?"

"Goddamnit, wake up and listen!"

"All right, Michael, I'm listening!"

"This is what you and I did this morning: we woke up early, made love, then took a shower together. I left the house about nine-thirty—later than usual—for the office. You got that?"

"If you say so."

"It's important, if anybody should ask."

"All right. Can I go back to sleep now?"

Michael slammed down the phone. Where were his fingerprints on the Cadillac—on the door handle? Yes, and on the dashboard, where he'd braced himself. Christ, if they ever found that car . . . The phone rang.

"Hello?"

"Mr. Vincent? Is that you?"

"Yes, who is this?"

"My name is Larry Keating; I sent you a screenplay? I'd like to set up a meeting."

"Call my secretary this afternoon." He hung up. The phone rang again, and he let it ring. He sat and let the phone ring until Margot got back.

"Is it all right?" he asked.

"It's all right. The madam can control the situation. She's extremely annoyed that this has happened, but she'll keep her mouth shut, and she'll keep the girl quiet, too."

"Good."

"I didn't get a chance to tell you earlier, but your appointment with the trade paper is tomorrow, for an interview and photographs."

"Fine," he said, then sat bolt upright. "No!"

"Tomorrow's bad? Your book was clear."

"I'll do it on the phone."

"Michael, they can't take pictures on the phone."

"No pictures. I haven't got time to mess with these people; tell the guy if he wants to talk to call me tomorrow morning."

"All right."

"And hold all my calls until I tell you. I've got some thinking to do."

"All right."

He tried to think but couldn't. Finally, he buzzed Margot. "Find out who's the chairman of the board of trustees of Carlyle Junior College, then make me an appointment as soon as possible." This was dangerous, but he had to do it now, or he would go completely crazy.

The chairman's name was Wallace Merton, and his office was in a downtown law firm. Michael was made to wait a few minutes, increasing his nervousness. When he was finally announced, he drew a deep breath and tried to relax.

"Good morning, Mr. Vincent, what can I do for you?" Merton asked, waving Michael to a chair. He clearly was not accustomed to spending time with strangers.

Michael sat down and set his briefcase on the floor. "Good morning, Mr. Merton; I won't take much of your time."

"Good."

"I am a producer at Centurion Pictures, and I am interested in the film rights to a property which I understand has been left as a bequest to the college."

Merton looked at him blankly. "I don't have the slightest idea what you're talking about."

"The estate of Mildred Parsons?"

"Oh, yes; that man Moriarty."

Best to tell as much of the truth as possible. "I saw him last week, but frankly, he was a little worse for the wear, and I couldn't make much sense of what he had to say. I did understand that the board of trustees had it in its power to sell the rights."

"Well, we didn't last week—only Moriarty did, but some hit-and-run driver ran him down in front of his house this morning."

"I'm very sorry to hear it."

"It seems most of my day has been taken up with Mr. Moriarty and his problems."

"If I'd known about this I certainly would have waited a decent interval, but as long as I'm here, may I explain myself?"

"Go ahead."

"I read the book recently and thought it might make a nice little art film, if I can fit it into our schedule. We normally have a couple of dozen projects like that floating around the studio at any given time."

Merton looked at Michael sharply. "I've done some business with you movie people in my time, and it sounds to me like you're trying to buy a valuable property cheap."

Michael stood up and put his card on the man's desk. "I'm sorry to have taken up your time,

Mr. Merton; you're obviously very busy today. If you have any interest in selling the rights, call me." He turned to go.

"Oh, sit down, Vincent," Merton said. "At least tell me what you've got in mind."

Michael sat down. "What I have in mind, sir, is offering you ten thousand dollars for a year's option against a twenty-five-thousand-dollar purchase price."

"Let's get this done, Mr. Vincent: twenty-five thousand against fifty. I have a fiduciary responsibility to the college to get a decent price."

"Twenty against forty. That's as far as I can go without the board's permission."

Merton stood up and stuck out his hand. "Done. Send me a contract and a check."

Michael shook the man's hand. "I'm sorry about Mr. Moriarty."

"Drunken oaf," Merton said. "He had a liver the size of a watermelon. He told me his doctor gave him six months, and that was nearly a year ago; I shouldn't think he'd have lived another month."

When Michael got back to his office there were two men in his waiting room.

"Mr. Vincent, these two gentlemen are police officers," Margot said. "They'd like a word with you."

25

Michael sat and looked at the two police officers. This was a new experience for him. In the past he had always avoided talking with policemen.

"I'm Sergeant Rivera," said the larger of the two men. "This is Detective Hall."

"What can I do for you, gentlemen?" Michael asked, more calmly than he felt.

"Are you acquainted with a lawyer named Daniel J. Moriarty?" Rivera asked.

"Yes, I am, if you can call it acquainted."

"What do you mean?"

"I mean that I met the man once, at his office, and he was roaring drunk. There was a bottle of Scotch on his desk as we spoke."

"When was this?"

"Late last week—Thursday or Friday."

"You were in his diary for Friday morning."

"That was it, I guess. I suppose this visit must be about his death."

The cop regarded him for a moment before speaking. "And how is it you come to know of his death, Mr. Vincent? He only died this morning."

"I spoke with Mr. Moriarty about acquiring the film rights to a novel called *Pacific Afternoons*. He controlled the rights, but as I said, he was drunk. He did manage to explain that all the rights to the work had been bequeathed to Carlyle Junior College, so earlier today I met with the chairman of their board of trustees, a lawyer named Wallace Merton. He told me that Mr. Moriarty had been run down by a hit-and-run driver."

"I see," the cop said, sounding disappointed.

"So, gentlemen, you now have my entire knowledge of Mr. Moriarty."

"Just one other thing, Mr. Vincent," the policeman said. "Did Mr. Moriarty refuse to sell you these rights?"

"He may have; it was hard to ascertain his meaning, given his condition. In any event, it seemed to me that if I was going to get anywhere, I'd have to talk with Mr. Merton."

"Were these rights very valuable to you, Mr. Vincent?"

"Not in a major way. The book was published in the nineteen-twenties and is little known today. A friend gave it to me to read last year sometime, and it occurred to me that it might make a film. I finally got around to looking into the rights. I didn't even know who controlled them until last week. If you don't mind my saying so, it seems that interviewing me is quite a long way from a hit-and-run incident."

"It was more than that," the policeman said. "Mr. Moriarty wasn't actually killed by the car. The driver got out and knifed him, just to be sure."

"Good God!" Michael said. "That's pretty brutal."

"Yes, it is."

"So I suppose you're interviewing anybody who had anything to do with him."

"That's right, and there are surprisingly few people who had anything to do with him."

"It's really ironic that he should be murdered," Michael said. "Wallace Merton told me that Moriarty was a dying man—a bad liver."

"That's what we learned from his part-time secretary. Mr. Vincent, can you tell me where you were between eight and nine o'clock this morning?"

Michael didn't miss a beat. "Of course. I got up later than usual this morning. I didn't leave the house until around nine-thirty, and I was in the office before ten."

"Is there anyone who can corroborate that?"

"Yes, my secretary can tell you what time I arrived here this morning, and the woman I live with can tell you when I left the house."

"And her name?" His notebook was poised.

"Vanessa Parks." He gave them the phone number.

"What kind of car do you drive, Mr. Vincent?"

"A Porsche Cabriolet."

"Color?"

"Black."

"Do you know anyone who drives a red Cadillac?"

"No. Everybody in this business seems to drive a foreign car—just take a look in the lot outside."

The policeman smiled. "I noticed." He looked around the room. "This looks like a room I saw in a movie once."

"This was the study in a nineteen-thirties movie called *The Great Randolph*."

"That's it! I knew I'd seen it somewhere."

"You're a movie fan, then?"

"Absolutely."

"Would you like a little tour of the lot?"

"I'd love it some other time, Mr. Vincent, but we've got a lot on our hands this afternoon."

"Call my secretary anytime, and she'll arrange it for you."

"And when can I expect to see *Pacific Afternoons* on the screen?"

"Oh, that's hard to say. I only bought the rights today, and a screenplay has to be written. I'd say a year, at the earliest."

"So you did get the rights after all?"

"Mr. Merton and I reached agreement very quickly. I don't think he'd ever had another offer. By the way, would you like his number?"

"Thanks, we already have it."

Michael stood up. "Gentlemen, if there's nothing further . . ."

The policemen rose, then stopped at the office door. "There were two men in the Cadillac," Rivera said.

"Oh? Any leads?"

"One or two. It was a professional job; we know that much."

"Sounds interesting. Tell you what, Sergeant, when you've made an arrest give me a call, and let's talk about it. Might be a movie in it."

"Maybe I'll do that, Mr. Vincent," Rivera said.

"Don't wait until you're ready to go to trial, though. Call me the minute you've made an arrest, before there's a lot of publicity." He smiled. "I wouldn't want to get into a bidding war."

The cop laughed and shook his hand. "A bidding war sounds good to me." He gave Michael his card. "Call me if you think of anything else I should know."

Michael gave him his card. "Same here. True crime stuff is always good for the movies." He waved and went back into his office.

He waited until he was sure they'd left the building, then called Vanessa.

"Hello?"

At least she was awake. "Hi, babe. You remember our conversation of this morning?"

"Yes," she said exasperatedly, "we made love and took a shower together, and you didn't leave until nine-thirty."

"You'll be getting a call from a policeman who'll ask you about that."

"What's this about, Michael?"

Stick close to the truth. "Last week I tried to

buy the screen rights to *Pacific Afternoons* from a lawyer named Moriarty. He wouldn't sell them to me, so I went to the lawyer who represents the college that owns the rights, and he sold them to me. Then Moriarty gets run down by a car—murdered apparently—and the cops came to see me, since I was in Moriarty's diary."

"So where were you this morning?"

Michael stopped breathing. "Didn't you wake up at all when I got up?"

"No."

He relaxed. "Well, I was right there, babe. I fixed myself some breakfast as usual, and I decided to read a script before leaving for the studio. That's why I was late."

"So why didn't you just tell the police that?"

"Because you couldn't back me up if you were asleep."

"Oh."

"See you later, babe. We'll drive out to Malibu for dinner, okay?"

She brightened. "Okay."

"I gave the cops the number; they'll call."

"Okay, I know what to say."

He hung up. "Margot," he called out, "get me Leo."

Leo took the call. "Yeah, kid?"

"Just wanted to let you know I've sewed up the rights to *Pacific Afternoons.*"

"How much?"

"Twenty grand against forty."

"You're my kind of guy. See you." Leo hung up.

Michael hung up, too. He was thinking of growing his beard again.

On the way home, Michael stopped his car at a phone booth and called a number Tommy Pro had given him.

A recorded voice answered. "Please enter the number of a touch-tone phone where you can be reached at this hour." There was a series of beeps.

Michael tapped in the number of the phone booth, then hung up and waited nervously. Ten minutes passed, then the phone rang. He snatched up the receiver. "Tommy?"

"Where are you calling from?"

"A phone booth on Pico."

"How are you, kid? What's up?"

"Tommy, you very nearly got me hung up on a murder rap. What the hell were you thinking of?"

Tommy was immediately apologetic. "Listen, I'm sorry about that, kid. The guy was recommended to me highly; who knew he was going to be a cowboy? Don't worry, he's already out of the picture."

"Tommy, people *saw* me in that car with him. The cops have already been to my office."

"That's natural; after all, you had a meeting with the guy, right? Just be cool and everything will be okay."

"Tommy, I don't know how you could put me in this position."

Tommy's voice hardened. "Your problem is solved, right?"

"Yes, but . . ."

"I gotta go." Tommy hung up.

Michael was left with the dead phone in his hand.

26

Michael sat at a table at a McDonald's on Santa Monica Boulevard and watched the door for Barry Wimmer. He recognized the short, bearded man from his own description and waved him toward the table. Wimmer stopped at the counter and picked up a Big Mac and fries first.

Michael shook the man's hand as he sat down.

"First meeting I ever took at McDonald's," Wimmer said.

"Morton's didn't seem appropriate."

Wimmer emitted a short, rueful laugh. "No, I don't guess you'd want to be seen with me at Morton's."

"Or any other industry hangout," Michael said.

Wimmer looked ill for a moment. "Thanks for reminding me," he said bitterly.

"When did you get out?" Michael asked.

"Four months ago."

"How are you making a living?"

"I've worked up a couple of budgets for friends," Wimmer replied, attacking the Big Mac.

Michael reached into the briefcase beside him and fished out a budget for *Pacific Afternoons*. "Tell me what you think of this," he said, handing Wimmer the document across the table.

Wimmer put down his burger and began leafing through the pages, chewing absently. He took his time. "This is as tight as anything I've ever seen," he said finally, "but it'll work if you can shoot outside L.A."

"I want to shoot in Carmel."

Wimmer nodded. "If you've already got a budget, why did you want to see me?"

"I've heard some good things about you."

"Not recently, I guess. My name's mud in this town."

"Very recently. I heard that you may have taken various studios for as much as five million dollars over the past ten years."

"I got sent away for two hundred grand," Wimmer said. "That's all I'll cop to."

"What did you do with all the money?" Michael asked. "I'm curious."

"I lived well," Wimmer said.

"You lived high, too, from what I've heard."

Wimmer smiled ruefully. "You could say that."

"Are you still using?"

"Prison didn't do much for me, but it got me off cocaine. There was a pretty good therapy program."

"Out of all the money you took did you save anything?"

Wimmer snorted. "If I had, do you think I'd have gone to jail for two hundred grand? I'd have made restitution."

"What are your plans for the future?"

"I was thinking of starting a private course for production management."

"That should buy groceries."

"And not much else."

"Are you interested in getting back into the business?"

"Doing what? Props?"

"As a production manager."

Wimmer stopped chewing and looked at Michael for a long time. "Don't fuck around with my head, mister."

"I'm quite serious."

"On this project?" He tapped the budget.

"On this project."

"You think you could trust me not to steal?"

Michael wiped his mouth and threw his napkin onto the table. "Barry, if you come to work for me, stealing will be your principal duty."

Wimmer stared at Michael, apparently stunned into silence.

"Let me ask you something," Michael said. "How did you get caught on the two hundred thousand?"

Wimmer swallowed hard and fiddled with his french fries. "I had a producer who was as smart as I was."

"I'm smarter than you are, Barry," Michael said. "And if you were stealing from my production, I would catch you at it."

Wimmer nodded. "I see," he said. "You won't catch me, is that it?"

"That's it," Michael said.

"We split what I can take?"

"Not quite. Not fifty-fifty."

"What did you have in mind?"

"I'll give you twenty percent of anything you can rake off the budget."

"What happens if we get caught?"

"Who's going to catch you, if not me?"

"Doesn't Centurion have any controls at all?"

"Of course they do, and very good controls, too. But from what I've heard, you're something of a genius at fooling the studios."

"You could say that," Wimmer agreed.

"What's the number at the bottom of that budget?" Michael asked, nodding toward the document.

"Eight million, give or take."

"What sort of budget would that be in this town?"

"Tight, under any circumstances; but who's your star?"

"Robert Hart."

Wimmer's eyes widened. "And your writer?"

"Mark Adair."

"Director?"

"A very bright kid from UCLA Film School."

"Then eight million is an impossible budget, even with a kid director."

"Would ten million be more in line?"

"Fifteen million would be more in line, if

everything were cut to the bone and Hart took points instead of salary."

"Suppose we settle at nine and a half million. We shoot the picture for eight million, and you, employing your special genius, flesh it out to nine million five. You think you could do that?"

"For twenty percent? In the blink of an eye."

Michael smiled. "That's what I thought."

"What do I get paid for the picture?"

"You'll work cheap. Nobody will be surprised; at this point you'd take just about any job, wouldn't you?"

"I would."

"You've never, ah, collaborated with anybody on something like this, have you?"

"No."

"Well, we had better get a couple of things straight. First of all, there will never be any transaction of cash between you and me. Every week, you'll go to the local Federal Express office and send eighty percent of the rake-off to an address I'll give you. I want you to remember at all times that I'm smarter than you, Barry; that's very important to our working relationship."

"Okay, you're smarter than me. I can live with that."

"My share of the money is going to be untraceable; I'll help you see that your share is, too. It is not in my interests for you to get caught."

"What happens if I do get caught? I mean, if you're underestimating Centurion's controls?"

"I assure you that I'm not, but I'll give you a

straight answer to your question: If you get caught, you'll take the fall. I'll testify against you myself; there won't be any way you can implicate me, and if you try, I'll make things even worse for you."

"You're a sweet guy," Wimmer said.

"Is anybody else in town going to hire you?"

"Nope."

"Then you're right; I'm a sweet guy—as long as things go smoothly. You fuck up, and you're back in jail; you fuck *me*, and—I want you to take this seriously, Barry—I'll see you dead. That's not a euphemism; it's a serious promise."

Wimmer stared at Michael.

"On the brighter side, you'll make some very nice money, and you'll be seen to rehabilitate yourself. I'm going to make a lot of pictures, and as long as our relationship works out, you'll have a job."

"That sounds good," Wimmer said.

"So we understand each other? I wouldn't want there to be any misunderstanding."

"We understand each other completely," Wimmer said firmly.

"Good." Michael extended his hand and Wimmer shook it. "Be at my office on the Centurion lot first thing tomorrow morning. I'll have a desk ready for you, and I'll leave a pass at the gate."

"Yes, sir," Wimmer said, smiling.

27

Monday night at Morton's. The *crème de la crème* of the motion picture industry sat in the dimly lit restaurant on Melrose Avenue and displayed their standing to each other. Michael and Vanessa sat with Leo and Amanda Goldman at a table between that of Michael Ovitz, head of the talent agency Creative Artists Agency, and that of Peter Guber, head of Sony Pictures. Michael had been introduced to and had exchanged desultory chat with both men. Being in their presence, on equal terms, gave him a satisfaction he had not felt since he had made his deal with Centurion.

After dinner, when the women had adjourned to the ladies' room, Leo put his elbows on the table and leaned forward. "There's a guy I'd like you to consider to direct *Pacific Afternoons*," Leo said. "His name is Marty White."

"I appreciate the suggestion, Leo," Michael said, "but I think I've already found a director."

Leo's eyebrows went up. "Who? How could you do that without my knowing about it?"

"Leo, I shouldn't have to remind you that I don't need your approval to hire a director."

"Jesus fucking Christ, I know that; what I don't know is why I didn't *know* about it. I know *everything* that goes on at my studio."

"So I've heard," Michael said.

"You couldn't take a meeting with somebody about that job that I wouldn't know about. Not with any director in town."

"This guy has never directed anything. That's why you don't know about him."

Leo leaned forward and made an effort to lower his voice. "You've hired some schmuck who *never directed a picture*?"

"Well, he's directed things at school."

"At *school*!"

"He's at UCLA Film School."

"You hired a *student* to direct this movie?"

"Leo, *I* was a student at film school when I produced *Downtown Nights*."

"That's different."

"No, it's not different; it's exactly the same."

"I think you've gone crazy, Michael."

"Did you screen the reel?"

"What reel?"

"Leo, I sent you the kid's reel last Wednesday."

"I didn't get to it yet."

"Well, if you had gotten to it, your blood pressure would be a lot lower right now."

"So, what's on the reel?"

"A scene from a Henry James novel that was so good I couldn't believe it."

"Just one scene?"

"A scene of eight pages with a long tracking shot, an orchestra, and seven speaking parts."

"Who's this kid?"

"His name is Eliot Rosen."

"Well, at least he's Jewish."

Michael laughed.

"Are you Jewish, Michael? I could never figure it out."

"Half," Michael lied. "My mother."

"What was your father?"

"Italian."

"What did they do about your religious upbringing?"

"I was a lapsed Catholic by the time I was six."

"If you were Jewish, you'd be perfect."

"You're going to love Eliot Rosen. He'll probably drive you crazy, but you'll love him. He may be the new Orson Welles."

Leo groaned. "You got any idea how much money was lost backing Orson?"

"Eliot is going to make you a lot of money; I'll see to it."

"Well, you're as tight with a buck as anybody I ever saw; if he works for you, he'll make money for me." Leo flicked the ash off his cigar. "I hear you hired a production manager from outside the studio."

"That's right, Leo; I wanted somebody who'd report to me instead of you."

"You hired Barry Wimmer."

"That's right."

"Michael, you gotta know he did time for stealing from a production."

"He was a cokehead. He's clean now."

"I'm worried."

"Leo, he's so grateful for the chance that he'll work three times as hard as anybody else would." Michael paused. "Cheap, too."

"I like that part. If he steals from me, I'll take it out of your end."

"Fair enough."

"What're you paying the kid Jewish director?"

"Two hundred thousand."

Leo smiled broadly. "Don't you let him fuck up."

"Leo, even if he fucks up he won't cost you nearly as much as Marty White would."

The women returned to the table, and as they sat down, Amanda Goldman's foot ran down the back of Michael's calf. He gave her a brief smile and filed that move away for later consideration.

28

Michael put down Mark Adair's first-draft screenplay of *Pacific Afternoons* and picked up the telephone.

"Hello?" a deep voice answered.

"Mark, it's Michael Vincent."

"What did you think?" Adair asked.

"I think it's wonderful. You've captured the book, both in structure and in intent, and you've made the book's dialogue work beautifully."

"But . . . ?"

"But nothing. I think it's shootable as is."

"No producer has ever said that to me," Adair said warily. "There has to be something else."

"There is something else, but it in no way detracts from what you've done."

"What is it?"

"Near the end, you've left out a crucial scene and substituted something that doesn't work nearly as well."

"Are you talking about the scene where the doctor sings to the girl and wins her heart?"

"I am."

"There are two reasons that could never work in this film, Michael."

"What are they?"

"First, it would come off as mawkish, sentimental, and unbelievable to a modern audience; second, you'll never get Bob Hart to do the scene."

"Mark, the scene is sentimental; I'll grant you that, but it is by no means mawkish—at least not the way we'll shoot it."

"Name me a picture where that sort of thing has worked."

"All right, *A Room with a View.*"

Adair was quiet for a moment. "There was no singing in that."

"No, but the period was one that accepted sentimentality as normal; the period of *Pacific Afternoons* is much the same, *and* the characters are not very different."

"What about Bob Hart? How will you get him to do it?"

"You leave that to me. When the time comes, I'll want your support to help persuade him, though."

"I don't know."

"Tell you what, Mark; I'll make a private deal with you. Put the scene back in—just as it is in the book—and if, when you've seen it on film, you don't think it works, then I'll shoot your substitute scene."

"You've made me an offer I can't refuse. Now

tell me what other criticisms you have of my script."

"I can't think of a thing. I'm sure Bob Hart— and especially Susan Hart—will have some comments, and the director may as well, but it won't be anything that damages what you've done. I won't let that happen."

"Who's going to direct?"

"A young director named Eliot Rosen. He's very smart and sensitive, and you're going to love him."

"I'll get right on a second draft."

"Don't write a second draft; just insert the scene, and leave everything else as it is."

"Bless you, my son." Adair hung up.

Michael replaced the receiver and reflected on how well everything was going. His intercom buzzed. "Yes?"

"Michael," Margot said, "Sergeant Rivera is here; I've told him you've got a tough morning, but he'd like to see you if you can manage it."

A trickle of fear ran down Michael's bowels. "Send him in," he said, keeping his voice calm.

Rivera was alone this time. "Thanks for seeing me," he said, extending his hand. "I won't take much of your time."

"Glad to see you, Sergeant," Michael said, shaking his hand and waving him to a seat. He held up Mark Adair's screenplay. "The first draft of the screenplay of *Pacific Afternoons* is in, and it's great. Looks like we'll be shooting in the spring."

"Good," the sergeant said, easing into a chair.

"I thought I'd bring you up to date on where we are on the Moriarty homicide."

"Great, I'm all ears. I haven't seen anything in the papers about it for a few weeks."

"I haven't released anything to the papers."

"Have you made an arrest?"

"No, and I'm not sure we will."

Michael guarded against feeling relief. "Why not?"

"Looks like a mob hit, pure and simple; a contract job."

"Moriarty had mob connections?"

"Maybe, maybe not, but somebody who's connected wanted Moriarty dead, I guarantee you."

"Tell me about it."

"The car was driven by a low-grade hood from Vegas named Dominic Ippolito—real scum."

"How'd you find that out?"

"Some hikers found Dominic dumped in the desert near Twenty-Nine Palms; his fingerprints were on file."

"Did you find the car?"

"Dominic was *in* the car. It was a mess—down a ravine four or five hundred feet."

"Is that it?"

"Not quite; we found some other prints in the car that were interesting."

Michael's heart nearly stopped, but he didn't blink. "Yeah?"

"The car was stolen; there were the car owner's prints, of course, and his wife's, but the other set was unusual."

"Tell me."

"They belonged to somebody named . . ." He took a folded sheet of paper from his pocket and glanced at it, then handed it to Michael. "Vincente Michaele Callabrese."

Michael found himself staring at his own birth certificate. "Who is he?" he managed to say. He put the paper on his desk so that Rivera wouldn't see his hands shaking.

"He's the son of Onofrio and Martina Callabrese, and he's twenty-eight years old. That's all I know; that much was on the birth certificate."

Michael, who had been imagining handcuffs, saw a glimmer of hope. "You weren't able to find out anything else?"

"Nothing, and that's very unusual. There is apparently no other piece of paper in the world on this guy—no Social Security number, no driver's license, no insurance—the guy has never had a credit card or a charge account. The only reason we know about him at all is that he had an arrest when he was eighteen, for car theft—the charges were dropped for lack of evidence—and he got himself printed. That put him in the FBI fingerprint files. There was no photograph on file; I don't know why."

Michael remembered it well. "You mean there's no way to track him down?"

"Nope. But he's almost certainly mobbed up."

"Why do you say that? Because he's Italian?"

"No, it's just that it's nearly impossible for anybody to live to be twenty-eight years old in this country and not have a lot of paper on him. The only people who have no paper on them are people who've been using forged or stolen paper all their lives, and that adds up to mob."

"So what does all this mean?"

"It probably means something like this: Moriarty has some dealings at some time with somebody who's connected, and something goes wrong; he makes an enemy. The enemy talks to somebody, money changes hands, and a contract is put out on the guy. Callabrese, or whatever name he goes by, is probably the mob contact. He was the second man in the car. He, or somebody he knows, hires Ippolito to make the hit, and Callabrese goes along to make sure it's right. Then, when it's all over, Callabrese puts a bullet into Ippolito and dumps him and the car in the desert, thus making it impossible for Ippolito to ever tell anybody who hired him. Only Callabrese wasn't smart enough to wipe his prints off the car. That tells me something about him."

"What?"

"That he's not the brains behind all this. Otherwise, he'd have taken more care to cover his tracks."

"I see." Rivera was right; he'd been stupid. But he'd been so frightened at the scene that he hadn't thought about prints until later. "So what's your next move?"

"I don't have a next move," Rivera replied. "But one of these days this guy Callabrese will make a mistake and get picked up. I've flagged his prints, so if he ever gets arrested again and is printed, I'll get a call from the FBI inside of a week."

"Sergeant, I'll be frank with you; it doesn't look like we've got a movie here. This is all too incomplete."

"I figured."

"But if you ever come across another case that looks good, I want to hear from you." Michael had meant this to dismiss the policeman, but Rivera didn't move.

"There's something I'd like to satisfy myself on," he said.

"What's that?"

"Well, it's interesting that this Callabrese guy has two names that are similar to yours— Vincente and Michaele."

"An interesting coincidence," Michael said. He was frightened again now.

"How old are you, Mr. Vincent?"

"Thirty."

"Do you have some paper that would document that?"

"Sure." Michael was ready for this; he opened the file drawer in his desk and rummaged through the personal file. "Here," he said, handing the policeman a birth certificate.

Rivera read it carefully. "You're thirty, all right, and Callabrese was born at Bellevue Hospital, whereas you were born at St. Vincent's." He looked up. "Are you Italian?"

Michael shook his head. "Jewish."

"I see you're growing a beard."

"I've had a beard off and on for years."

"I wonder if you'd be willing to do a lineup for me."

"Are you kidding?" Michael said. "I saw a movie when I was a kid where a guy agreed to do that, and he got picked out, even though he was innocent."

"Well, you're within your rights," Rivera said, standing up.

"It isn't that I'm standing on my rights," Michael said, walking him to the door. "I just don't have the time for something like that. I'd waste half a day, and that's a lot of money in this business."

"Sure, I understand." He held out his hand. "I'll let you know if I come up with another case that might make a movie."

"You do that," Michael said. "And Sergeant?"

"Yes?"

"Could I have my birth certificate back?"

"Oh, sorry," Rivera said, handing back the paper.

"I'll be happy to make a copy for you, if you need it," Michael said.

"Oh, no, no; just an oversight."

Some oversight, Michael thought, as he watched the homicide detective go. The certificate was real, on file—Tommy Pro had seen to that years ago. But now Michael's fingerprints were on it. He sat down at his desk and took a few deep breaths. He hoped to God that Rivera was satisfied.

Margot came in with the mail. "This is everything that isn't junk," she said, placing the pile on his desk.

"Thanks." He rummaged around his desktop and through the drawers.

"What are you looking for?" she asked.

"My letter opener."

"You're always losing things; I'll find it while you're at lunch."

When Michael came back from lunch, the letter opener was on his desk.

29

Michael looked across his desk at his director. Eliot Rosen was tall, skinny, and ill-shaven. At this moment he was exploring a nostril for something.

"Eliot," Michael said, "promise me that when Bob and Susan Hart get here you won't pick your nose."

"Sorry," the young man said, blushing. Eliot blushed a lot.

"I've shown them your reel, and they're impressed, but they still want to meet you. There's a lot riding on this meeting, Eliot."

"I know that," Rosen said.

"Remember, you're not just talking to the actor but to his wife as well. Susan Hart is the hardest to handle of the two, and I don't want you to mess this up by kowtowing too much to Hart. Include her in everything you say, and if you can muster some charm, that would help, too."

"I'll do my best," Rosen said.

"If there's an argument about *anything*, follow my lead, do you understand?"

"Listen, I have opinions, too."

"Not at this point you don't. If you have an opinion that might spark some controversy with the Harts, express it to me first, and privately. If it's a point I think we can win, then I'll carry the ball, okay?"

Rosen nodded. "Okay," he said sullenly.

"Eliot," Michael said placatingly, "you're at the beginning of what I think is going to be a big career. Don't screw it up by alienating a powerful star and his influential wife. If they want something that's bad for the movie, I'll protect the movie, don't worry. And when we get to the part about the singing scene, don't say anything; just nod agreement."

"I've got a lot of problems with that scene," Rosen said.

"Eliot, we've already been over this; the scene stays in, and I don't want to hear another word about it."

"All right, all right, you're the boss."

"Don't resent it, Eliot; everybody has a boss around here, except Leo Goldman, who is, effectively, God. Leo has given me a lot of freedom, and I'm not going to let anybody compromise that, especially a first-time director."

"All right, all right."

"Don't worry, this picture is going to establish you." He smiled. "After *Pacific Afternoons* I won't be able to afford you."

Rosen smiled. "I like that idea."

There was a brief knock on the door, and Margot showed in Robert and Susan Hart.

Michael went to Susan first, giving her an affectionate hug and kiss, then he shook Bob's hand warmly. "I'm so glad to see you both," he said, "and I can't wait to hear your reactions to the screenplay. And may I introduce Eliot Rosen?"

The young director shook both their hands. "Your work has given me a great deal of pleasure," he said to Bob Hart. "I'm thrilled to be on this picture."

Hart accepted this praise graciously, and everybody took a seat on the facing sofas before the huge fireplace.

"I remember this set," Hart said. "I loved the movie, and I loved Randolph. I always wanted to play the part."

Michael smiled. "That's a very good idea," he said. "When we've finished *Pacific Afternoons*, we ought to explore the possibilities." He leaned forward on the sofa. "Now," he said, "tell me what you thought of the screenplay."

"I just loved it," Hart said.

"There are problems," Susan interjected.

Michael picked up a copy of the script from a stack on the coffee table. "I want to hear about every one of them, starting from the beginning."

Susan Hart, speaking without notes, went through the screenplay, scene by scene, noting criticisms large and small. Michael noted that nearly every one of them was aimed at increasing the size of her husband's part and augmenting his dialogue. He agreed with Susan immediately on more than half her points and promised to consult with Mark Adair on the rest, then get back to her.

"Finally," she said, "the singing scene has to go."

Michael did not react immediately, but turned to her husband. "Bob, how do you feel about that scene?"

"I can do it," Hart said quietly.

"But he won't," Susan said firmly. "Bob has devoted the past twenty-five years to building an image that has become solid gold. I won't allow him to do something that would shatter that image in the minds of his public; we'll back out of the film first."

"Let me tell you how I feel about that, Susan," Michael said to her, then directed himself almost entirely to Bob Hart. "Bob is at a turning point in his career; he has mined the vein of police, western, and action movies brilliantly, and he has reached a point where to continue exclusively in that vein would simply be repetition. If he does that, even the fans and critics who have loved all of it are going to begin to fade away. Another thing: it has been a long time since a script has really drawn on all of Bob's talent as an actor."

"That's very true," Hart said. His wife glanced sharply at him.

"Bob has resources that his public has not seen yet, and this film is going to stun them, I promise you. Here we have a somewhat retiring but thoroughly masculine character with many, many facets. He proves his manhood when he stands up to the trainer who has been abusing horses, and he shows remarkable sensitivity in the scenes with his child patients. Still, he is unable to express himself to this woman he fears may be too young for him. *But*, in this one terribly moving scene, he wins her heart forever. Now what can be wrong with that?"

Susan Hart spoke up. "Certainly, what you say about the scene with the trainer and those with the children is true, and certainly, the doctor has to win the girl, but why the hell does he have to *sing*?"

"Because he is an incurable romantic, Sue, and this is an incurably romantic film. That is its great strength, and that is what is going to create enormous word of mouth for this film. What's wrong with singing?"

Susan drew herself up and began to reply, but she was, uncharacteristically, interrupted by her husband.

"It wouldn't be the first time I've sung," Bob Hart said.

Susan turned and stared at him. "What?"

"Long before we even met, darling, I was trained for the musical stage; in fact, that was where I thought my career would lead."

"You never told me that," she said, astonished.

"It never came up. Before I joined the Actors Studio I was concentrating mainly on finding a part in a musical. It was Lee Strasberg who saw the dramatic talent in me and who changed my direction."

"For which we can all thank him," Michael said. "Let me ask you, Susan, have you heard this piece of music?"

"No, and that's not the point," she replied.

"I want you to hear it right now," Michael said. He picked up the phone. "Margot, please send in Anton and Hermann."

Anton Gruber and Hermann Hecht entered the room and everyone settled in to listen.

Anton played an introduction, then Hermann began to sing. Michael glanced surreptitiously at Susan Hart from time to time, but her face was a blank mask. When Hermann had finished, everyone applauded, then the musicians left.

Michael turned to Bob and Susan. "Well?"

"I can sing it," Hart said. "It's within my range. I'll have to do a lot of vocalizing; get back in shape."

"Susan?" Michael asked.

"I grant you it's beautiful," she said, "but why does it have to be in German?"

"Tell you what, Susan, let's shoot it, then decide," Michael said. "I promise you I'm not going to make a fool of Bob. If you don't like it when it's done, we'll shoot an alternative scene."

She turned to her husband. "Do you really feel comfortable with this?"

Hart shrugged. "Let's see how it goes."

"All right," Susan said, "we'll look at it on film, then decide. But nobody, and I mean *nobody*, in the industry sees the scene until we've approved its inclusion."

"That's fine with me," Michael said. "Eliot?"

"Fine with me, too," Rosen said. It was the first time he had spoken.

"I'll get back to you on the screenplay after I've talked to Mark," Michael said. The meeting adjourned.

When the Harts had gone, Eliot Rosen spoke again. "Do you really think she'll sit still for that scene?" he asked. "She looks like a pretty tough cookie to me."

"Trust me," Michael said. "Anyway, the scene is what kept her from getting around to questions about you."

"I'm beginning to like the scene," Rosen said.

30

Michael stood in the center of Leo Goldman's enormous office and basked in the glow of adulation. A hundred of the film industry's movers and shakers—producers, studio heads, actors, directors, and journalists—filled the room. They had all just seen the first screening of *Downtown Nights*, and there was nothing but praise in the air.

Michael's beard had grown fuller now, and he felt reasonably safe in this crowd, although he had spent the first ten minutes of the after-screening party checking out every face in the crowd. None of them was the man in the Mercedes who had witnessed the murder of Daniel J. Moriarty, and none of them was the woman in curlers across the street.

He was receiving the congratulations of one of the town's hottest directors when Leo's secretary tugged at his elbow.

"What is it?" Michael asked, trying not to sound irritable.

"The security guard at the main gate is on the phone and wants to talk with you. Apparently there's someone who claims he knows you trying to get onto the lot."

Michael excused himself from the conversation and went into the outer office to take the call.

"Mr. Vincent, this is Jim at the front gate. There's a man here named Parish who says he's the director of your picture; he wants to come to the screening."

"Chuck Parish?" Michael asked. This was inconvenient.

"That's the one."

Michael thought for a moment. "Jim, give him directions to my office; I'll meet him there."

"Yessir."

Michael hung up the phone and left the building. He walked quickly toward his office and arrived just in time to see Chuck Parish climbing out of a battered sports car. As Michael approached, Parish tripped getting out of the car and fell on his face. A briefcase that had been in his hand bounced and came to rest a few feet away.

Michael picked up the briefcase, then helped the young man to his feet. "Careful there, Chuck; you took a bad spill." He looked terrible, Michael thought.

"Goddamned car," Chuck said. "Can't get used to it; belongs to a friend."

"Come inside." Michael unlocked the door, turned on some lights, then led Chuck into his office. "That's a pretty bad scrape on your fore-head," Michael said. "Let me get something for it." He went to the liquor cabinet, poured some vodka on a tissue, then returned and dabbed at Chuck's forehead until the scrape was clean. The smell of the alcohol blended in with whatever Chuck had been drinking.

"Do you think I could have some of that stuff in a glass?" he asked.

"Sure." Michael filled a glass with ice and poured vodka over it. "Tonic?"

"Just ice will do."

Michael gave him the drink and showed him to one of the facing sofas. "I didn't know you were in L.A. Why didn't you call me?"

"I've been here a couple weeks," Chuck said, taking a big gulp of his vodka. "Heard there was a screening of my movie tonight."

"There was, earlier," Michael replied. "It was over an hour ago. I wish I'd known you were in town; I'd have invited you."

"Bad timing, as usual," Chuck said. "How'd they like it?"

"The reaction was mixed," Michael lied.

" 'Mixed,' huh? So it's going nowhere?"

"Too early to tell."

"How's the lovely Vanessa?" he asked bitterly.

"All right, I guess," Michael replied, then changed the subject quickly. "How are things going? What are you working on?"

"I've written another screenplay," Chuck said, staring into the cold fireplace.

"Good; I'd like to read it."

Chuck opened his briefcase and tossed Michael some bound pages.

Michael looked at the cover. "*Inside Straight*. Nice title; what's it about?"

"I'd rather you'd read the whole thing without my telling you too much."

"All right; I'll try to get it read over the weekend."

"I can't wait that long."

"Beg pardon?"

"I want to sell it to you now."

"But I haven't read it yet."

"It's better than *Downtown Nights*," Chuck said. "You can trust me on that."

"I don't doubt it, Chuck, but I can't buy it without reading it."

"Why not? Don't you have any authority around here? I can't imagine you making a deal, Michael, that didn't put you in the driver's seat."

"I have the authority, Chuck, but don't you think it's a little unfair to ask me to buy it sight unseen?"

"I need the money, Michael."

Michael was stunned. "Chuck, the last time I saw you, you had something like three quarters of a million dollars in cash. What do you mean, you need the money?"

"I just need it."

"Why?"

"There are a couple people pressing me."

"What sort of people?"

"Very insistent people."

"What happened to all the money, Chuck?"

"Well, there were a couple of bad investments and some slow ponies. And there was this very expensive lady," Chuck said. "She and I picked up this little habit."

"Coke."

Chuck nodded. "God, I just don't know how the money could have gone so fast."

"I would have thought that after seeing what happened to Carol Geraldi you'd have stayed away from coke."

"Look, it's nothing I can't handle. I'm going into rehab next week—got a spot nailed down at a clinic up the coast. I just need to pay a few debts and get myself tided over until I can start the program, you know?"

Michael flipped quickly through the screenplay. There was no way to judge it so quickly, but it looked well organized, at least. And Chuck Parish was a very talented writer.

"How much do you want for it?"

"Jesus, I don't know. I'm into a shark for over fifty grand, and there's a connection or two who's looking for another thirty or so."

Christ, Michael thought; he really was in deep.

"How about a quarter of a million?"

"Chuck . . ."

"I know, I know, you haven't even read it. Believe me, Michael, it's my best work. It's terrific."

"How soon do you need the money?"

"Now."

"Now? Chuck, it's nine o'clock in the evening; I can't get a check cut at this hour."

"First thing tomorrow morning, then?"

"I can't pay you a quarter of a million dollars for this sight unseen."

"How much?"

"You really owe eighty grand to these people?"

"At least."

"All right, Chuck, I'll give you a hundred thousand for it, sight unseen."

"I'll take it," Chuck said without hesitation.

Michael went to his desk and found a standard boilerplate rights contract, then came back to the sofa. He placed the contract on the table and handed Chuck a pen. "Sign right here," he said, pointing.

"There are a lot of empty blanks," Chuck said.

"I'll fill them in later."

"When do I get the money?"

"I'll get a check cut first thing tomorrow morning."

"I need cash, not a check."

"All right, meet me at the studio's bank at the corner of Wilshire and Beverly Glen at, say, eleven. No, make it noon."

"Noon. You promise?"

"Of course."

Chuck signed the contract.

Michael took the contract back to his desk and put it into a drawer. "Chuck, I'd like to talk longer, but I've got to be somewhere."

Chuck stood up. "I want to direct it," he said.

"I'd like you to direct," Michael said, "but I can't commit on that right now."

"Where's my copy of the contract?"

"I'll complete it and bring your copy to the bank. Now you'll have to excuse me, Chuck."

They shook hands and Michael walked him to his car. "Noon tomorrow," he said.

"Noon tomorrow."

Like hell, Michael thought. Not unless this is a real winner. He waved good-bye, went back to Leo's office to say good night to everybody, then went back to his office, found a legal pad and a pen, adjusted a reading lamp, and stretched out on a sofa. *Now let's see if this thing is any good*, he thought, opening the screenplay. If it's not, Chuck will have a long wait at the bank.

Two hours later, Michael put down the screenplay and leafed through his notes. Chuck had been right; it needed some work, work that he could do himself, but it was terrific. *Inside Straight* was going to be his next picture, right after *Pacific Afternoons*. He drove home feeling great.

31

Michael got to the office early the next day and began working up Chuck's contract. As soon as Margot came in he gave her the signed copy and asked her to fill in the blanks, then he called Leo Goldman.

"Great screening, huh?" Leo chortled.

"It seemed to go well."

"Well? It went terrific, kid; I'm smelling Academy Award nominations!"

"I'm glad to hear it."

"How's *Pacific Afternoons* going?"

"Extremely well. We'll have a finished script very soon."

"By finished, do you mean approved by Susan Hart?"

"I do."

"Good going. She's not easy to handle, but you're doing a great job. Let me give you a tip about the Harts: Bob is a lot weaker than he seems. He's been through a couple of drying-out programs, and he does fine for a while, but as soon as he's faced with a role that scares him, he's back on the bottle. His particular weakness is fine French wines. Susan made him sell his cellar at auction earlier this year, and the sale brought over a million dollars. The man had the largest collection of 1961 red Bordeaux in the United States; he'd been collecting them for years. I bought some of them myself, before the auction, but I can't serve them when the Harts come over. The man is helpless in the presence of a Mouton Rothschild."

"He seemed quite confident at our first script meeting; very much in control, not yielding to her."

"The man's an actor, and a good one; remember that. Susan is not a monster, she just wants to avoid any situation that might get Bob drinking again. She puts a lot of effort into that. When you start shooting, whatever you do, keep Bob away from wine."

"I'll keep it in mind." He certainly would.

"Any idea what you'll do after you wrap *Pacific Afternoons*?"

"That's why I'm calling, Leo; I've bought a script—only last night, in fact."

"What is it?"

"It's called *Inside Straight*, and it's about a friendly weekly poker game where three of the players conspire to take one of the others for everything."

"Who wrote it?"

"Chuck Parish, the guy who wrote *Downtown Nights*."

"Sounds good; what did you pay?"

"Two hundred thousand, and it would be worth half a million if some agent were shopping it around."

"Great!"

"One thing, Leo, Chuck is in some sort of a bind, and he wants his money in cash. I told him I'd meet him at the bank this morning with a check that he can cash right away."

"Have you got a signed contract?"

"Yep."

"Have you got the screenplay in a safe place?"

"I do."

"I'll call Accounting and get your check cut; I'll call the bank, too, and tell them you'll want to cash it."

"Tell them we'd like a private room for the transaction."

"You got it. Listen, kid, do you want me to read the screenplay before you do this?"

"I'd love you to read it when I fix a few things, but believe me, it's not necessary now. I don't want to option it, either."

"I trust your judgment, kid. Your check will be ready in an hour."

Michael was at the bank at 11:30 with his own briefcase and a cheap plastic one. He sought out the branch manager and introduced himself.

"I'm glad you called ahead," the manager said. "We needed some time to put that much cash together." Michael handed the man both briefcases. "Ask your people to put a hundred thousand in each one," he said. "I'm expecting a Mr. Parish, and I'll give you the endorsed check as soon as he arrives."

"I'm glad you brought two," the manager replied, taking the cases. "We didn't have a lot of hundreds, so most of it is in twenties and fifties." He showed Michael to a conference room and left with the briefcases. He was back in five minutes. "I'll have to have the check, of course, before I turn the money over to you."

"Of course," Michael replied. "Why don't you keep the money at your desk until I get the check endorsed by Mr. Parish?"

"Glad to." The manager left with the two briefcases.

Chuck arrived at five minutes before the hour and was shown to the conference room; he didn't bother with pleasantries. "Did you bring the money?"

Michael took an envelope from an inside pocket. "I've got the check right here; you'll have to endorse it." He took the check from the envelope, turned it face down on the conference table, and gave Chuck a pen. "Sign right here."

Chuck hurriedly signed the check; his hands were shaking, and he looked even worse than he had the evening before.

"I'll be right back," Michael said. He left the room and took the check to the manager's desk. "Here's your endorsed check," he said.

The manager examined it. "Do I have your assurance that you know this man to be who he says he is?"

"You have it."

The manager handed over the two briefcases.

Michael returned to the conference room with both cases. He entered, placed his own case on the floor beside the table, then put the plastic one on the table top. "I want you to count it," he said to Chuck.

Chuck opened the case, shuffled briefly through the money, then closed it. "Looks okay to me; I'll trust you."

"It's all there," Michael said. He took more papers from his jacket pocket. "Here's your copy of the contract with my signature." He handed the folded papers to Chuck, who put them in his own pocket. Michael produced another sheet of paper and placed it on the table. "I'll need you to sign a receipt, and then the money's yours."

Chuck signed the receipt without looking at it, then stood up. "Thanks, I'm out of here."

"Chuck, before you go, there's something you had better understand."

"Yeah?"

"The contract and the receipt state the amount as two hundred thousand dollars."

"What?"

"I've put that figure in for my own reasons, and for all practical purposes I have just given you and you have just received two hundred thousand dollars."

"I don't understand."

"Don't worry, it'll help you get your price up in this town. You can always show people a contract that says two hundred thousand instead of a hundred. And it would be in your own best interests, if anyone should ever ask, to say that you got two hundred thousand."

"Michael, are you stealing money from me?"

"Chuck, if you ever say anything like that to me again—or to anybody else—you and I will have done business for the last time. Now, if you're unhappy in any way, you can put that briefcase back on the table, I'll give you back your contract, and we'll call it a day." He waited for an answer.

"I'm happy, Michael," Chuck said. "After all, who else would give me a hundred grand for a screenplay he hadn't even read?"

"That's right, Chuck," Michael said. He smiled. "Just remember, you and I are both going to be around for a long time; we've already made some money together, and we'll make a lot more."

Chuck shook his hand and left. Michael waited five minutes, then picked up his own briefcase and left, waving good-bye to the banker.

Michael got into the Porsche and drove downtown to his own bank, the Kensington Trust. Derek Winfield received him in his office.

"I'd like to make a deposit," Michael said.

"Of course," Winfield replied. "I'll just have this run through a counting machine to confirm the total." He left the room with the briefcase for a few minutes, then came back and handed Michael the empty case and a receipt. "Is there anything else I can do for you?"

"I'd like to know my current balance," Michael said.

"Of course." Winfield took a key from his pocket and inserted it into a computer terminal on his desk. He typed a few keystrokes, looked at the screen, then typed a few more strokes. A printer on a side table hummed and produced a sheet of paper. Winfield handed it to Michael. "Interest will be paid tomorrow on the past week's earnings," he said. "This amount doesn't include that."

Michael looked at the sheet of paper and smiled. "Thank you," he said. "I'm very pleased."

"I'm glad," Winfield replied. "And today's deposit will be earning from tomorrow."

Michael left Winfield's office whistling. It was difficult to know how things could be any better.

32

Special Agent Thomas Carson of the Los Angeles office of the Federal Bureau of Investigation leaned over the counter and pressed his ear to a headset. Lined up along the twelve-foot counter were half a dozen Ampex reel-to-reel tape recorders, moving spasmodically.

"It's his second trip to the bank," the technician said, twitching the volume slightly so Carson could hear better.

"What happened the first time?" Carson asked. "Remind me."

"My memory is that he deposited a large sum of money, but you'll have to check the transcripts to be sure. Callabrese's name is in the log for that date, and the log should be cross-referenced by now."

"Thanks, Ken," Carson said. "I'll look up Mr. Callabrese." He went to the files, found the name, and referenced the date; then he went to another filing cabinet and extracted the transcript. He sat down and read it thoroughly, then reread the file on the Kensington Trust. There was a weekly meeting with the bureau chief in a few minutes, and Carson was light on input; this would give him something to talk about. He went to the computer room and requested a profile on Vincente Callabrese, waiting for the printout. He was not the first, he noted in the logbook. An LAPD detective named Rivera had gotten in ahead of him. He called Rivera.

"This is Tom Carson over at the FBI," he said.

"Hi."

An unenthusiastic response. Why did cops hate the FBI so much? He had never understood it. "I just ran a guy named Vincente Callabrese through the system, and I saw you did, too. What have you got?"

"His fingerprints were on a car used in a crime. A mob hood from Vegas named Ippolito stole a car and ran a guy down with it. Contract job. Callabrese's prints were on the dashboard."

"And what do you surmise from that?"

"I surmise he was in the car. A witness said there was a second man."

"Where do you go from here?"

"Nowhere," Rivera replied. "The guy's a complete zero in the system; no paper of any kind. All I can do is put a flag on his record and wait for him to get arrested. It'll happen sooner or later; it always does."

"Right, Detective Rivera," Carson said. "Thanks for your help."

"Hey, wait a minute," Rivera said. "I showed you mine; now you show me yours."

"Oh, we've got even less than you have," Carson said. He could hear Rivera swearing as he hung up the phone.

Carson stopped by his desk to check his messages, then tucked the file under his arm and walked down the hall toward the large corner office that housed his chief. There were two other department heads present—personnel and investigation; Carson was head of surveillance.

Carson endured the personnel report in silence and the investigation report with interest, then it was his turn.

"What have you got for me, Tom?" the chief asked.

"You'll recall, chief, that we've had a tap on the offices of the Kensington Trust since last May."

"No, I don't," the chief replied curtly. "What the hell is the Kensington Trust?"

Carson was going to have to make this good. "They're an investment bank based in London, with offices around the world; what the Brits call a merchant bank."

"So?" The chief looked at his watch. The man had come out of the major crime side of the Bureau, and financial stuff bored him. He liked mob stuff, though; Carson knew that.

"We've suspected them for a long time of a major laundering operation, but they're very slick, and it's been hard to nail down anything. However," he said quickly, before the chief could interrupt, "now we think there's a significant connection with La Cosa Nostra."

Suddenly the chief was all ears. "Oh? Tell me about it."

"A few months ago, a new face turned up at Kensington's offices, name of Callabrese."

"And he's mob?"

"We believe him to be." Carson had precious little evidence to support this conclusion, but he had the chief's interest for the first time in weeks, and he wasn't going to let this opportunity pass. "In the first of his two visits to the Kensington offices Callabrese opened a new investment account with seven hundred and sixty thousand dollars. A hundred thousand was in cash, and the rest was in a cashier's check on a New York bank."

"Which bank?"

"We don't know that, and we'd have to subpoena their records to find out. I don't think it's worth doing just yet."

"Go on."

"Callabrese specifically requested that his money go, and I quote, 'on the street.'"

"Jesus, Carson, that could mean Wall Street. What's the big deal?"

"You'd have to listen to the tapes to get the nuances, chief, but I don't think he meant Wall Street. He said he expected a return of three percent a week, and Kensington's L.A. manager said he thought he could manage that."

The chief nodded. "That sounds like loansharking," he said, "but we don't have enough evidence to prove it, do we?"

"Not yet, chief, but even if we did, I wouldn't want to go after Kensington. I think the bank is important because it could lead us to some really big-time stuff. It's more important as a conduit of information for us than as a target for a bust."

"I see your point," the chief said, nodding. "How much longer have we got on the court order?"

"Three weeks," Carson replied.

"Have we got a cooperative judge?"

"Cooper; he's pretty good."

"Wait two weeks and then go back for a six-month extension," the chief said. "I'll sign the request."

"Yessir," Carson said happily; this had been exactly what he had wanted. He hated to see a wiretap order expire; it made him look bad.

"What happened on Callabrese's second visit?" the chief asked.

"He brought another hundred thousand in cash."

"Well, he's got to be mob; nobody walks around with that much cash."

"On his first visit, he mentioned a New York connection, but no names. I'd give odds he's connected, though."

"With a name like Callabrese? Sure he is. Did you run him through the system?"

"Yes, and he's there, but it's a low-grade presence. He was printed on a juvenile arrest eleven years ago, but nothing since. An L.A. homicide detective had run a request recently; I talked to him about it. Turns out Callabrese's prints turned up on a car that had been stolen by a Vegas mob guy and used in a hit-and-run murder. This guy came up dry on a background check—there's no paper at all on Callabrese."

"Then he's mob," the chief said, excited now, "and it doesn't sound like he's just passing through. Did you order a photograph?"

"There isn't one on record. The local precinct must have screwed up. I've flagged his file, though. If he gets arrested, I'll hear about it."

"Add Callabrese to the watch list," the chief said. "I want the name cross-referenced to both banking and loan-sharking."

"Yessir."

The chief stood up. "Thank you, gentlemen. Next week at the same time."

Carson went back to his desk feeling pretty good. Odds were he wouldn't hear from Callabrese for a while, but it was a name he could use in weekly meetings for weeks to come. "Thank you, Vincente Callabrese," he said, "wherever you are."

33

The ringing telephone woke Detective Ricardo Rivera. He rolled over and looked at the bedside clock: 6:30. And he didn't have to be in until 11:00. Shit.

"Hello?"

"Hello, Ricky."

He should have known. "Cindy," he said, exasperated, "why the hell are you calling me at six-thirty in the morning?"

"I guess you know why," she said.

"Goddamnit, I'm not on until eleven; I could have slept another three hours." She had lived with him long enough to know that once he was awake he couldn't go back to sleep.

"Sorry, I wanted to be sure and catch you."

"How's Georgie?" He'd always hated the name, but she had insisted on naming him after her father. George Rivera just didn't work for him.

"He broke a finger playing football yesterday."

"Are you sure it's broken?"

"Sure, I'm sure; they put a cast on it in the

emergency room. He'll have to wear it for six weeks."

"Badge of honor," Rivera said, smiling in spite of himself. He'd had a cast on his arm once, and he'd gotten a lot of mileage out of it with the girls.

"I had to write a check for the hospital," she said. "We hadn't used up the deductible yet."

He cringed inside. "How much?"

"Three hundred and twenty dollars."

"Christ! You'd think he'd broken his back!"

"They had to x-ray and everything. It's not really out of line, considering what medical stuff costs these days."

"Did you have that much in the bank?"

"That's why I'm calling. I've got to make a deposit today to cover the check, and I haven't got it."

"Let it bounce once," he said. "Payday's the day after tomorrow."

"I can't do that, Ricky," she said. "I'm not screwing up my credit record now that I'm on my own. The order says you pay for medical."

"All right," he said. "I'll stop by a branch this morning on the way to work."

"Thanks," she said. "And Ricky?"

"Yeah, your check will be on time; don't worry."

"Is that the truth, Ricky?"

"Yes, it's the truth."

"Because you've been late three times, and it's really screwed up my life every time, you know?"

"It'll be on time."

"My lawyer says that if you're late again I shouldn't let you see Georgie this weekend."

"So you're going to hold me up with the kid?"

"Not if I get the check on time," she said.

"It'll be on time, I promise."

"And you promise to make the deposit this morning?"

"Yes, I promise."

"Thanks, Ricky; I'll see you this weekend."

Rivera got out of bed and rummaged in the bedroom desk for his checkbook; his balance was three hundred and thirty-one dollars. He'd have eleven bucks left after he wrote her the check. He looked in his trousers pocket; twelve bucks there. It was TV dinners until payday. He sat down at the desk, took a fistful of bills from the top drawer, and added them up on the calculator. After the bills and Cindy's check, he'd have just under a hundred dollars to last him until the next payday.

Ever since the divorce, over a year ago, he'd had no money. Even his small part of their savings had been frittered away paying the most basic bills. He wasn't making it, and that was a fact.

They'd lived decently when they were married; there was a pretty nice house in the Valley and two cars. She'd gotten the house and the station wagon, but he was making the payments on both, of course. They'd accumulated some savings, but the judge had given her most of it. He knew her well; if he didn't keep up the payments, she'd go for sole custody of the boy, and she'd probably get it, too.

He sighed heavily. His life was in the toilet, and he didn't like the swim.

He stopped at the bank and deposited the three hundred and twenty dollars into her account, and he arrived at his desk early. There was a message to call Chico; he walked over there instead.

Chico was bent over a photographic negative of a thumbprint, inspecting it carefully with a magnifying glass. Rivera waited until he straightened up to speak.

"How you doing, *amigo*?" he asked.

"Ricardo, my boy, how you?"

"Okay. You got something for me?"

"Yeah; sorry I took so long."

"That's okay, there was no rush. It's off the books, anyway; I'm just satisfying my own curiosity."

Chico poked through a drawer and came up with a plastic Ziploc bag containing an elongated silver object. There was a fingerprint card stapled to it. "I got a match on the right index," he said. "That what you wanted?"

"Well, it confirms my guess," Rivera replied wearily, "but it doesn't get me anywhere, really. I can't prove when the prints got where they did."

"That's the way it goes," Chico said, handing him the bag.

Rivera accepted it. "Thanks, *amigo*; I owe you one." He walked back to his desk, and his heart was beating faster. He had the sonofabitch, he had him cold. Now he had enough for an arrest and a lineup.

He sat down at his desk and thought carefully about this. If he played his cards right, there was light at the end of his own particular tunnel. He picked up the telephone and dialed the number.

"Hello," he said. "This is Detective Rivera, LAPD. I'd like to see him as soon as possible."

"Please hold," the woman said.

"Michael, that Detective Rivera is on the phone again. He wants to see you as soon as possible."

Michael thought for a moment. "Margot," he said, "remember when I lost my letter opener a while back?"

"Yes," she replied.

"Where did you find it?"

"I didn't. I just went over to Supply and got you a new one."

"I see," he said. "Ask Detective Rivera if he's free for lunch."

34

Michael got to the beach half an hour early. He'd borrowed Margot's little BMW, and he parked it at the extreme northern end of the parking lot, by itself. He got out and trudged through the sand toward the sea, then stopped halfway and looked back toward the highway. The beach was lightly populated at this hour on a weekday; that was good. A couple of hundred yards to the north was a small concrete block building containing toilets. He walked over to it and checked the men's room: three urinals, two stalls, and a sink. He reached behind him and made the pistol stuck in his belt more comfortable; then he left the building and returned to the parking lot.

Rivera was on time. Michael watched him park his car and approach; he smiled and extended his hand. "Good to see you, and thanks for meeting me out here; it was a lot more convenient for me."

Rivera shook his hand but didn't speak.

"Let's take a stroll while we talk," Michael

said. He started up the beach toward the toilets, and Rivera kept pace with him. The wind was at their backs. "What's up?" Michael asked. "Made any progress on your case?"

"Funny you should ask," Rivera said. "It's solved; I wrapped it up this morning."

Michael felt nauseous. "Congratulations! Tell me about it."

"You want me to lay the whole thing out for you, or you just want the results?"

"Lay it out for me," Michael said. Another hundred yards to the toilets.

"It went something like this," Rivera said, puffing a little; it was hard walking in the soft sand. "Our man Callabrese was some sort of a mob guy in New York. Mob guys always have false I.D.'s—Social Security cards, driver's licenses, that sort of thing—that's why there was no paper anywhere on Callabrese under his own name. So, anyway, Callabrese gets the hots for L.A. He comes out here and goes into a legitimate business, and he's doing pretty good. Then Moriarty gets in his way. The lawyer has something Callabrese wants, and Moriarty won't sell it to him. Callabrese doesn't like this, and he reverts to type. He calls somebody, who calls somebody in Vegas, who sends Ippolito down to L.A. to deal with Moriarty. Ippolito steals a car, meets Callabrese somewhere, probably so he can ID the guy, and they park on Moriarty's street and wait for him to surface. He comes out of the house to get in his car, Ippolito runs him down, then gets out of the car, goes back, and puts a knife in him.

Callabrese watches all this from the car, and two neighbors get a good look at him."

Fifty yards to the toilets. "Yeah, go on."

"Then Callabrese and Ippolito part company, and somebody, a third party, probably, takes Ippolito out to the desert and whacks him, so he can never finger Callabrese. But Callabrese has made a stupid mistake; he has left some fingerprints in the car."

"So how do you find him?" Michael asked. Twenty yards to the toilets. Nobody near.

Rivera stopped and turned toward Michael. "I think I know where to put my hands on him."

Michael took him by the arm and propelled him gently forward again. "I've got to take a leak," he said.

Rivera began walking and continued talking. "All I've got to do, see, is pick this guy up, fingerprint him, and put him in a lineup. I'll have firm fingerprint evidence, which puts Callabrese in the car, and two eyewitnesses who'll put him at the scene. Bingo! A first-degree murder conviction. Remember, we've still got the death penalty in California."

Ten yards to the toilets. "I've got to stop in here for a minute," he said. He walked into the toilet and stood at a urinal. Rivera followed him and did the same. Good. This was reckless, Michael knew, but there was no other way. He finished at the urinal, zipped up his fly, and took a step backward. His right hand went to the small of his back.

There was a scraping noise from the door, and a man and a small boy entered. Where the hell did they come from? Michael pretended to be stuffing in his shirttail. Rivera stepped to the sink, rinsed his hands, and walked out of the restroom. Michael followed. What was he going to do now? He started back toward the parking lot. It would have to be in the car; maybe that was best anyway.

The two men trudged silently through the sand for a moment, then Rivera continued.

"So, I've got my man," he said. "You think there's a movie in this?"

"Maybe," Michael said.

"I've always been interested in the movie business," Rivera said.

"Yeah? What in particular interests you?" Maybe there was another way.

"Oh, production, development, that sort of thing."

"You might be very good at it, ah . . . what's your first name?"

"Ricardo; my friends call me Rick."

"Well, Rick, there's always room in the movie business for fresh talent."

"I thought there might be, Michael," Rivera replied. "In fact, I noticed there are a couple of empty offices in your building."

"That's right; I'm still staffing up. I'm going to need a production assistant and maybe an associate producer. You interested?"

"I might be," Rivera said.

"What do you think you could bring to the job?" Michael asked.

"Well, I've worked on lots of interesting cases

that might make movie material," Rivera replied. "And I could serve as a technical consultant on cop films."

"That's very interesting," Michael said, "and you're obviously a bright guy. You might do very well in the movie business."

They were nearly to Rivera's car now. "Is that an offer?" he asked.

"I'd have to be sure of what I'm getting," Michael replied.

"Shall I be absolutely frank?" Rivera asked.

"Of course. I appreciate frankness."

"You'd still be in the movie business, for one thing," Rivera said.

"How would I know I was secure in my position?" Michael asked.

"You'd have my personal guarantee," Rivera said.

"But how can you guarantee such a thing?"

"Well, you see, I would ordinarily have my partner involved in a case like this—you met him the first time we came to your office—but he's on his two-week vacation, so I've developed this evidence on my own."

"I see; and where is this evidence?"

"Right this minute it's in a safe in my lawyer's office. That's so if I should die from anything other than natural causes, my lawyer could take the appropriate action."

They were approaching Rivera's car. He was probably lying, Michael thought, but he couldn't take the chance. "Rick, I think you might be very useful to me. Let's make a deal." How much did a detective make, fifty, sixty grand? "Why don't you come to work for me as an associate producer. I'll give you an office in my building, and you can develop cop stories for me."

"Sounds good," Rivera said. "And I could provide, ah, security for your productions, too."

"Good idea. How about a hundred grand a year?"

"How about a hundred and fifty?"

Michael laughed. "You drive a hard bargain." He had to make a decision; he was either going to have to blow the cop's brains out right now or bring him on board. What was it Lyndon Johnson used to say? It was better to have an enemy inside the tent pissing out than outside the tent pissing in.

"I think I'm a pretty good bargain," Rivera said. "After all, if I take this job, I won't be in a position to make that evidence available to the department, not without compromising myself. I think having me aboard would be very good insurance, and a hundred and fifty grand isn't big money in the movie business. I'd want more, of course, when I'm worth it."

"Of course," Michael said. "The sky's the limit in the movie business." He made his decision. "You've got a deal, Rick; when can you come to work?"

"Almost immediately," Rivera said. "I'll put in my retirement papers as soon as we've signed a contract."

"I'll get something drawn up today," Michael said.

"Oh, I would like a little something up front, just to seal our deal," Rivera said. "How about twenty-five thousand in cash, under the table? Let's call it a signing bonus. I wouldn't like to have to pay taxes on it."

"I think we can arrange that," Michael said, shaking his hand. "Why don't you come around tomorrow about five, and I'll have a contract for you. You can start as soon as you can get out of the police department."

"That sounds good," Rivera said, sticking out his hand. "As Bogart said to Claude Rains, I think this could be the beginning of a beautiful friendship."

Michael took the hand. "I certainly hope so," he said. *Right up until the moment I see you dead*, he thought.

35

Michael shifted the Porsche down into second gear and turned off Sunset onto Stone Canyon. He glanced at Vanessa, who sat silently in the passenger seat.

"Look, this is supposed to be a celebration tonight; do you think you could try and cheer up a little?"

"Some celebration," Vanessa said sullenly.

"*Downtown Nights* got a nomination for best picture, for Christ's sake! Can't you be happy about that?"

"Yeah, and so did Carol Geraldi! In *my* role! *I* could have had that nomination!"

"Are you blaming *me* for that? It was Chuck who dumped you from the part."

"That's not the way I hear it," she said through clenched teeth. "In fact, I hear it quite differently."

"I don't know what the hell you're talking about." They passed the Bel-Air Hotel; they were nearly at the Goldmans' house.

"I just happened to run into Chuck at the Bistro Garden," she said. "You didn't even tell me he was out here."

"Chuck. Great. The idiot has blown three quarters of a million dollars since we made the picture, and he's turned himself into a junkie. I'm surprised he can afford the Bistro Garden."

"He's looking very well, as it happens; he's just out of rehab and seems very together."

"Swell; I'm glad to hear it."

"You didn't tell me you'd bought his screenplay."

"I haven't told anybody; I'm still working on it."

"He seems to think you've cheated him somehow."

Michael slammed on the brakes and brought the car screeching to a halt. *Cheated him?* Let me tell you the truth about that. Chuck came to me in dire need of money; he had blown all the money he'd made on *Downtown Nights*, and he was into the loan sharks and pushers. I gave him *two hundred thousand dollars* for his screenplay, *sight unseen*, because I respect his talent and wanted to help him. Do you think there's anybody else on the face of the earth who would have done that?"

"He also told me about how you brought Carol Geraldi into the movie, and how I got dumped."

"All right, I'll tell you exactly what happened. Chuck came to me at lunchtime one day during rehearsals and said that he didn't think you could hack the part, that you weren't right for it. I said I thought that you weren't superficially right, but that you were a good enough actress to carry it off. He insisted that we find somebody else for the part; he was the director, and I couldn't really argue with him, so I went out and found Carol Geraldi, who was down and out, and I convinced Chuck to use her.

"I hardly knew you; you were nothing to me at the time, and the director wanted another actress. If Chuck has told you anything else, he's lying."

Vanessa said nothing.

He reached over, took her by the shoulders, and turned her toward him. "Listen to me," he said. "I've taken you out of a modeling career and given you the role of a lifetime in *Pacific Afternoons*, playing opposite one of the biggest stars in the world. I've installed you in a beautiful apartment, directed your career, and I'm paying you five thousand dollars a week, which, I might add, you're blowing on clothes and an expensive car. I've done all this on nothing more than instinct that you'll make a fine actress and because I love you, and what I'm getting back is that you're angry with me because a director dropped you from a part you weren't really suited for and gave it to another actress who could turn it into an Academy Award nomination." He reached around her and opened the passenger door. "It's time for you to decide where your true interests lie, Vanessa; it's time to decide whether you want to be with me or with Chuck Parish; it's time to decide whether you really want the part in *Pacific Afternoons*. There's the door; either get out and go your own way or close it and apologize to me."

Vanessa hung her beautiful head for a moment, then reached over and pulled the car door closed. She turned back to him, snaked an arm around his neck, and kissed him. "I'm sorry, Michael," she said.

"How sorry?" This was an old game with them.

Her hand went to his crotch and began massaging. "I'm an ungrateful bitch. You've been wonderful to me, and I want you to know how much I love you for it." She unzipped his trousers and pulled him free. Her head went down into his lap, and her lips closed over him.

Michael leaned back against the headrest and ran his fingers through her hair. "Sweet girl," he said.

Vanessa concentrated on her work, moving her head up and down, making little noises.

It had been a long time since she had done this, and Michael had almost forgotten how good she was at it, how much she knew about pleasing a man, how much she could do with lips and tongue. He came violently, but she held onto him, sucking, kissing, stroking, until his spasms ceased.

She tucked him back into his trousers and zipped him up. "Am I forgiven?" she asked, kissing him lightly on the ear.

"You're forgiven," Michael replied. He put the car in gear and drove up Stone Canyon toward the Goldman house and the adulation that awaited him.

36

Michael eased the Porsche into the turn-around of the Goldmans' driveway and handed the keys to the valet parker. Cars were lined up in the driveway waiting their turn.

They were greeted at the door by an English butler. "Everyone's out around the pool, sir," the man said.

They followed the music outdoors and joined a crowd, the core of which was the Monday night mob at Morton's, where Michael was now a regular. Amanda Goldman broke away from a group, hugged Vanessa, and planted a firm kiss on the corner of Michael's lips. For an instant her tongue found its way surreptitiously into his mouth. She seemed to get just a little hotter each time he saw her. "You both look wonderful," she gushed, "and congratulations on your nomination, Michael." She turned to Vanessa. "I know that this time next year we'll be giving a party for you. I can't *wait* to see *Pacific Afternoons*."

Michael thanked her. "Where's Leo?" he asked.

"At the other end of the pool, I think," Amanda replied. Vanessa saw one of her girlfriends and wandered off.

Amanda took Michael's arm and tugged him toward the house. "Before everybody gets hold of you, come inside. I've never shown you the wine cellar, have I?"

"The wine cellar?"

She towed him quickly down a hallway, then down a narrow flight of steps; at the bottom, she flipped a switch, and a room about fifteen feet square opened before them. The walls were stacked from floor to ceiling with rows of bottles, and the contents of each rack were clearly labeled.

"Amanda, this is very impressive, but what the hell are we doing down here?"

"I just wanted a moment alone with you," she said, stepping close to him and putting her arms around his waist.

"That's a very nice thought," he said, smiling. "And just why did you want to be alone with me?"

"I've wanted to be alone with you since the first moment I set eyes on you, at Barbara Mannering's in New York."

"That's the nicest thing anybody has said to me all day."

"Every time you're around, all I can think about is getting you into bed."

"Now, Amanda," he said, "don't you think that would be a little dangerous in the circumstances? After all, I work for your husband."

"Let's get something straight," she said. "I have

no interest in leaving Leo for you, so you're not under any pressure. All I want is to be fucked crazy now and then. If we can keep it on that level I think we can enjoy ourselves quite a lot."

"I like the idea, I must admit. And I like the terms."

"Don't call me, I'll call you," she said. "And I mean it, I *will* call you."

"Not at home, and when you call the office, use this number." He took a pen and wrote it on the palm of her hand. "Margot doesn't answer that line; it goes straight to my desk."

"Ah, the lovely Margot," she said cattily. "Have you fucked her yet?"

"Certainly not," Michael replied with mock sternness. "Margot's a little too close for comfort."

"That never stopped her before," Amanda said.

"It's strictly business with Margot and me," he said.

She turned to the rack behind her and extracted a bottle. "Here's a little reminder of our bargain," she said, handing him the bottle.

"Château Mouton Rothschild, 1961," Michael read from the label. "One of Bob Hart's favorites, Leo tells me."

"Poor Bob," Amanda said, pouting. "Can't drink anymore. Leo bought that wine from him, you know." She took his hand. "Now let's go socialize before they search the house for us."

She took him from group to group, introducing him, while he accepted congratulations. Finally she put him with a writer from the *Los Angeles Times.* "Michael, this is Jack Farrell. Be nice to him, or he'll say something awful about your pictures." With a squeeze of Michael's hand, she left them alone.

"I thought *Downtown Nights* was wonderful," Farrell said.

"Thank you; we worked hard on it."

"What's happened to the director—what's his name?"

"Chuck Parish," Michael said. "Are we off the record here?"

"Of course; this is a social occasion."

"Chuck's had a bad time, I'm afraid; the money he made on the movie is all gone—fast women and white powder. He turned up at Centurion a while back, desperate for money, and wanted to sell me his new screenplay."

"You didn't buy it?"

"I did buy it, and sight unseen."

"That's incredible; what did you pay him for it?"

"Two hundred thousand."

"Christ, did Leo know you hadn't read it?"

"That's between you and me," Michael said.

"So where's Parish now?"

"I got him into a rehab program, and to his credit, he finished it. I hope he can keep it together this time, but . . ." Michael shook his head regretfully. "I've had to tell him that I can't buy treatments from him, only finished work. That way, you know, he produces. The worst possible thing you could do to a guy like that would be to give him money up front. It would go to some pusher, and he'd never finish anything."

"I see your point," Farrell said, looking sympathetic. "I think it's a fine thing that you would help him when he's in that kind of shape. In this town, people just dump junkies, write them off."

Michael spotted Leo at the other end of the pool. "Excuse me, will you? I want to catch up with Leo."

"Sure. Listen, can I call you sometime and get the latest on your projects?"

"Of course, any time."

"I'll call you."

Michael waved, then walked over to the bench where Leo was sitting, blowing smoke rings from his cigar toward the high hedge. "How goes it, boss?"

Leo slapped him on the knee. "Just the man I'm looking for. First of all, a formal congratulations on your nomination."

Michael held up the bottle of wine. "I've already been rewarded by your lovely wife."

"She showed you the cellar, huh?"

"I was very impressed. I'll save this bottle for a special occasion."

"Good, there are going to be a lot of them. By the way, I was very impressed with your presentation of *Pacific Afternoons*. Script, storyboards, costumes, production design—it all looks great. And on a nine-and-a-half-million-dollar budget, too. It's a fucking miracle!"

"It's the way I plan to shoot everything, Leo. I think too much money gets spent in this town."

"My philosophy exactly, kid. We're going to make beautiful music together."

"You bet," Michael replied.

"Listen, kiddo, I think the studio owes you a little reward. Why don't you find a house for yourself, something nice. The studio will buy it, then sell it back to you for fifty cents on the dollar."

"Leo, that's very generous."

"No, it's not; it's good business. You and I are going to make a lot of money together, kid."

"I believe we are."

"You start looking for a house tomorrow. Call Marie Berman, she's the best real estate lady in town." He scribbled the name on the back of his card. "Remember, now—something nice. You can go to, let's say, five million."

"You're a prince, Leo."

"I'm a king, kiddo; *you're* a prince."

Michael liked the sound of that.

37

Michael was already dressed when Vanessa woke up. "It's Saturday," she said. "What are you doing?"

"I've got some things to clear up at the studio before we leave for Carmel tomorrow," he said, brushing his hair briskly.

"I thought we'd have lunch today," she said, pouting.

"Not today, Vanessa."

"Where did you and Amanda disappear to at the party last night?" There was petulance in her voice.

"She wanted to show me Leo's wine cellar." He slipped into a linen jacket and inspected himself in the mirror.

"Did you screw her?"

Michael looked at her. "In a wine cellar?"

"That wouldn't matter to you; it wouldn't matter to her, either."

"Vanessa, you're beginning to sound like a

wife." He had considered and rejected this option long ago.

"So? What's wrong with that? I want to be a wife."

"Vanessa."

"Why not, Michael? We'd be the golden couple of Hollywood."

"We can be that without being married."

"If you're working today, why are you all slicked up?"

"I'm casually dressed, Vanessa; it's a Saturday, remember?"

"I want to go to the studio with you."

"And what would you do at the studio but keep me from working? You'd be bored stiff."

"I want to go."

"No. I'll see you later." He walked out of the bedroom before she could reply. The place was a mess, he noticed on his way to the front door, and the maid had come only yesterday. Vanessa would live like a pig if he'd let her. She really was beginning to be a pain in the ass.

He gave the Porsche to the doorman at the Beverly Hills Hotel and found the coffeeshop. Marie Berman was waiting for him. He sat down and ordered a Danish and coffee.

"So," the real estate agent said, "you want to see houses in the four-to-five-million-dollar bracket?"

"I've thought about it, and I've changed my mind."

"What do you mean?"

"I don't want to look at houses; I want to look at one house."

"One house?"

"Just one. Sift through your mental files and find the best house in town for under five million."

She looked thoughtful. "What do you want, exactly?"

"I want big rooms, sunshine, nice gardens, a pool, and a tennis court. I'd like the guest rooms to be away from the master suite."

"How do you feel about the beach?" she asked.

"Love it."

"Finish your breakfast."

He followed her car out the Pacific Coast Highway through Malibu. He kept expecting her to stop at one of the hundreds of beach houses, but she kept going. Finally, she turned left and stopped at a security guardhouse. The guard raised a gate, and they drove in.

He followed her past a number of beautiful homes, then she turned into a circular drive and stopped before a very impressive contemporary house. They got out of their respective cars.

"Do you know where we are?" she asked.

"I'm fairly new in town; tell me."

"You're in Malibu Colony. This little peninsula contains the biggest and best houses; it has the best beach and the best neighbors."

"Looks good," Michael said. "Let's see the house."

She fiddled with a key safe hanging on the front doorknob, then opened the door. Inside, the hallway ran straight through the house to the beach. They walked through, her high heels clicking on marble floors. On the ground floor there was a huge living room, kitchen, dining room, and, best of all, Michael thought, a large library. It would make a spectacular home office.

She led him down a stairway. "Wine cellar through there, temperature-controlled year-round, and here—" she threw open a set of double doors. Beyond was a screening room with two dozen seats and the latest projectors.

Upstairs there was only one enormous suite, with bedroom, sitting room, kitchenette, two dressing rooms, and two baths; there was also a sauna, and a big whirlpool tub on a high deck overlooking the Pacific.

She led him back downstairs and outdoors. Enclosed by a high wall were a two-suite guest-house, a pool, and a tennis court. Michael had never played any sport except for stickball and handball, but tennis appealed to him. He liked the clothes, for one thing, and he liked to watch beautiful women play.

"There are servants' quarters on the other side of the house, off the kitchen," she said.

"How much?" Michael asked.

"This house cost seven million dollars to build three years ago. The owner was a studio head who got chopped. It's been vacant for nearly a year."

"Sounds too rich for me," Michael said regret-fully.

"Leo Goldman is a good friend of mine," she said. "I'd like to do him a good turn. I happen to know that the bank that holds the mortgage wants out very badly. The market in big houses has gone to hell in this recession. If I make them an offer that covers most of the mortgage and my commission, I think they'd be willing to take a loss."

"What would it take?"

"You're not going to be able to get a mortgage for this place in today's climate," she said. "It would have to be all cash on closing."

"How much?"

"Offer them four million six," she said, "and a quick closing."

"Make the offer," Michael said. "I can close immediately."

"I'll call the bank president at home." She walked into the kitchen and produced a small cellular phone from her handbag.

Michael walked around the pool, peeked into the cabana. He walked onto the tennis court and inspected the surface. Perfect, like everything else about the house. He looked back toward the kitchen and saw Marie Berman gesticulating, pacing the floor. He glanced at his watch; she had been on the phone for five minutes. She hung up.

Michael watched as she came through the sliding doors toward him. *It didn't work,* he thought.

She stopped in front of him. "If the studio will close on Tuesday, you've got a deal."

Michael's heart leapt. "I'm delighted to hear it," he said, smiling broadly.

She handed him the keys. "As far as I'm concerned, the place is yours from this moment. Who's going to decorate it for you?"

"Who's the best?"

"James Fallowfield," she said. "*If* you're willing to spend at least half a million." She dug into her purse. "Here's his number."

"Does he work on Saturdays? I'm leaving town tomorrow for three weeks."

"Maybe."

Michael handed her back the card. "Call him for me. Tell him I'll spend a million dollars if he's here in an hour."

She whipped out her little phone and dialed. "James? It's Marie. Good, and you? Glad to hear it. Listen, I have a new client for you, but he's in a hurry. No, listen to me, James; it's a million-dollar budget. Right. Malibu Colony in an hour; there's a black Porsche parked out front. Your client's name is Michael Vincent." She hung up. "He's on his way."

"Thanks, Marie, I appreciate that."

"Don't mention it; I appreciate the commission. Should I call Leo about the closing?"

"If you would. He'll know where to reach me if you need to talk to me. And Marie, I don't want *anyone* to know about this but Leo and me. I don't want to read about it in the trades."

"I understand. If you don't need me further, I've got a house to show in Bel-Air."

"I'll be fine, thanks."

They shook hands and she left the house.

While he waited for the designer, Michael

toured the house again. It looked even better than before.

James Fallowfield arrived half an hour later.

"The budget is one million dollars, and not a penny more—and that includes your fee," Michael told him.

"My fee is ten percent of whatever you spend, and I'll get you a lot of stuff at cost plus ten."

"Okay. Six weeks from now, I want to walk in this house and find it furnished to the hilt—dishes in the cupboards, towels in the baths, books on the shelves, pictures on the walls. I don't want to have to go shopping for a thing."

"No problem," Fallowfield said. "Any preferences as to style?"

"Rich, elegant, subdued; soft, comfortable furniture. I'd like a Steinway grand in the living room. Don't buy everything new; I want the place to feel lived in. I want to walk in and feel that I've always lived here."

"Will there be a woman living here?"

"Yes, but she won't be involved in the decorating."

"I won't have to get a woman's approval on anything, then?"

"No, just mine." It was easier this way; he'd surprise Vanessa when *Pacific Afternoons* wrapped.

"That will save an enormous amount of time."

Michael wrote in his notebook, then tore out the page and handed it to Fallowfield. "I'm going to Carmel tomorrow; this is where I'm staying. Send me sketches of what you're doing; the bills go to my office, to Margot Gladstone. I want a detailed accounting of everything as you go, then Margot will check everything off as it's delivered."

Fallowfield looked at his watch. "I'd better get started," he said.

"You do that."

The man left, and Michael walked around the house again. Perfect.

38

Michael stood on the beach at Carmel and watched Robert Hart approach on horseback. Vanessa waited for Hart in the foreground of the shot. The sun was a huge red ball sinking into the Pacific behind them, lighting the scene to perfection. Hart dismounted, kissed her lightly, then took her hand and led her and the horse down the beach toward the façade of the cottage that George Hathaway had designed.

"Don't cut," Michael whispered to Eliot Rosen. "Shoot whatever's in the camera; we can use this footage behind the titles."

Eliot nodded. "Good. It's perfect, isn't it?"

"Couldn't be better."

"That's it," the camera operator called out. "Want to do another one before the light goes?"

"Print that and wrap," Eliot called back.

The man gave a thumbs-up sign.

Michael took Eliot's arm and walked him down the beach toward the cottage. "You've done a fine job up here; I want you to know that."

Rosen blushed. "Thanks."

"When we start the interiors at the studio next week I want you to deal a little differently with Bob Hart."

"What do you mean?"

"All during the exteriors you've been properly deferential to Bob, and that's good, given your relative positions in this business. Also, most of the exteriors have shown the doctor in charge of things, confident. But in the interior scenes, the doctor is less certain of himself, because he doesn't know if the girl can ever want him. Bob, given his natural mien, will appear confident and in charge in almost any scene, and you cannot let him do that in the interiors. I want you to crack the whip with him, rattle him; don't let him get away with a thing; do an extra take or two, even when it's unnecessary."

"I don't know if I can treat Robert Hart that way," Eliot said. "Do you think he'll sit still for it?"

"He will, because he knows he should. Susan won't."

"Oh, shit," Eliot said. "I have to tell you, I'm scared to death of her."

"And it shows. I'll keep her off your back as much as I possibly can, but if she starts getting to you, just tell her, as calmly as you can, that you're the director, and what you say goes. If she won't take that, tell her to see me. I'll back you all the way."

"All right, if you say so," the young man said. "Michael, I haven't told you this, but Susan has been at me about the singing scene. She really doesn't want Bob to do it."

"I know, and nothing you or I can say to her will change her mind. But we *are* going to shoot it."

"I'm worried that her attitude will erode Bob's confidence in his ability to do it."

"That can work to our advantage, Eliot. The doctor begins the scene shakily anyway, then gains confidence. Bob can bring it off; I'll see to it."

"I don't know how you're going to do that," Eliot said, "but I wish you luck."

"You crack the whip on everything else; leave Bob in that scene to me."

When the crew moved back to L.A., Michael's offices were a hornet's nest of activity. Besides himself, Margot, and Rick Rivera, Michael had two production assistants on board, and he was working every day in the editing room with Eliot Rosen, the film editor, and her assistant, editing the exterior footage. The business of making *Pacific Afternoons* exhilarated Michael, and his concentration was complete.

But when he finally left the studio late in the evenings, he had Vanessa waiting for him at home. She hadn't had a lot to do in the exteriors, and she had been fine then, but now that the burden of shooting rested as much on her as on Robert Hart, she was nervous, tense, and bitchy. Michael had read lines with her for a while, but finally, when her insecurity had driven him

nearly mad, he'd hired one of the supporting ac-
tresses, an old pro, to work with her, and he took
to sleeping in his office.

Leo always sat in on the dailies with Michael, Eliot,
and Margot, who took notes. He was protecting
his investment, and he seemed pleased. Near the
end of shooting, he asked Michael to stay behind
in the screening room when the others left.

"Michael, I think it's going beautifully," Leo
said.

"I'm glad you think so, Leo." He thought he
knew what was coming, and he was not wrong.

"Kiddo, Susan Hart came to see me this
morning."

"Right on schedule," Michael said, smiling.

"I think she may have a legitimate concern,
Michael. She really doesn't think Bob can bring
off the last scene, and God knows, she knows
him better than anybody. She was frantic this
morning; I've never seen her like that."

"She's been getting short shrift from Eliot,
and I haven't been very sympathetic, I guess. I'll
try to placate her."

"I don't think you can do that, not if you
shoot that scene."

"For Christ's sake, Leo," Michael said irritably, "I made a deal with her; I told her that if she
and Bob weren't entirely happy with the scene,
I'd shoot an alternate. What more can I do than
that?"

"Maybe you ought to just shoot the alternate
and forget the singing scene."

"No, absolutely not."

Leo lit a cigar and blew smoke at the screen. "I think the problem is, she doesn't want footage to exist in which Bob makes a fool of himself. She's worried that it might get around town. When Bob was drinking, he wasn't exactly everybody's sweetheart; he has enemies."

"I see."

"I hope you do. You're going to have to find a way to get past Susan on this, or she's not going to let Bob do the scene."

"I'll work on it."

"You better, kiddo."

Michael sat in a rehearsal studio and listened to Robert Hart sing *"Dein ist mein gauzes Herz."* Anton was at the piano, and Michael thought it went well. Hart, in fact, sang better than Michael could have hoped. His voice was a light baritone and quite pleasing. Anton liked it, too, he could see. Susan Hart was there, and she motioned Michael outside.

"Michael," she said when they were in the hallway, "I don't want Bob to do this scene."

"Susan, we have a deal."

"Not anymore, we don't. The scene is driving Bob crazy. You don't see it, but I hear about it when we get home. I won't let him do it, and that's final."

"Didn't you think he sang well?" Michael sighed. "All right, Susan. We wrap the day after tomorrow. I'll cut the scene; we'll shoot the alternate."

"Good," she said, pecking him on the cheek. "When do I see it?"

"I want Mark to do a polish first. How about ten o'clock Friday morning, my office? We have to do a set change, and we won't be ready to shoot until after lunch."

"You promise?"

"I promise. The scene will be waiting for you."

She gave him a big smile, then walked down the hall toward the ladies' room.

Michael watched her go. He was thinking hard.

39

Michael slept in his office again on Thursday night, and on Friday morning, the last day of shooting on *Pacific Afternoons*, he held an 8:00 A.M. meeting with Eliot Rosen and the production manager, Barry Wimmer.

"Barry, I want you to go now and get the set ready for the drawing room scene."

"Which drawing room scene—the singing one or the alternate?"

"We're going to do them both—the alternate first."

"Has anybody told Bob Hart?"

"Leave that to me. I want Eliot to be able to light the set in an hour. We shoot at ten-thirty. Eliot, the schedule calls for three cameras for today, right?"

"That's right. I wanted to get Bob on one, then use the other two for simultaneous reaction shots from Vanessa and the little audience."

"In the singing scene, we'll use all three cameras on Bob, then shoot the reaction shots later. Tell the operators, Barry."

"Whatever you say," Barry said, rising.

"Make sure Bob doesn't hear about it until I'm ready to tell him."

"Right." Barry left.

Eliot looked frantic. "Have you told Susan about this?"

"She's due here at ten, and she'll be fifteen minutes early. I'll break it to her then."

"You'll keep her off my back?"

"She won't be at the shooting."

"How are you going to keep her off the set?"

"Leave it to me, Eliot. Now go talk with your people and make sure the cast and crew are ready at ten-thirty sharp. Have Anton standing by to play piano; find him a costume."

Eliot left, shaking his head.

Michael went to his briefcase, found a small bottle of Valium, and shook two into his hand. Reconsidering, he added a third. He found a coffee cup in the wet bar and, using the butt of his fat Montblanc fountain pen, crushed the pills into a fine powder. He added a few drops of hot water from the tap and stirred until the tranquilizer had completely dissolved; then he poured the liquid into a bar glass and returned it to its place on the shelf. If this didn't work, he'd slug her, if he had to.

At a quarter to ten, Margot showed Susan Hart into Michael's office. He put her on the sofa and gave her the pages to read. "Hot off the fax machine from Mark," he said. These were the pages he had removed from the first draft of Adair's script. She began to read.

He went to the wet bar. "Something to drink?"

"No thanks," she said, reading rapidly.

"Fruit juice? Perrier?" Come on, lady, he thought; the alternative is a quick chop to the neck.

"Oh, all right, I'll have a V-8."

He took down the prepared glass, opened the juice can, and poured the contents into the glass, giving it a quick stir with a spoon. Then he poured himself a Perrier and went to the couch. "Here you are," he said, placing the glass in her hand.

Susan sipped the juice idly and continued to read. Finally, she put down the pages and smiled. "I think it's so much better than the singing scene, don't you?"

"If you say so, my darling."

She drank more of the juice. "What time are we shooting?"

"One o'clock sharp. They're putting the new set together now."

"Why don't we go over and take a look at it?"

"I promised George Hathaway we wouldn't see it until it was done. If you have any objections, there'll be time to make changes."

"Good." Susan yawned. "Sorry, I didn't sleep very well last night."

You'll sleep well today, Michael thought. "Relax. I'd like you to read something, if you have time."

"Sure. Something for Bob?"

"Not really. I'd just like another opinion." He handed her the screenplay for *Inside Straight*. "You're the first to read it—not even Leo has seen it."

She took the script. "I like the title."

"Just read the first act, and tell me what you think."

"Sure."

"If you'll excuse me for a moment, I've got to attend to something."

"Go ahead, I'll read." She sipped the V-8.

"More juice?"

"No, this is fine."

Michael left the office and closed the door.

He waited ten minutes, then returned. Susan Hart sat on the sofa, her head on her chest, snoring lightly. Michael put a cushion at the end of the sofa, lowered her head gently onto it, then lifted her feet onto the couch.

He went to a cupboard, removed a gift-wrapped box, and left the building. He walked quickly down the street to the bungalow occupied by Robert Hart as a dressing room, knocked, and was invited to enter.

Bob Hart was sitting at his makeup mirror reading a newspaper. "Come in, Michael," he said. "We ready to shoot?"

"In a few minutes, Bob." He held out the package. "This was on your doorstep."

"Who from?" Hart asked, accepting the package.

"I don't know. Go ahead and open it."

"I hear we're shooting the alternate," Hart said. He tore away the ribbon and foil wrapping, then opened the box.

"That's right."

"Where's Susan?"

"She's in my office, reading a script."

The actor looked into the box gave a little gasp. "Jesus H. Christ," he said, "look at this." He held up a bottle of wine.

"I don't know much about wines," Michael said. "Is it something good?"

"It's a Château Mouton Rothschild 1961; a lot of knowledgeable people would say it's the greatest wine of this century."

"I've certainly never tasted anything like that," Michael said. "I suppose you'll save it for a special occasion."

Hart removed two glasses and a corkscrew from the gift box. "Have some right now," he said. "Taste it for me; tell me what you think."

"I'd love to," Michael said. He watched as Hart lovingly removed the cork, wiped the lip of the bottle, and poured a glass. He swirled the red liquid in the glass and sniffed it deeply.

"Magnificent nose," he said. He handed the glass to Michael.

Michael accepted it, held it to the light. "Beautiful color," he said. He sniffed the glass. "You're right; it has a wonderful bouquet." He tilted the glass back and sipped the wine. "My God," he said. "I've never tasted anything like it!"

"Is it truly wonderful?" Hart asked, his envy obvious.

"You know, Bob," Michael said, "in this scene the doctor is supposed to have had a couple of glasses of wine."

"I shouldn't," Hart said regretfully. "I'm on the wagon."

"Of course," Michael said, watching the actor closely.

"Still, if it would help the scene, I don't suppose half a glass would hurt."

Michael picked up the bottle and filled the second glass. "I don't see how it could possibly hurt," he echoed.

Hart sniffed the glass again, then took a sip, sloshing it around his mouth. "Perfectly wonderful," he pronounced. "A hint of blackcurrants, wouldn't you say?"

"I would." Michael had no idea what blackcurrants were.

Hart took another sip. "Fills the mouth; and a very clean finish. God, what memories this brings." He took another, deeper draught of the wine. "Ahhhhhh," he breathed. "You know, Michael, I have been more worried about the singing scene than I may have let on."

"Oh? It certainly never showed."

He drank from his glass, and Michael refilled it. "Yes, I'm afraid I let Susan carry the can on that one. I mean, it went well enough in rehearsal, but I was worried. It's been thirty years since I sang in front of an audience—even an audience of actors."

"Well, nothing to worry about now."

"I know, but I really would have liked to see it

on film. I mean, I wouldn't like for anyone else to see it, but I would have found it interesting."

"If you like, one of these days we'll shoot a test."

"Yes, maybe." Hart emptied his glass.

Michael walked onto the set with Bob Hart and called Eliot Rosen over. "Do one quick take of the alternate," he said. "No more."

"All right, everybody," Rosen called to the cast and crew. "Let's shoot one; this is not a rehearsal."

They went through the scene: the doctor interrupted a recital, with Vanessa at the piano, and made his speech to her.

"Cut!" Eliot called. "Print it! That's a wrap, it's all we need."

There was a buzz as the actors rose from their seats.

Michael walked onto the set. "Just a minute, everybody!" He turned to Hart. "Bob, I wonder, just as a little treat for us all, if you'd sing *'Dein ist mein ganzes Herz'* for us."

"Yes, yes," some of the supporting cast cried.

Hart, who was showing a little pink under his makeup, looked around as if to see if his wife were present. "Well, all right; I'd love to. Just give me a moment." He walked out of the lighted area.

Michael was waiting for him. He handed the actor a glass of wine, then raised his own. "Your good health."

"Thank you, Michael," Hart said, raising his own glass. He emptied it, then turned back to the set. As he walked on, there was a round of polite applause from the supporting players.

Michael looked at Eliot Rosen, who nodded. All three cameras were trained on Hart. "Just for fun, let's shoot it," he said.

"Whatever you say," Hart replied with a wave of his hand.

Anton, dressed in period costume, took his place at the piano.

"Quiet, please!" the assistant director called out. A hush fell on the stage.

"Roll cameras," Rosen said quietly.

"Speed," each operator called back.

"Action."

Hart waited a moment, then made his short speech. He nodded to Anton, who played a short introduction, then the movie star began to sing.

Michael stood entranced. The music had the same effect on him as it had the first time he'd heard it, and as he looked around, it was clear that the audience of supporting actors was rapt, too. Hart, as the doctor, played the scene expansively, singing his heart out, and as the song drew to a close, tears could be seen running down his cheeks. The little audience burst into spontaneous applause, something that had not been in the script.

Eliot Rosen waited a full minute before calling, "Cut! Wonderful, Bob! For all of us, thank you so much."

Michael took him aside. "Shoot the reaction shots now, to playback. Wrap it as soon as you can, and get the film to the processors. I want to work on this tomorrow." He went forward, separated Bob Hart from the little throng of actors who were fawning over him, and walked him toward his dressing room.

"Bob," he said, "that was a thrilling moment for me. I only wish your public could have seen that scene."

"I only wish Susan could have seen it," the actor replied. "But don't tell her I did it."

"Don't worry, Bob. Mum's the word." Michael left Hart at his dressing room door and began walking toward where his car was parked. As he got into the car he glanced back and saw Vanessa knocking at Hart's door. Hart opened the door, and she went inside.

Michael was unaccustomed to being cuckolded. He drove back to his office in a quiet fury.

40

Michael watched as Bob Hart leaned over his wife and kissed her on the lips. "Come on, sleeping beauty, wake up."

Susan Hart opened her eyes and looked at her husband. "Hello. Is it time to shoot?"

"We've already done it," the actor said. "Got it in one take; I think it'll be good."

She sat up, rubbed her eyes, and looked at Michael. "Why didn't you wake me?"

"You were exhausted; I didn't have the heart."

"You didn't sleep well last night, you know," Hart said to her.

"That's right; I was so tense about this last scene. When can I see it?" she asked Michael.

"Not until Monday," he replied. "I've told everybody to go home and relax. We're on schedule, so there's no need to work this weekend."

She suddenly looked sharply at her husband. "Bob, have you been drinking?"

"Just a glass of wine," the actor replied. "A fan sent a bottle."

"You shouldn't have," she said worriedly.

"It's all right. Come on, let's go home."

Michael saw them to their car. When he got back, Rick Rivera was waiting for him. "I hear it went well," the former detective said.

"It did. What did you want to see me about, Rick? I'm very busy."

Rivera laid some pages on Michael's desk. "I've done a treatment based on a case I had a couple of years ago. I'd like your reaction."

"I'll get to it as soon as I can," Michael said. "Now if you'll excuse me . . ."

"Sure." Rivera left Michael's office.

Michael glanced at Rivera's treatment, then dropped the pages into a drawer.

The phone rang. "Michael," Margot said, "it's James Fallowfield; will you speak to him?"

"Yes." Michael was excited about the call. After weeks of looking at photographs of furnishings, of approving fabric and paint samples, the new house was approaching completion. "James? How are you?"

"I'm extremely well, Michael. Let's see, it was six weeks ago tomorrow that you gave me the assignment, wasn't it?"

"That's right."

"It's finished. When do you want to see it?"

"I can be there in an hour." Michael hung up and walked out of his office to Margot's desk. He handed her a key. "Margot, I'd like you to find a couple of men and a van on the lot, then go over to my apartment and remove my clothes and take them to the new house."

"It's ready?" Margot asked.

"It is."

"Shall I move Vanessa's things, too?"

"No."

Margot looked surprised. "As you wish." She found her purse and left the building, passing Barry Wimmer on the way out.

"Barry, my office," Michael said. Once inside, he closed the door. "How much?" he asked.

Barry dug a piece of paper from his pocket and handed it to Michael. "A little over a million three," he said. "I kept twenty percent as agreed and shipped the rest as you instructed."

"It should have been a million five," Michael said.

"I could have done it, but it might have been noticed," Barry said. "I used my best judgment."

"All right," Michael said. "Is Eliot still shooting the reaction shots?"

"Yes. He's done the supporting cast; Vanessa's shots are next."

"Go and see Eliot. Tell him to keep Vanessa working for another couple of hours."

"She's a quicker study than that."

"Just do it."

"All right. By the way, we're throwing a little wrap party when Eliot finishes Vanessa's shots. Will you come?"

"Thanks, but I can't. Give my best to everybody, and send me the bill."

"Right; thanks."

Michael took Rick Rivera's treatment from his desk drawer. "Read this over the weekend, will you?" he said, handing Barry the pages. "I want to know what you think."

"Sure, I'll be glad to."

"Barry?"

"Yes?"

"Has Rick ever shown any interest in the budgets?"

"He asked me what we were spending for *Pacific Afternoons*."

"Did you tell him?"

"It was no secret."

"If he ever asks you about budgets again, I want to know."

"Sure."

"That's all."

The production manager left.

As he drove toward Malibu Michael felt the same thrill of anticipation that he had felt when he was on his way to L.A. for the first time. He had never owned anything but clothes and a car; now he was about to become a homeowner.

The guard at Malibu Colony admitted him quickly, and Michael drove toward his new house. He parked in the circular drive and opened the front door with his key. Although he had approved of everything that had gone into the house, Michael had made a point of not visiting the place while James Fallowfield was doing his work, so it was as if he were entering the place for the first time.

The designer met him in the hall and walked him through the house. Michael followed him silently, drinking in the atmosphere of his new home. Everywhere there was handsome, comfortable furniture, plush rugs, good pictures. Already the house seemed an extension of him.

When they had finished, Fallowfield faced him anxiously. "You haven't said a word," the designer said.

"It's absolutely wonderful, James," Michael said. "You've done exactly what I asked you to do."

Fallowfield exhaled sharply. "Thank God. You scared me badly there. I've never had a silent client."

Michael walked the man to the front door and stuck out his hand. "Thank you so much," he said.

"There's champagne in the fridge," Fallowfield said, then left.

As Michael was about to close the door, a van pulled up, followed by Margot's BMW. Michael showed the men where to put his clothes, then came back downstairs. He looked through the house until he found Margot standing in his study, staring.

"It's very beautiful," she said. "In a strange sort of way, Fallowfield has made the place like you."

"How so?"

"I don't know—it's very handsome, even sexy, but it tells me very little about you."

Michael liked that. "Excuse me, I have to make a call; don't leave." He picked up a phone, dialed the studio, and asked to be connected to the sound-stage where Eliot was still shooting. When the director was on the phone, Michael asked, "Are you finished?"

"Only just," Eliot replied.

"How did it go?"

"Beautifully. Vanessa was very good."

"I want the film back tomorrow morning, and I want a rough cut by Monday at nine."

"We can do that," Eliot said.

"Congratulations; you did a fine job."

"Thank you, Michael. You were very supportive."

"I won't be at the wrap party. Please thank everyone for me; tell them they did a superb job."

"All right."

"And let me speak to Vanessa."

Vanessa's voice was tired but happy. "Hello, Michael? Where are you?"

"I had to leave the studio. You've done a good job, Vanessa; you'll get a lot of offers when the film starts to screen."

"Aren't you coming to the wrap party?"

"No. I'm otherwise occupied, I'm afraid."

"Michael, you sound funny."

"It's time for you to do Hollywood on your own, my dear."

"What?"

"I've moved out of the apartment."

"Michael, I don't understand."

"You and I don't need each other anymore. You'll do just fine on your own."

"Michael . . ."

"The lease on the apartment has another six weeks to run; that'll give you time to find a new place. I'm doubling your salary under our contract. If you need anything, call Margot."

"Michael . . ."

"Good-bye, Vanessa." He hung up. When he turned, Margot was staring at him oddly.

"That was . . . very strange," she said.

"Come into the kitchen," he said. He led the way, then found a bottle of champagne in the refrigerator. He began opening it. "There's a lot of food in the icebox," he said. "Will you join me for dinner?"

"Michael, what exactly does this invitation mean?"

He found two glasses and poured the wine. "Nothing profound; just a good dinner and an evening of uninhibited sex between two people who know each other well. By Monday morning, we'll have forgotten all about it."

She smiled. "In that case, I'd be happy to accept."

He handed her a glass. He'd always enjoyed older women, and he'd always wondered what she'd be like in bed.

41

Michael went to the studio on Saturday, leaving Margot lying by the pool, and saw the dailies of the last day of shooting. He was astonished at how powerful Bob Hart's performance was in the singing scene, even without reaction shots. The editor, Jane Darling, and Eliot Rosen watched with him.

"It's extraordinary, Michael," Eliot said. "You were right."

"Jane, I want you to keep the reaction shots of the supporting cast to a minimum," Michael said. "I don't want anything to detract from the performance we've just seen."

"What about Vanessa's shots?" Eliot asked.

"They're important to the scene, of course, but the scene is Bob's, not Vanessa's, so don't use any more of her than is necessary to convey his conquest of her."

"Conquest?" Jane Darling said. "I hadn't thought of it that way."

"It's a conquest pure and simple," Michael said.

"The male point of view, I suppose."

Michael laughed. "Exactly that. Jane, how close are you to a rough cut?"

"Close. All that's left to do is organize this scene."

"Can I screen the whole thing Monday morning?"

"Oh, I guess I can work tomorrow," she said.

"I'll send you large amounts of flowers if you do."

"How can I resist?" she said dryly.

When he got back to the new house, Margot was gone.

Michael arrived at his offices at nine o'clock sharp on Monday morning. He exchanged greetings with Margot as he usually did, and there was not a hint of anything other than business in her mien. That was the way he wanted it. "Get me Leo," he said.

"Morning, kiddo," Leo yawned.

"Rough night, Leo?"

"A late one. Poker with the boys."

"You up for a screening of the rough cut of *Pacific Afternoons*?"

"Already? You better believe I'm ready. Eleven o'clock in Screening Room A?"

"See you then." He buzzed Margot. "We're screening the rough cut at eleven in A. I want you to round up enough people to fill the room, and go heavy on the secretaries."

"Can I come?"

"I wouldn't do it without you. And get the Harts for me."

Susan Hart sounded tired. "Hello, Michael."

"Good morning, Sue. Can you and Bob make a screening of the rough cut at eleven?"

"Bob's, ah, not very well," she said. "I'll be there, though. How does it look?"

"We'll see it together. I'm sorry Bob isn't well."

"Michael, what exactly happened on Friday?"

"What do you mean?"

"I mean, I fall asleep, which I never do in the daytime, and Bob ends up drinking wine with you."

"Bob invited me to have a glass," Michael said.

"Where did he get it?"

"It was delivered to his bungalow. Some fan sent it, he said."

"That's what he said."

"Susan, is there something wrong?"

"Didn't you know about Bob's, uh, problem?"

"I'm sorry?"

"Bob can't handle alcohol. He'd been on the wagon for months."

"He did say that, but I didn't infer that he had a problem."

"All right, I'll see you at eleven."

"Screening Room A." He hung up.

Barry Wimmer appeared at the door. "Got a minute?"

"Just about that. Come in."

Barry handed him some pages. "I read Rick's treatment over the weekend."

"And?"

"It's interesting stuff; certainly worth your time to read. To tell you the truth, I could never figure out what Rick does around here. He's looking better to me now."

Michael tapped the pages. "This is what he does; he's my resident expert cop."

"Well, I like it. A good writer could whip it into something really taut and exciting."

"I'll read it first chance I get." As Barry left, Michael reflected that maybe Rick Rivera wouldn't be a total liability after all. Certainly this treatment, if it was as good as Barry said, could help justify having Rick on the payroll. Leo had been asking questions about that.

Michael picked up Leo at his office and walked him to the screening room. Margot had done her job well; the room was packed.

"What is this, a sneak preview?" Leo asked as he entered the room.

Everybody laughed.

Michael looked around for Susan Hart, then saw her in the fourth row, where Leo liked to sit. "Leo," he whispered.

"Yeah?"

"If Susan tries to talk before it's over, shut her up, will you?"

"Yeah, okay."

Michael followed Leo into the row and sat down. The fourth row had little writing desks attached to the soft seats, and Leo sat down and picked up a pencil. Michael pressed a button on the arm of his chair and said, "All right, roll it."

Five minutes into the film, Michael got up and stood against the wall, watching the faces of his audience. He didn't need to see the film; he needed to see their reactions. The audience was very still.

He stood against the wall for most of the film's running time, and he knew from the faces that he had made a good film. What he didn't know was if he had been crazy to force a big-time movie star to do a scene that might make laughingstocks of them all.

As the scene began, Susan Hart looked over at him with an expression of pure hatred. She whispered something to Leo and started to get up.

Leo put his hand on her arm and pressed her back into the seat, holding a finger to his lips. On the screen, Robert Hart began to sing.

Michael looked up the rows of viewers, mostly women, and watched their faces as Bob sang. There was a look of pure wonder on each of them, but Michael's great surprise was Leo Goldman as Hart finished his song. Leo's face was shiny with tears.

The editor had cleverly put a piano track of the song under the final scene, when Bob and Vanessa walked down the beach toward the cottage, and as the screen went dark, the little audience stood and applauded.

It took Michael a few minutes to get to Leo, as they were both crowded by women who wanted to congratulate them. He caught a glimpse of Susan Hart's face through the crowd, and it was stony with anger.

Finally, only Michael, Leo, Susan, Eliot, and Jane, the editor, were left in the screening room.

"Michael," Susan Hart said, "I want to see the alternate scene."

"There is no alternate scene," Michael said.

"You shot it, I know you did."

"I burned the negative this morning."

She turned to Leo. "Are you going to let him get away with this?"

"Susan," Leo said, "am I crazy or something? Didn't you just see the movie I saw?"

"Of course I saw it."

"Didn't you like it?"

"I didn't like the singing scene."

"Didn't you hear the reaction of those women?"

"Michael packed the screening."

"So what? Those secretaries are people; they go to the movies."

"I've been tricked," Susan said. "I don't know quite how it was done, but I won't be made a fool of."

Leo put his arm around her shoulders. "Susan," he said firmly, "thank Michael."

42

From an article in *Vanity Fair*:

As Academy Award time approaches again and the usual prognostications paper the trades and the daily newspapers, more than a little attention is being paid to a "little" film and its rather mysterious producer, relative newcomer Michael Vincent. The film is *Pacific Afternoons*, adapted by Mark Adair from an obscure 1920s novel of the same name by a spinster named Mildred Parsons.

The movie has received four nominations, for Best Picture, Best Actor, Best Actress, and Best Screenplay Adapted from Another Medium. Not since *Driving Miss Daisy* has a low-budget film attracted such rave notices or, for that matter, such box office. *Variety* reported last week that the picture has had a domestic gross of more than $70,000,000, and if it does well at the Awards, insiders say it could end up doing more than $150,000,000 worldwide. This is especially good news for its producer, because if sources at Centurion Pictures are correct, his contract gives him ten gross points if he keeps his budgets under $20,000,000. *Pacific Afternoons* is reported to have cost less than $10,000,000 to shoot, plus as much again for prints and advertising.

Michael Vincent arrived in Hollywood a couple of years ago with only one movie under his belt, the much-lauded *Downtown Nights*, which was nominated for Best Picture but didn't win, and for Best Actress. The late Carol Geraldi, who died of a drug overdose shortly after completing work on the film, won a posthumous Oscar with a performance that everyone said would have revived her moribund career if she had lived. *Downtown Nights* was written and directed by a New York University Film School student named Chuck Parish, but it was the film's producer who has, unaccountably, received all the praise. Vincent sold the just-completed film to Centurion's Leo Goldman and simultaneously made a production deal for himself with the studio.

Vincent is currently shooting *Inside Straight*, another screenplay by Chuck Parish, and his next project is said to be a cop drama brought to him by an ex-homicide detective who is now an associate producer with Vincent. This time, Vincent is directing.

Leo Goldman, who could be said to have discovered Vincent, is bullish on the thirty-one-year-old producer. "He's another David Selznick," Goldman said in a telephone interview. "I've never worked with a young producer who had so great a grasp of what goes into making a movie—*and* he keeps

costs down. I don't think anybody else could
have shot *Pacific Afternoons* on the budget Michael
did."

True enough, Vincent is adept at shooting on a
shoestring. His secret seems to be to get good people
to work for very little. For instance, Robert Hart,
whose usual fee these days is in the $3,000,000
range, is said to have done *Pacific Afternoons* for under half a million, because Mark Adair was writing
the screenplay, and because the part gave him an
opportunity to do something strikingly different.
Adair, too, is said to have worked for a fraction of
his usual fee. Neither man would comment on
what he was paid.

Another way Michael Vincent is able to keep
costs down is by using unknown talent. He picked
Eliot Rosen, the director of *Afternoons*, right out of
UCLA Film School, on the strength of an eight-
minute scene Rosen shot for a class. And Vanessa
Parks, the beautiful young actress who has been
nominated for her work in the film, was a little-
known model when Vincent met her. He placed
her under personal contract to him on a salary of
$5,000 a week, and after *Afternoons* he doubled
her salary. He also moved her into a Century City
penthouse with him.

So it would seem that everybody is delighted
with Michael Vincent—Centurion and all the
people who have worked with him. Except that
isn't the case. It seems that almost everybody who
works with Vincent does well out of it in one way,
but loses out in another. Witness the salaries Vincent paid Hart and Adair, compared to the money

Vincent himself has made on the film. Vincent also seems to leave human wreckage in his wake. Carol Geraldi, who was, during the time she worked on *Downtown Nights*, a serious heroin and cocaine junkie, is now dead; Robert Hart, who had been on the wagon for some months after years of a drinking problem, was back at the Betty Ford Clinic for a tune-up three days after completing his outstanding work on *Pacific Afternoons*.

Vanessa Parks is another such case. While $5,000 a week sounds like a lot of money, it is only about a quarter of a million dollars a year, and even though Vincent has doubled her salary, her performance in *Afternoons* and her nomination have pumped her asking price up to two million or more. She has the fastest-developing career of any actress since Julia Roberts, but Vincent stands to gain the most from her success, since he owns her contract and negotiates all her deals.

Is this all just good business on the part of Vincent? Well, consider this: When Vanessa Parks signed her contract with Vincent, he took all her living expenses—clothes, a new Mercedes, everything—out of the weekly salary he was paying her. Then, during the shooting of *Pacific Afternoons*, he bought a fabulous new house in the Malibu Colony without mentioning it to Parks, and minutes after she finished shooting her part in the film, he called her and told her that he had moved out of the Century City apartment, and that she had only a few weeks to find a new place to live. After that, he declined to take her phone calls unless the subject was strictly business. Parks is now back with Chuck Parish, who was her boy-friend when she met Vincent.

But earlier in this piece it was said that Michael Vincent was mysterious. Consider this: Vincent is happy to give interviews to the press, on the condition that no photographs are taken of him, his office, or his house, and that there be no discussion of his personal life. The only photograph extant of the producer is the illustration for this article, and that was taken from the TV screen when he accepted Carol Geraldi's posthumous Oscar. His acceptance speech—"I didn't know Carol Geraldi before shooting *Downtown Nights* and I never saw her again afterwards, but she touched all our lives with her talent"—is the Gettysburg Address of acceptance speeches, and he dodged the usual photographs and interviews after the ceremonies, heading straight for Swifty Lazar's after-Oscar party at Spago, where he felt he had to be seen.

When one looks into Michael Vincent's background independently, one finds nothing; a blank. It is known that he is a native New Yorker, but no one knows where he attended school and college, except for his part-time stint as a student at the NYU Film School, or where he worked before joining Centurion. His parents, whose names appear on his birth certificate, a public record, are apparently dead, since they cannot be located.

So the mysterious Mr. Vincent lives silently in his Malibu Colony mansion (practically a gift from Centurion), and the only person in whom he seems to confide even a little is his executive assistant, Margot Gladstone, a beautiful, fiftyish former actress who also once worked for Leo Goldman. Gladstone guards the gates, and she is effective.

Leo Goldman and Centurion, as might be expected, are deliriously happy with Michael Vincent, as the total grosses on his two completed films are well over a hundred million dollars, on an investment of less than thirty-five million. Recently Goldman invited Vincent to join Centurion's board of directors. "Except for me," Goldman says, "our board was financial people and captains of industry. I felt it was time we had another filmmaker on the board."

So the mysterious Vincent sails on toward major Hollywood success, perhaps even immortality, and who cares about the jetsam left in his wake? Granted, it's an industry of sharks, but Michael Vincent is, even in Hollywood, something special.

43

Michael put down the magazine and stared out at the sea. He kept telling himself that this was part of the business, but he could not put down the fear inside him. They had been checking out his background, and that was very frightening indeed. They hadn't found much, because he had anticipated such an inquiry, but if anybody smart ever had a reason to find out about him, the truth would eventually be known.

He turned his mind toward the past and observed Vinnie, the mob collector, on his rounds—breaking fingers and noses, forcing money out of people, getting blood from turnips. That had been his job. Vinnie was another person from another time; he in no way resembled Michael, who was everything Vinnie had ever wanted to be.

The phone rang, startling him. He was doing a lot of his work at home now, and Margot could ring him directly and put any caller through. Only a handful of people had his home number.

"Hello?"

"Hiya, kid," Leo said. "I know you don't deign to come into the office these days, but I trust you will show up for the board meeting at two."

"I'll be there, Leo."

"I'm looking forward to introducing you to the guys, and they're looking forward to meeting the producer who is putting so much money in their pockets."

Michael had never been to a board meeting; he had no idea what happened in one. "What am I supposed to do, Leo?"

"Just agree with me, kid; vote my way."

"Is there something to vote on today?"

"You'll hear about it at two. See ya." Leo hung up.

Almost immediately the phone rang again, and this time it was the special ring that identified a call from the front gate.

"Mr. Vincent, there's a lady here to see you," the guard said.

"A lady?" Michael was irritated. He had been dating half a dozen starlet types, but he didn't like them showing up at the house unannounced. "What is her name?"

"She said to tell you Amanda."

Suddenly Michael wasn't irritated anymore. "It's all right; send her in." He walked quickly through the house to see that everything was neat. It was; it was always meticulously organized.

The front bell rang, and he went to the door. Amanda Goldman stood there in a wisp of a silk dress, her blonde hair falling around her shoulders, looking very beautiful.

"Good morning, sir," she said. "Is it too early for deliveries?"

"Deliver yourself inside," Michael said, smiling and kissing her softly. "You've been a long time coming."

"I thought the anticipation would do you good," she said. "Show me your house."

Michael led her around the ground floor, down to the screening room, out to the pool and tennis court.

"Now show me upstairs," she said.

Michael showed her upstairs.

Amanda nodded with approval as she walked around, then, when he showed her the upstairs deck with the hot tub, her eyes brightened. "Now this is what I'm in the mood for," she said. She reached behind her neck, undid something, and the little silk dress fell around her feet. She was wearing nothing underneath.

Michael was immediately thankful for the Southern California female's obsession with beauty and fitness. Amanda Goldman, in her early forties, must have looked much the same fifteen years before, he thought.

"Join me?" she asked, stepping into the hot tub.

Michael joined her.

The board of directors of Centurion Pictures convened at a little after 2:00, after some desultory chat among the participants. Michael had shaken hands with all of them before entering the boardroom, but Leo, nevertheless, made a formal introduction.

"It is my great pleasure to welcome today our newest director, Michael Vincent. I expect Michael to bring to this board the intelligence and creative thinking of a first-rate filmmaker, and, in addition, a lot of good old horse sense."

There was a round of polite applause.

Leo remained standing. "Gentlemen, this is a special rather than a regular meeting of this board; I have called this meeting to consider a takeover offer."

Michael was startled, but he immediately began thinking what this might mean to him; he didn't think he liked it. It was plain from the expressions on the faces of the other directors that they were surprised, too.

"I would be very surprised," Leo said, "if none of you had heard this was in the wind. These things have a way of getting around."

A gray-haired man at the opposite end of the long table spoke up. "Well, I sure as hell haven't heard anything about it, Leo, and I think I'm as well-connected as anybody else here."

"Harry," Leo said, "if you haven't heard about it, nobody's heard about it."

There was a murmur of amusement around the table.

"The offer comes from the Yamamoto Corporation of Tokyo," Leo said. He mentioned a very large figure.

Michael suddenly wished he owned some Centurion stock.

"Yamamoto?" a director asked. "I tend to get these Japanese companies mixed up."

"The Yamamoto Corporation has wide interests—electronics, of course, real estate in this country and Europe, a car-manufacturing operation in Thailand, pharmaceuticals and the record business in Europe. They seem to think that a major American film studio would be compatible with their other holdings."

"If they're offering that, they'll offer more," Harry said from the other end of the table. "I move we tell them to stick their offer up their sideways Oriental asses."

"There is a motion on the table to decline the offer," Leo said. "Do I hear a second?"

"Second," a voice said from down the table.

"All in favor," Leo said.

There was a chorus of ayes.

"All opposed?"

Silence.

"Harry's motion is carried unanimously," Leo said.

"Leo," Harry said, "just because I don't like their offer doesn't mean that I couldn't be persuaded to like the right number."

"Harry," Leo said, "I want you and every member of this board to know that I will never accept an offer from a Japanese company. I don't mean to sound racist, but the little bastards already have Universal and Columbia, and anyway, Centurion is just not for sale."

"Everything's for sale, Leo," Harry said, "even Centurion."

"Not as long as I control fifty-four percent of the voting shares," Leo said.

Harry said nothing.

"Now, gentlemen, there being no other business before this board, we are adjourned. Scatter to the four winds this afternoon, but remember, dinner is on me tonight. My house at seven."

The directors stood and shuffled from the room, chatting among themselves.

Ten minutes later, Michael was alone with Leo in his office. "Tell me something, Leo," he said. "Those men have come from all over the country for this meeting, haven't they?"

"They have."

"I know you must have a good reason for this, but I think if I were one of them and I were summoned out here for a five-minute board meeting, I would be somewhat pissed off."

"I do have a reason," Leo admitted. "This is not the last we're going to hear from this Yamamoto bid. This particular group of Japs is one tough bunch of sonsofbitches. I wanted my board to know that I am not going to brook any leaning toward accepting such an offer. Not as long as I control fifty-four percent of the stock."

"Why not, Leo?"

"Because this studio is me. It is my life. It is what I do and who I am. I'll sell when I'm on my deathbed—if the offer is stupendous."

"I see."

"Good, because I'll want you on my side, finding good business reasons to hang on to this studio."

Michael walked to the door. "I'll keep that in mind."

"See you at my house tonight," Leo said, giving him a little wave with his cigar.

44

Rick Rivera sat by the pool behind the house in West Hollywood and regarded the young woman who slept, naked, on the chaise next to him. She was slim, brown everywhere, and oily to the touch. It was only five o'clock on a Saturday, he reflected, and he had already banged her twice.

Rick lay back and reflected on the changes in his life since he had come to know Michael Vincent. He was only renting the house, sure, but he had an option to buy if he could come up with a substantial down payment. Cindy and the kid were taken care of now; no more squawks from her at alimony time, although she had been dropping big hints about a new car.

His sex life was athletic, thanks to his position in the movie business. The starlet as a life form would outlive the cockroach, he thought. As long as there were movies, there would be pretty women who wanted parts. If a hydrogen bomb fell on L.A. and wiped out all the studios, the next day those girls would be drifting in from Nebraska and Alabama, picking among the ruins, looking for a producer to fuck for a walk-on. He heaved a sigh of great contentment.

The cordless phone rang.

"Hello?"

"Mr. Rivera?"

"Yes."

"This is Miss Callahan at the Bank of America."

A little knot of tension formed inside his stomach.

"Yes?"

"You're a month late on your Visa payment," she said. "When may we expect payment?"

"Oh, I'm sorry about that," he said. "My secretary must have overlooked it. I'll see that she gets you a check next week."

"By that time you'll be into the next billing cycle, Mr. Rivera. If you're going to go on using the card, I'll have to have a payment by the close of business on Tuesday."

"Sure, sure, no problem. Sorry about being late."

"Given the way the mails are these days, perhaps it would be best if your secretary took your payment to a branch."

"I'll see that she does," Rivera said. He hung up the phone. Payday wasn't until next Friday; he'd have to take the payment to a branch at the last minute and hope the check didn't clear before he got his paycheck into his account.

The afternoon was ruined for him. A whole Saturday of sex and contentment ruined by a bill collector. It was amazing, he thought: when he'd been on the force, he'd been living from paycheck to paycheck, just barely getting by. Now he was pulling down a hundred and a half a year, and he was *still* living from paycheck to paycheck. At a different level, of course; he was driving a BMW instead of a Toyota, and his current address was a better one, but still, he was living right at the line. What he needed was to pump up his income, say, another fifty thousand a year. That would do it; that would put some money in the bank every month after the bills were paid.

Michael was spending one of his rare days at the office, working through a pile of phone messages and mail that had built up over the past weeks. He had cut the negative on *Inside Straight*, and it was good. It might not pull down a nomination for best picture, but it would make money and, with his points, and with the money Barry Wimmer was skimming off the top for them both, he'd be richer next year. The phone buzzed.

"Yes?"

"Rick would like to see you," Margot said. "He says it's important."

He sighed. "All right, send him in." Rivera was a pain in the ass.

Rick came bustling in and laid a fresh script on Michael's desk. "Just back from the typists," he said. "A shooting script, I reckon. When do we go?"

"We've wrapped on *Inside Straight*," Michael

replied. "I'll put it into preproduction next week, if the script's right."

"Who's going to direct?"

"I am."

"Good, good. From what I've seen on the dailies of *Inside Straight*, you're going to be a top director."

Why did he have to sit here and take this syrup from this annoying ex-cop, Michael wondered. He'd like to give him the chop right now. Granted, he had finally gotten a shootable script out of Rivera's treatment, but that was the only productive work Rivera had done since he had crowbarred his way into Michael's offices. "Thanks, Rick. Was there anything else?"

Rivera got up and closed the door, then sat down again. "I got this call over the weekend," he said.

"Yes?" Michael asked irritably.

"From an FBI agent in the L.A. office," he lied.

Now Michael worried, but he tried not to show it. "And?"

"This agent says he did a records search on a guy named Callabrese, and he found out that I had done the same a while back."

"Why would he do that?" Michael asked, alarmed now.

"He wouldn't say, exactly; he just wanted to know if I had found out anything else about this guy—something that might not be in the FBI records."

"Come on, Rick, don't string this out; what do

you think the guy has got?" There couldn't be anything, Michael told himself. He had never committed a federal crime; he had never done anything that would bring him to the attention of the FBI, not in L.A.

"Well, I happen to know that this particular agent runs the wiretap operation in the L.A. office," Rivera said. "I think he might have picked up the Callabrese name that way."

"What else?" Michael asked.

"That was it," Rivera replied. "He said to call him if I ever heard anything."

"Fine; don't worry about it. I've got some calls to make, Rick."

"Ah, Michael, I was wondering—you're going into production on my movie pretty soon. Doesn't that rate a raise?"

"Listen to me, Rick. You've been on board here for a long time; I've paid you a lot of money, and you've come up with exactly one treatment. All you do is hold casting sessions for nonexistent films and screw whoever will go for your line. You might just give some thought to what you'd be doing now if you weren't working for me, if I weren't around to prop you up."

"Listen, Michael, I didn't mean . . ."

"Sure you did, Rick; you thought you could hold me up for even more money, didn't you? Well, if you want to keep making what you're making, you'd better start coming up with some filmable ideas, do you understand me?"

"Sure, Michael, I'll get right on it."

"See that you do, and I don't want to see any more bimbos in your office. Run your casting scams somewhere else, you got it?"

Rick was backing out of Michael's office. "Sure, Michael, whatever you say. And listen, there was this case I had a few years back . . ."

"Write a treatment and have it on my desk by the end of the week," Michael said.

"Sure thing, Michael."

"And if you hear from this FBI agent again, I want to hear the conversation."

"I'll report to you right away, if I hear from him."

"Put a recorder on your phone. I want to hear the tape."

"Sure, Michael, right away." Rivera backed out and closed the door.

Michael sat and thought. After a moment, he knew that there was only one place he'd ever used the name Callabrese in L.A.

He left the office, got into his car, and drove until he found a working pay phone. He looked up a number in his pocket address book and dialed. The phone was answered by a beeping noise.

"Message for Mr. T.," he said. "Call V. tonight from a good phone."

He hung up, got into his car, and drove back to the studio.

45

Michael stood at the front door and watched the stretch limousine follow the road from the security gate to his driveway. The car stopped, and the chauffeur leapt out and held the door for Tommy Pro, followed by a blonde.

Michael met them on the walk and hugged Tommy. "Jesus, man, you've slimmed down!" He held Tommy back and looked him up and down. "A new tailor, too; you look great!"

Tommy grinned. "Two grand a pop, *paisan.*" He turned and introduced the blonde. "This is Sheila."

"Hi, Sheila," Michael said.

"Hello," the girl said. She was nervous and looked a little sick.

Michael turned to the chauffeur. "Take the bags in and to your left and out to the guesthouse by the pool."

"Hey, hey," Tommy said, looking around the house. "This is a number one pad; this is better than the Bel-Air Hotel!"

"I thought you'd enjoy staying with me," Michael said, starting the tour of the house.

"Tommy," Sheila whispered, tugging at his sleeve.

"Oh, yeah," Tommy said. "Vinnie, did a messenger bring a package for me?"

"Right here," Michael replied, reaching for a fat brown envelope on a hall table.

Tommy took the package and held it out toward the girl, then snatched it back. "Don't overdo it," he said. "We're going to the Academy Awards, and you're not going to be stoned out of your tiny mind."

"I won't, Tommy," she said meekly.

He handed her the package, and she trotted toward the guesthouse after the chauffeur. Tommy shook his head and laughed. "Junkies gotta have their junk."

"Is she going to be okay, Tommy?" Michael asked.

"Sure, sure. She just had a long trip; she'll be fine when she's fixed." He looked at Michael's worried face and laughed. "Don't worry, baby, I'm not gonna stick you with another bummed-out broad."

Michael gave him the tour of the house, and after suitable praise from Tommy, he took him out onto the terrace overlooking the ocean. A man in a white jacket materialized.

"May I get you something, gentlemen?" he asked.

"Just a vermouth on the rocks," Tommy said.

He turned to Michael. "I gotta stay off the hard stuff; my weight, you know."

"I'll have a Pellegrino," Michael said.

"You, too, huh?" Tommy laughed.

"It's not a booze town," Michael explained. "After a while you get used to paying five bucks for water."

They settled into wicker chairs and looked out over the Pacific Ocean.

"This is really something," Tommy said, shaking his head. "A whole ocean at your doorstep. A *blue* ocean, too. You know what you gotta do to get by the ocean on Long Island these days? Millions, and then all you get is the gray Atlantic."

"You're looking really well, Tommy," Michael said. "I've never seen you so skinny."

"Well, you gotta make an impression these days, you know?" He leaned forward. "I got a personal trainer comes to the house three times a week. Maria can't believe it."

"How is Maria?" Michael asked. "And the kids?"

Tommy waved a hand. "Ah, she's Maria, always bitching, you know? The kids are great. Little Tommy got himself busted," Tommy said, laughing.

"What?"

"Went joyriding in somebody's Mercedes. Imagine, a twelve-year-old kid stealing a Mercedes!"

"That's good," Michael said, remembering that his own car-stealing record was why this meeting was taking place.

"Listen, I'm really looking forward to this Academy Awards thing. How'd you swing it?"

"I'm a member of the Academy now," Michael said. "Your seats won't be down front, though. That's reserved for the nominees. You'll be in the rear third of the orchestra."

"Listen, that's just great. I don't want to be anywhere near you, anyway. I don't want you and me connected just yet, you know?"

"Tell me how it's going in New York," Michael said.

"It couldn't be going better," Tommy replied. He took his drink from the silver tray and waited until the butler had left. "English?"

"Irish; they're the best."

"I'm impressed, boy."

"So tell me about New York."

"Well, you must have read in the papers, even out here, that we had kind of a shakeout in the family."

"Yeah, I saw that Benny Nickels and Mario B. got it."

"Coming out of a restaurant on Park Avenue, no less."

"And you profited from this event?"

"Did I ever! I pulled all of Benny's people and about half of Mario's into my operation. The Don is very, very happy with me these days."

"And how is the Don?"

"Ailing. His liver, you know? He always drank too much."

"What happens when he goes?"

Tommy smiled tightly. "I happen."

"That sounds great."

Tommy looked around. "You do what I tell you about this place?"

"Yes, it was swept this morning. Nothing, believe me. Nobody has a handle on me out here."

"Except the FBI," Tommy said.

"Not even them. My source says that the agent that runs the wiretap unit in L.A. picked up on Callabrese. Like I told you on the phone, there's only one place in this town where that name was ever used."

Tommy nodded. "The bank. I had somebody talk to Winfield. He's taking precautions."

"Tommy, I don't know whether to leave my money with that guy. What do you think?"

"How much you got with him?"

"About three million, four."

"Hey, that's good. You left the interest in, huh?"

"Nearly all of it. Once in a while I need a little untraceable cash, you know?"

"Don't I know?" Tommy laughed.

"Anyway, you're secure here. Malibu Colony is a very, very private place."

"Good, good." Tommy leaned forward again. "Listen, I'm so proud of you, kid; you're doing just great. I read about you all the time."

"You saw the *Vanity Fair* piece."

"Yeah; that was a little rough."

"Things are quieting down. I gave a quarter of a million to an industry AIDS charity—anonymous, you know? It was in the trades the next day."

Tommy's jaw dropped. "You *gave* away a quarter of a million?"

"A cheap investment. Now I'm known in the business as a philanthropist. Only trouble is, every charity in town has come out of the woodwork. I give ten grand here, twenty grand there."

"You can afford it, baby, with three and a half mil on the street."

"Tommy, that's the smallest part of it. I've made nearly fifteen million on my points on three movies, and there's more to come."

"How much of it you got left?"

"Well, after taxes, expenses, you know; maybe four million in the market, besides what's on the street."

"Taxes," Tommy said, shaking his head. "Imagine you and me paying taxes."

"You, too?"

"Listen, I've got a very nice line in legitimate stuff now. I run a dozen little businesses out of a holding company. We got offices in an office building—everything. And we pay taxes! It's driving the feds nuts."

"That's got to be the future," Michael said. "Legitimate."

"I'm always looking for an investment," Tommy said. "In fact, some friends of mine have brought up the subject of Centurion Studios."

Michael nearly dropped his drink. "Centurion?"

"Yessir. I've made some contacts in Japan. They've got their own little Cosa Nostra over there, only they call it the *yakuza*."

"That's very interesting," Michael said.

"In fact, they've got the jump on us in going

legit. For years they've been working their way into big, big corporations over there. Just between you and me, they've got Yamamoto sewed up tight."

"Yeah?"

"And they think there's a lot of money to be made in the movie business."

"They're right about that," Michael said. "Universal and Columbia are already in the Japanese bag."

"My friends think they can make even more money than those studios by using, shall we say, tried and true methods?"

"That's very interesting," Michael said.

"And you're on the Centurion board."

"Went to my first board meeting the other day."

"And?"

"Leo Goldman let the board know that he would never sell, especially to the Japanese. He owns fifty-four percent of the voting stock, you know."

Tommy smiled slightly. "Not owns; *controls*. Big difference." He got up. "Well, I'd better freshen up. We'll talk some more about this later." Tommy went back into the house, leaving Michael alone.

Michael sat and watched the waves break on the beach, trying to figure out what this could mean for him.

46

Michael was picked up by a studio limousine in the afternoon and driven to the Dorothy Chandler Pavilion for the Academy Awards presentations. Leo had tried to get him to escort an actress starring in one of Centurion's films, but Michael insisted on going alone.

His car had a pass taped to the front window that allowed it to drop its occupants at the front door, where the television cameras were. Michael made his entrance right behind Meryl Streep and her husband, and the television interviewer in front of the stands didn't recognize him. He liked that. Since the *Vanity Fair* piece, he had thought it good to cultivate the "mystery man" image, while doing anonymous good works that were always made public.

Once inside the Pavilion he met Leo and Amanda and worked the crowd, with Leo introducing Michael to half the stars in town. Shortly an announcement was made.

"Ladies and gentlemen," an amplified voice

said. "Will you please take your seats; we go on the air in twelve minutes."

Michael sat with Leo and Amanda ten rows back from the orchestra. As the music came up for the beginning of the telecast, he put on his heavy black-rimmed glasses. Even with Rick Rivera neutralized, he was terrified of being recognized by a witness to Moriarty's murder.

Michael looked to his right and saw Vanessa Parks and Chuck Parish sitting directly across the aisle. He nodded, but both of them ignored him.

After ten minutes of monologue by the master of ceremonies and another ten of dancing and singing, the awards began. There were only four that Michael had the slightest interest in: the nominations that *Pacific Afternoons* had earned—Best Actress, Best Actor, Best Picture, and Best Screenplay (Adapted). In fact, he cared deeply only about Best Picture, because the Oscar would come to him.

Leo leaned across Amanda and whispered, "I don't know if you noticed this last year, but it always seems to take longer here than it does watching it on television."

Michael could but agree. He was intensely bored with the pageant unfolding in the huge auditorium. His mind ran from his banking relationship with the Kensington Trust to the coming screenings of his new film to Tommy Pro's surprise announcement of his involvement with the Japanese who were bidding for Centurion. He wondered what Tommy meant by his statement that Leo controlled, but did not own, a majority of the studio's shares.

He was startled from his reverie by the reading of Vanessa's name, and he watched as a scene from *Pacific Afternoons* was projected onto a huge screen. There was the usual business with the envelope, and another actress's name was read out. He glanced across the aisle at Vanessa and saw her pale and rigid, clapping noiselessly for the winner. As soon as the winning actress had made her speech, Vanessa and Chuck got up and left the auditorium. Graceless, Michael thought; that would be written about, and he hoped it would not reflect badly on the film.

More dancing and singing, more hilarity from the emcee, then the award for Best Actor was announced. Michael looked around and found the back of Bob Hart's head three rows in front of him. He knew well how controlled the expression on the actor's face would be as the nominees' names were read and the clips of their performances shown. Bob's was shown last, and there was a burst of applause at the end of it. That must mean something, Michael thought. The people clapping were the ones who had voted.

A willowy actress, winner of last year's Oscar, read: "And the winner is Robert Hart for *Pacific Afternoons*." The name of the film was drowned out in the roar of approval from the audience. Hart made his way down the aisle and up to the podium.

"I will be as brief as my conscience will let me," the actor said to the audience. "First of all, I must thank my wife, Susan, without whom I never make a move, as you all know." There was applause for Susan, then Hart ran down a long list of names. "Finally," he said, "I must thank the man without whose foresight and wise guidance *Pacific Afternoons* could not have been made." He drew a breath.

Michael suddenly felt all warm inside. He was smiling in spite of himself.

"Leo Goldman," Hart said, then, holding the Oscar aloft, he left the stage in triumph.

Michael was stunned. Amanda's hand gripped his arm, and Leo leaned across her. "That was a shitty thing to do," Leo said.

Michael took a deep breath and tried to keep a pleasant expression on his face. His impulse was to flee the theater, but he calmed himself and waited.

Finally, finally, the award for Best Picture was up, and Michael watched through glazed eyes as the clips from the films were shown. He had just endured a personal insult witnessed by a billion people all over the world, and his mind was on how he could possibly get out of the auditorium without meeting the eyes of anyone present.

"*Pacific Afternoons*, producer, Michael Vincent," someone said. Michael continued to stare at the back of the seat in front of him. Suddenly Leo was banging him on the back and shouting, "Get up there, kiddo, you won!"

Michael stood, dazed, and a shove from Amanda started him down the aisle. He climbed the steps to the stage slowly, as if exhausted, and accepted a peck on the cheek from an actress he had admired all his life.

The applause died down as he stepped to the podium and cleared his throat. "I have already thanked repeatedly and profusely everyone associated with the marvelous experience that was *Pacific Afternoons*, including the perfectly wonderful Leo Goldman, so it only remains to thank all of you for conferring this award, and the Academy for presenting it. Good night." Someone took his elbow and guided him offstage.

Weak and perspiring from the double shock of Bob Hart's insult and winning the Oscar, Michael suddenly found himself in a backstage room with what seemed like a thousand photographers. Bob Hart was just concluding his remarks before a bank of microphones, and, collecting his wits, Michael strode across the room and flung his arms around the astonished movie star. "Take that, you son of a bitch," he whispered into Hart's ear; then he stepped back and pumped the actor's hand while a thousand flashguns recorded the event.

The bemused Hart was led away from the microphones by someone, and Michael found himself facing more press than he could ever have imagined existed.

Michael ignored their shouted questions and

raised his hands, one of them clutching the remarkably heavy statuette, for quiet. "Ladies and gentlemen," he said. "I am too stunned to answer questions, so I will just say that this award was made possible by superb performances by Vanessa Parks and Robert Hart and a wonderful job by a new director, Eliot Rosen. Without their work, I would not be clutching this Oscar, never to let it go."

He left the microphones and pushed his way through the mob, saying "thank you" repeatedly. There was no point in returning to his seat, since the Best Picture award ended the ceremonies, and he could hear the final music rising. Instead, he looked for the stage door that led to where the limousines were parked. He spotted an exit sign and headed for it, but someone took his arm and pulled him into what must have been the stage manager's office. Michael was prepared to fend off another reporter, but instead a man held up a wallet with an identification card.

"Mr. Vincent, I am Special Agent Thomas Carson of the Federal Bureau of Investigation." He nodded at the other man. "This is Special Agent Warren. We'd like to talk to you."

"What the hell is this?" Michael asked angrily.

"Perhaps I should say Vincente Callabrese?"

Michael was terrified, but he maintained his composure. "What are you talking about?"

"That is your real name, isn't it?" the agent asked.

"My name is Michael Vincent," he replied, "and I resent this intrusion."

"Are you refusing to talk to us?" the agent said, and there was something threatening in his voice.

"I most certainly am," Michael replied, uncowed. "If you wish to speak to me you may call my office during business hours. Is that perfectly clear?"

"Perhaps you'd rather come down to our offices to talk?"

"Am I under arrest for something?" Michael demanded.

"Not exactly."

"Then get the hell out of my way," Michael said, brushing past the two men and out into the hallway. He spotted the exit sign again and headed for it.

Outside there was a sea of limousines; Michael searched frantically for his, but they seemed to be identical.

"Mr. Vincent?" a voice called out, and Michael spotted his chauffeur.

"Yes, yes," Michael said, heading for his car.

"Congratulations, sir," the chauffeur beamed.

"Let's get out of here," Michael said, diving into the back seat of the car. "Take me home."

The chauffeur turned and looked over the seat. "Don't you want to go to the Lazar party at Spago?"

Michael hesitated. If he didn't show for the party, the papers would be full of it the next morning. He had to brazen it out. "All right, take me to Spago, but drive around a little; I don't want to be the first one there."

He sank back into the seat and tried to get ahold of himself.

47

Michael was home before midnight. He said good night to the chauffeur, tipped him a hundred dollars, and let himself into the house. The servants were asleep in their quarters, and the lights were off in the guesthouse.

He had barely managed to be civil to his hosts and the other guests at the Lazars' party; his mind had been racing the whole time, working on the FBI angle. They knew his real name, and they knew that Rick Rivera knew his name; they must also know why Rick knew it. He did not have much time.

He walked out to the pool and past it to the guesthouse, knocked on the door, and entered. Tommy and Sheila were still out. It did not take him long to find what he was looking for; he grabbed the brown envelope and stuffed it into a pocket. He went to the kitchen, rummaged around until he found some plastic freezer bags, then took two of them out to the beach, put one inside the other, and filled it with sand. Back in the house, he rolled the bag into a sausage shape and taped it closed. Under the sink, he found a pair of rubber kitchen gloves and put them into his pocket.

The security guard went off at midnight, and the gate opened automatically as the Porsche approached. He drove slowly into L.A., taking the freeway and exiting at Sunset. Soon he was in West Hollywood, searching for the address. He found it at a little past one o'clock.

The block was dark and quiet as he drove past the address and parked at the end of the street. He walked back to the house and stopped on the front porch; no lights were on. He rang the bell.

Shortly a light went on somewhere at the back of the house, and a moment later a bleary-eyed Rick Rivera opened the door.

"Michael? What the hell?"

"I need to talk to you, Rick."

"Sure, sure, come on in. Congratulations on the Oscar; that's really great. Can I get you something to drink?"

"Are you alone?"

"Absolutely."

"No girls in the house?"

"Not a one." Rick turned toward the bar.

"Nothing for me," Michael said. "You have something."

"Well," Rick said, pouring himself a stiff bourbon, "with what I've already had tonight, another one can't hurt."

"I won't take much of your time, Rick; there's something I have to know."

"Right."

"I heard from the FBI tonight, backstage at the Academy Awards."

"No kidding?"

"What have they got on me, Rick?"

"I told you, I think they picked you up on a wiretap."

"What, exactly, did they pick up?"

"I don't know. I just know that the agent who called me, Carson, is head of the wiretap unit."

"What did they ask you, exactly?"

"They asked me why I had run a check on Callabrese."

"And what did you tell them? Exactly."

"I told them that I had found the Callabrese prints on the car that ran down the lawyer."

"What else?"

"That was it."

"Rick, you said that you took the fingerprint evidence with you when you left the force, is that right?"

"That's right." Rivera spread his hands. "Look, Michael, I'm not going to give you up; it's insurance, that's all."

"What, exactly, does the evidence consist of?"

"The fingerprint card showing the prints lifted from the car, and the card with the file prints faxed in by the FBI."

"Is the card showing the prints lifted from the car the original?"

"Yes."

"Are there any copies?"

"No."

"Is there any other record showing the evidence you found on the car?"

"No."

"Your partner doesn't know about it?"

"No. He was on vacation when this came up."

"And where is the evidence now?"

"I told you, it's with my lawyer."

"I see." Michael walked over to the door and opened it. "Come over here; there's something I want you to see."

Rivera walked to the open door and peered out into the dark street. "What?"

Michael took a good backswing and, remembering his early experience, caught Rick across the back of the neck with his homemade cosh.

Rick's knees buckled and he fell in a heap. Michael dragged him away from the door, closed it, then massaged the ex-detective's neck to help prevent any bruising.

Michael made a quick tour of the house, switching on lights as he went, then switching them off behind him. He went back to the living room, heaved Rivera onto a shoulder, carried him to the bedroom, and dumped him on the bed. He stripped off Rivera's bathrobe, leaving him dressed only in jockey shorts, then tucked the man into bed.

He removed Sheila's brown envelope from his pocket, donned the rubber kitchen gloves, and opened the package. Two pharmaceutical vials of morphine were inside, along with half a dozen disposable syringes and a length of light rubber hose.

Rivera made a gurgling sound, and his eyelids fluttered. Time to hurry. Michael completely filled a syringe with morphine, then stood behind Rivera, winding the rubber hose around his arm from the same direction that Rivera would have done himself; the vein came up nicely. Rivera jerked and opened his eyes, staring at Michael.

Quickly, Michael inserted the needle into the vein and emptied it. Rivera opened his mouth as if to speak, then his eyes glazed over, and his head rolled to one side. Michael left the needle in the vein, took Rivera's other hand, and put his fingerprints on the syringe. He put Rivera's prints on the other syringes and the morphine vials, too, then put them into the bedside drawer.

Still wearing the rubber gloves, Michael began a systematic search of the house. After ten minutes he got lucky; in a small desk in the den he found an interoffice mail envelope marked LAPD, and inside were two fingerprint cards and Rivera's notebook, the kind carried by all police officers. He closed the drawer, turned off the light, and returned to the bedroom. He rearranged Rivera's body to look more natural, then, as a final touch, he turned on the TV to a late movie. Leaving the bedroom light on, he retraced his steps to the front door, making sure that he had left no trace of his visit; then, looking up and down the empty street, he closed the door behind him and heard the latch grab.

Slowly, he walked back down the street to the Porsche, got in, and started the car. Before switching on the lights he checked the rearview mirrors; not a light on in any house on the street. Taking care to remain inside the speed limit, he drove back to Malibu.

He let himself in through the security gate with his card and drove to the house, parking in the garage. The lights in every house in the Malibu Colony were out, he noted.

Inside, he went to the kitchen, replaced the rubber gloves under the sink, and found a packet of matches. He walked out the back of the house and along the beach in the moonlight, emptying sand from the plastic freezer bag as he went. A hundred yards down the shore, he walked to the water's edge, made sure he was alone, struck a match, and lit the police envelope. He held it carefully as it burned, and when it was down to ashes, he dropped it into the water. The tide was ebbing, and fragments of ashes went out with it.

He walked back to the house and, as he was about to go upstairs, Tommy let himself into the house with his key, Sheila trailing him. He walked over to Michael and gave him a big hug.

"You sonofabitch, you did it!" Tommy cried, shaking Michael like a rag doll.

"Congratulations, Michael," Sheila said. "Tommy, I want to go to bed now." She looked ragged.

"Go ahead, sweetheart, I'll be there in a minute." The two men watched the blonde twitch out of the house.

"Tommy," Michael said, "I'm afraid I borrowed Sheila's stash; a friend was in need."

"All of it?" Tommy asked, surprised.

"His need was great. I hope you can replace it without too much difficulty."

"No sweat, *paisan*," Tommy said. "I'll fix it in the morning."

"I'm bushed, Tommy. Let's talk at breakfast in the morning."

"Right." Tommy planted a big kiss on Michael's cheek and headed for the guesthouse.

Michael trudged up the stairs, drained of adrenaline and energy, sure of having covered his tracks.

48

Michael had already finished breakfast on the terrace overlooking the Pacific when Tommy came out of the guesthouse, still in pajamas and a silk robe.

"Good morning, Vinnie," he said.

"Morning, Tommy."

The Irish butler appeared, and Tommy ordered breakfast. When he had gone, Michael put his hand on Tommy's arm.

"I need your help," he said.

"Sure, anytime. What do you need?"

"Two things: I need an alibi from the time I got home last night a little before twelve until about two-thirty. How about, you and Sheila got home at, say, twelve-thirty, and you and I talked until two-thirty, then we both went to bed."

Tommy shook his head. "You don't need me in this; the cops hear my name, and they're all over you." He thought for a moment. "Here it is. Your houseguests were Sheila Smith and Don Tanner from New York. It happened the way you just said."

"Who is Don Tanner?"

"Straight guy, as far as the cops are concerned; works for me in a legitimate business. Don't worry, he'll play."

"All right, that sounds good."

"What else?"

"Can you get a message to Winfield at the Kensington Trust without the feds overhearing?"

"Sure; what's the message?"

"Tell him it was like this: I deposited over three quarters of a million with him two years ago, then pulled it out last April. Then tell him to pull everything I've got off the street and wire it to his branch in the Cayman Islands."

"Consider it done. Listen, Vinnie, I talked to you a little yesterday about our thing with the Japs."

"Yeah."

"It boils down to this: How would you like to be the head of a major studio?"

"Of Centurion?"

"That's the one."

"That's a very interesting idea, Tommy."

"Well, you are what I've got in mind. With an Academy Award under your belt, and with your record on keeping costs down, I can sell you to the Japs, no problem."

"What about Leo's control of the voting stock?"

"This is how it is: Goldman owns less than ten percent of the stock personally. His wife is the key. She's an heiress—her old man was into everything, and before he died, he set up a trust for her. That trust owns forty-five percent of Centurion's voting stock."

"Yeah, but Leo controls it."

"Here's the thing—there are three trustees who control Mrs. Goldman's trust; they appoint a representative who sits on the board and votes the stock. Mrs. Goldman has a big say, too; that's why Leo Goldman is the trust's representative."

Michael nodded. "Go on."

"Now the guy who heads the trustees is named Norman Geldorf. He's an investment banker who was a friend of Mrs. Goldman's father; he's also into some stuff with us."

"What kind of stuff?"

"Doesn't matter; it's all legitimate; Geldorf is a very legitimate guy. Thing is, though, the family has a *lot* of legit money invested with him, so I have his ear, and if I can show him how Mrs. Goldman's trust can benefit from a takeover of Centurion, he's in the bag."

"But won't he listen to Amanda Goldman? Won't he consider her wishes?"

"That's a consideration, sure. She has to be made to see the light." Tommy smiled and spread his hands.

Michael blinked. "You mean you want *me* to talk Amanda into voting her stock against Leo?"

"That would be very helpful."

Michael shook his head. "Listen, Tommy, you're getting into the realm of the impossible here."

"Impossible? Not with your talent with women.

Jesus, Vinnie, with your yen for dames, I'd be surprised if you weren't banging her already."

"That's beside the point," Michael said quickly. "And have you considered Leo's pull with the board? It's a closely held corporation. If the trust owns only forty-five percent of the stock, that means Leo and the other board members together control a majority, and Leo handpicked every one of those guys."

"You let me worry about that," Tommy said smugly. "You get on the good side of Amanda Goldman and start creating a few doubts about how Leo is running the store. Just a few. If you can gain her confidence then, worse come to worse, if we have to, ah, displace Goldman, then you'll be the only game in town."

Michael looked sharply at Tommy. "Wait a minute; Leo Goldman has taken pretty good care of me. I'm not about to pour a pair of cement shoes for him so you can drop him in the Pacific."

"Easy, kid," Tommy said. "It's never going to come to that. But you have to remember something: Leo Goldman is a Jew; he's not one of us, he's out for himself. The only reason he's backing you is because he knows you'll make money for him. Those people are just like us; they only care about their own kind. It's human nature."

"I don't want anything to happen to Leo," Michael said.

"Then get him to see the light."

Michael put down his coffee cup. "I've got to get to the office; I'm expecting the feds to call on me."

"Yeah?"

"Something to do with the bank, I think."

"Tell them Don Tanner sent you there, that the company he works for does some legitimate business with them. He's in town for the awards show."

"Tell me more about Tanner, in case they ask."

"He's corporate counsel for a film distribution company, small time, nothing you'd know about, but you can tell the feds that's how you met." He took a pad and pen from the table and wrote down Tanner's address and phone number in Los Angeles.

"Will I see you tonight?"

Tommy shook his head. "Nah, this was a one-nighter for me; I've got to be back at business in the morning. We're getting a noon plane."

The two men stood up and embraced.

49

It was after lunch before the two FBI agents showed up at Centurion Pictures. Michael showed them into his office.

"All right, what can I do for you?" he asked.

"We need your help," Carson said.

"If you needed my help you shouldn't have approached me last night," Michael replied. "I did not appreciate that."

"Tell you the truth," Carson said, "I don't much give a shit whether you appreciated it or not. You're between a rock and a hard place, mister, and you're going to help us whether you like it or not."

Michael glanced at his watch. "I'm going to give you just one minute to start making sense, and if you don't, then you can talk to my lawyer."

"I'll lay it out for you, Callabrese."

"My name is Vincent. It was legally and properly changed in New York State six years ago, for personal reasons. Lots of people change their names."

"All right, you're Vincent, but I know a homicide detective can put you away on a murder one charge; all it takes is a word from me."

"You're insane."

"You left your fingerprints all over the car when you ran down Moriarty."

"The lawyer? Detective Rivera told me he was killed by some Mafia hoodlum. They found him dead somewhere."

"Rivera didn't mention the Callabrese prints, I guess, because he didn't know you were Callabrese. When I tell him, he'll know, and I'll tell him unless you cooperate with me."

"Cooperate with you on what?"

"Bringing down the Kensington Trust."

"What has the Kensington Trust got to do with me?"

"You're doing business with them; they're funneling your money to the street sharks."

"You make less and less sense, Carson, and I'm running out of patience."

"Then I'll have a word with Rivera," the agent said, rising, "and then we'll see about your patience.

"Let me make it easy for you," Michael said. He pressed a button on the speakerphone. "Margot, will you please go to Rick Rivera's office and ask him to come and see me right away?"

"Yes, Mr. Vincent," Margot said.

"Wait a minute," Carson said. "You mean to tell me Rivera works for you?"

"And has for about a year and a half," Michael said.

"Doing what?"

"He's an associate producer, specializing in police stories."

"Horseshit. You bought him."

"I go into production next month on his first story," Michael said. "He's a valued associate."

Margot buzzed back. "Mr. Vincent, I'm afraid Mr. Rivera isn't in yet."

Michael sighed. "I'm afraid that's not unusual," he said. "He's been out of the office a lot recently."

"Let's get back to the Kensington Trust," Carson said. "What business have you done with them?"

"When I first came out here a couple of years ago, I deposited something over seven hundred thousand dollars with them."

"Where'd you get the money?"

"I earned it. On a film called *Downtown Nights*."

"What else?"

"Sometime later I deposited another hundred thousand with them, then in April of last year I withdrew all my funds and closed my account."

Carson looked surprised. "Why?"

"I wasn't terribly happy with the service. I moved my funds to two brokerage accounts. Would you like the names of my brokers?"

"Yes."

Michael took a legal pad from his desk and wrote down the names. He wondered if they knew yet that Rivera was dead.

"Another thing," Carson said, "where were you between midnight last night and two A.M. this morning?"

They knew. "At home. From the Awards ceremony, I went to Irving Lazar's party at Spago, but I left early; I was home before midnight."

"Can you support that statement?"

"Of course; I had houseguests. They were already home when I got there, and we stayed up talking until about two-thirty."

"Who were these guests?"

"Don Tanner, a lawyer for a film distributor, and his girlfriend, Sheila Smith. Would you like their number?"

"I would."

Michael wrote down Tanner's number on the pad, then shoved it toward Carson. "That's it, gentlemen; I don't have any more time for you."

Carson and Warren stood up. "We'll be back," Carson said.

"No, you won't," Michael said, remaining seated. "Not unless you have a warrant for my arrest. Otherwise, we'll meet at my lawyer's office."

"You're a slick number, Callabrese," Carson said, "but we're on to you now."

"The name is Vincent," Michael said. "Get out."

The two agents left, and after they had gone Michael lowered his forehead to the cool glass top of his desk. He was covered. They had nothing.

50

Michael and Amanda Goldman lay naked on the upstairs back deck of the house, baking in the midafternoon sun. They had already made love once. Michael dribbled oil on her back and rubbed it in gently.

"Mmmmm," Amanda sighed. "I don't think I've ever known a man who knew women so well, Michael. You never miss an opportunity to please."

"I'm glad you think so," Michael said softly.

"If I weren't married, you'd be dangerous."

"You mean to Leo specifically, or just married?"

"I mean to Leo. If I were married to anybody else, I'd be thinking about leaving my husband for you."

"I'm glad you couldn't leave Leo for me. I love the man; he's been absolutely wonderful to me."

"Don't take it too personally," she said. "It's not as if he isn't making a lot of money out of the relationship."

"Funny, another friend of mine pointed that out not long ago."

"Who?"

"Just a friend; somebody who doesn't know Leo, who was just making an objective observation."

"Your friend is a shrewd judge of character. People like Leo get as good as they give."

"Leo has always struck me as generous."

"Generosity is a two-way street. Surely you aren't naive enough to believe that anybody in this town, in this industry, has the slightest whit of unrequited generosity in his soul. You read in the trades about somebody who's made some big donation to some charity. Chances are he's doing it because somebody he wants to do business with is involved with the charity."

"So what do you and Leo give each other? How do you reciprocate?"

"Well, let's see; Leo gives me a status in this town that only two or three other men could. There's hardly anybody in the country that I couldn't have at my dinner table on a couple of days' notice—right up to, and including, the president of the United States."

"What could you offer the president of the United States, besides a good dinner?"

"Leo could put together a million dollars in campaign contributions to the party in a week, and with his left hand. Every politician in the country knows it."

"What else does Leo do for you?"

"Status is everything in this town," she replied.

"I can pick and choose among our invitations—and we're invited everywhere. I can lunch with a Nobel laureate; I can give a boost to any charity I choose. Leo makes all that possible."

"And I suppose his money doesn't hurt."

"Money has nothing to do with what Leo does for me. I'm richer than he is."

"I didn't know."

"Leo is the perfect man for a rich woman to be married to, you know; he's an excellent tender of my money. Since we've been married, he's increased my fortune many times over. If we were divorced, I'd have to pay him alimony."

"How did he do this?"

"With the studio."

"Your money is invested in the studio?"

"My money practically controls it. The trust my father set up for me owns nearly half the stock, and Leo's bit puts us over the fifty-percent mark. Not many people know that; Leo likes for the town to think that he's in personal control."

"I guess that must keep him in line."

She laughed. "It certainly does. I can promise you, in all the years we've been married, Leo has never slept with another woman. He knows that if he did and I found out about it, I could cut his dick off, and the size of a man's dick is everything in this town." She laughed even louder. "A woman I knew, who before she died was a very important hostess in this town, was being wheeled into the operating room for surgery, and she said to her husband, who was walking along beside the gurney, 'Whatever they do, don't let them cut off my dick.'"

Michael laughed appreciatively. "And what is it you give Leo, besides money?"

"I'm the smartest and best hostess in this city, maybe the country. You should know; you've been to my house often enough. I make Leo look like the king he likes to think he is. I cater to his every vanity. I order his clothes, I choose his food and wines, and of course, there's the sex."

"How is that?"

"Well, we've been married a long time. Leo is happy with an occasional blow job, and I'm an ace at that, as you well know."

"I know. Doesn't he do anything for you?"

"Why do you think I'm fucking you?"

"I'm glad to be of service."

She rolled over. "I didn't mean to sound hard; it's more than just sex. If I let myself, I could fall very much in love with you." She shrugged. "Hell, maybe I already am."

"That's the nicest thing I've heard since I came to L.A."

"I'm glad you think so."

"What do you think of me?" Michael asked. "I'd really like to have your blunt opinion."

She looked up at him. "I think you're more than just a young man on the make. I think that, in a few more years, you could become a legendary moviemaker, right up there with the best of them. I think, if you play your cards right, you could rule this industry."

"Thank you, I have to agree."

They both laughed.

"Amanda, apart from loving me, do you like me?"

She smiled. "I do."

"That's a relief," he sighed. "I'd like to think I'm more to you than a good fuck."

"You are."

"Do you trust me?"

"Probably as much as I trust anybody."

"Then there's something I have to tell you."

"What?"

"I wouldn't have brought this up, but I had no idea about your financial involvement in the studio."

"What is it, Michael?"

"I think there's major trouble brewing at Centurion."

"What kind of trouble?"

"Has Leo told you about the Japanese offer?"

"Yes. He said it was inadequate."

"Suppose they made it good enough? What do you think Leo would do?"

"I hope he would take it."

Michael shook his head. "I don't think he would take it under any circumstances."

"*Any* circumstances?"

"I think Leo likes running the studio so much that he's too emotionally involved to make a good business decision."

"God knows, he loves running the studio," she agreed.

"There's more to this. Leo is getting into a

couple of very expensive projects—the sort of thing that he's always saying he doesn't like."

"You mean the science fiction film?"

"Yes. I'm alarmed at the amount of development money that's gone into it without a finished script. Then there's the Vietnam movie; it would have to be shot in the Philippines, and you know how shaky the political situation is there."

"Well, he's always felt strongly about Vietnam, but that does sound risky."

"I think there's some restiveness among the board members about those two films and about the Japanese offer."

"How much restiveness?"

"It's hard to say. I'm operating on instinct here."

"And what do your instincts tell you?"

"That the potential exists for a major debacle. If Leo proceeds with both these projects, while at the same time refusing even to consider an offer for the company that interests the board, then . . ."

"Then, what?"

"Then there could be a boardroom rebellion."

"So what? Leo and my trust together have an absolute majority."

"That's not the only consideration. Centurion borrows to finance its films, just like all studios. In fact, its debt is heavier than most. If several board members decided to sell their stock to the Japanese outfit, the banks are going to take it as an indication of a lack of faith in Leo's management, and things could get very shaky indeed."

"Are you seriously worried about this, Michael?" She looked very worried indeed.

"Look, I'm sorry; Leo's no fool; he can handle the situation. I shouldn't have brought it up."

"No, no, I'm glad you did. I should know about these things, and Leo isn't telling me."

"For God's sake, don't bring this up with Leo. He might figure out where you got the information."

"I've got to do something," she said.

"Don't say a word to Leo, whatever you do. I'll keep you posted on developments. Then, if things get serious enough, you can say that you were approached by some of the board members, who gave you the information."

"That's very sweet of you, Michael," she said, stroking his cheek. "I know how loyal you are to Leo. I know you would never do anything to hurt him."

"Of course not. I'd like to keep him out of trouble, but he's just not willing to take anybody's advice about the situation. I hesitate to say it, but I think there's a touch of megalomania in Leo these days."

"There always has been," she said.

"Let's change the subject."

"What subject did you have in mind?"

He leaned over and bit a nipple lightly.

"Ooooh," she moaned. "*That* subject."

51

Michael sat in Leo's private screening room, adjacent to his office, and watched the studio head's latest personal production, *Drive Time*, a comedy.

"What do you think?" Leo asked when the lights came up.

"I think it's going to do business," Michael said.

"Is that it?"

"Leo, I won't bullshit you; it's like *Inside Straight* in that it's not going to pull any nominations, but it's going to do business. It's a good movie; I liked it."

"Good," Leo said, sounding relieved. "I'm getting some flak from Harry Johnson about my personal stuff. He and I have never agreed on movies; now he's hoping I'll fall on my face with the sci-fi movie." He beckoned to Michael. "Come on in my office for a minute."

Michael followed Leo into his huge private office. The storyboards for the science fiction movie were stacked against a sofa. The movie still had no name.

"Have you seen these, Michael?" Leo asked, waving his cigar at the storyboards.

"Of course, Leo; I was at the presentation yesterday, remember?"

"Oh, yeah, yeah. I want your honest opinion. If I can make the movie that's on these storyboards for, say, eighty million—and that figure is strictly between you and me—what do you think it'll do in the U.S.?"

"Leo, have you ever known me to be overoptimistic about grosses?" Michael asked.

"No, never."

"Good. So believe me when I say I think it'll do a hundred and seventy-five million domestic. God only knows what it'll do worldwide, maybe two hundred fifty million?"

Leo's eyes lit up. "That's what I think," he said. "You know damned well I'm down on blockbusters, but this one I'm willing to bet the farm on."

"You may have to, Leo."

"You mean the board? They'll bitch and moan until they see the grosses, then I'll be their hero again."

"I think you're right, Leo. If I were in your shoes, I'd go the whole hog."

"Well, that's something coming from you, kiddo, stingy as you are with a budget."

"You can't do low-budget sci-fi," Michael said.

"I'm thinking of putting the Vietnam film into turnaround," Leo said.

"Why?"

"Well, you know how nuts the Philippines have been, politically."

"They've had a successful election," Michael said. "The right man won; the communists seem to be in retreat. It might be a good time."

"You think so?"

"Do you know anybody in the State Department?"

"Yeah, as a matter of fact."

"Call him; ask him to talk to somebody on the Philippines desk; see what's happening."

"Good idea. I'd really hate to stop work on the film; I think it could be great."

"So do I. It would be worth a little hassle in the Philippines to get a great movie made."

"Johnson, that cold-eyed Scandinavian son of a bitch, was on the phone this morning about these two films. I don't know what's got into the old bastard; he always used to back me on everything. It's not like we're losing money."

"Fuck him," Michael said. "Make the movies you want to. Why else be the head of a studio?"

"You're right about that, kid," Leo said with vehemence. "That's why I could never sell this place. Do you have any idea what it's like to be able to make any movie you want, and without *anybody's* permission?" He walked over and sat down at his desk.

"Almost," Michael said. "You've been that good to me."

Leo reached into his top desk drawer and removed a small revolver, gold-plated. He flipped the cylinder open and showed Michael that it was loaded. "You know what I'd do if I had to let somebody like Johnson tell me what movies I could or couldn't make?" He held the pistol to his temple.

"Leo . . ." Michael said.

Leo pulled the trigger.

Michael was halfway out of his chair before he realized that the gun had not gone off.

"Heh, heh," Leo chortled. "Had you going, didn't I?" He tossed the revolver across the desk to Michael.

Michael opened the cylinder and extracted a cartridge. It looked real enough, though it felt a little light.

"Special effects made them for me years ago," Leo said. "The pistol is one of only two made special by Smith and Wesson. Eisenhower owned the other one."

Michael took the silk handkerchief from his breast pocket and carefully wiped the pistol. "It's beautiful, Leo." He placed the weapon on Leo's desk.

"Oh, I've got the real ammo, too," Leo said, holding up a handful of loose cartridges, then dropping them back into the drawer with a clatter. "If ever some nutcase gets through security and into this building, I'd like to have a piece nearby, you know?" He put the weapon back into the drawer.

"I hope you have a permit, Leo."

"Sure I do; I can even carry it as a concealed weapon, but I'm not as paranoid as all that."

"I'm glad to hear it. Guns are dangerous."

"You're right, of course. I mean, I'm no NRA enthusiast like Chuck Heston, for instance, but I think a man ought to be able to own a piece for his own protection."

"A responsible man, yes," Michael replied. He looked at his watch. "I'd better get back to my office; I'm due to look at the first advertising ideas for *Inside Straight*."

"Let me know when they're ready for me to see," Leo said.

"Sure," Michael replied. He left Leo's office wondering what it would be like not to have to go to anyone for approval of anything, ever.

Margot gave him his messages. "I put the ad people in your office," she said.

"Right," Michael replied, flipping through the messages.

"How did the screening go?" Margot asked.

"I thought it was okay. Leo put a gun to his head when it was over."

Margot laughed. "The gold-plated one?"

"That's the one."

"He's been doing that for years, every time he wants to make a point."

Michael looked at her. "Why don't you come over this weekend and cook you and me dinner?"

"Why not?" Margot said, smiling.

Michael was spending a lot of afternoons with Amanda, but he still enjoyed Margot on a Saturday night.

52

Michael walked into the Beverly Hills Hotel, through the main lobby, and out into the rear gardens. A housemaid directed him to Bungalow Four. A Japanese man answered the door.

"I am Michael Vincent."

The man bowed, then ushered Michael into a living room. At one end of the room a large dining table was surrounded by several men, all but three Japanese. Harry Johnson stood up and approached Michael, his hand out.

"Hello, Michael," he said, beaming. "Thank you so much for coming."

Michael nodded noncommittally.

"Please let me introduce you to these gentlemen."

Everyone at the table stood.

"This," said Johnson, indicating a white-haired Japanese man, "is Mr. Matsuo Yamamoto, head of the company that bears his name."

The Japanese bowed. "How do you do, Mr. Vincent," he said, and his English was vaguely British.

"How do you do?" Michael replied, bowing slightly as he had been told to do.

"This," Johnson continued, "is Mr. Yamamoto's consultant, Mr. Yasumura."

A stocky, low-browed man standing next to Yamamoto bowed, but said nothing.

There were three other Japanese, two of whom seemed to be management types; the third seemed somehow less business-oriented. Johnson then introduced the two Caucasians standing at the table.

"This is Norman Geldorf, chairman of Geldorf and Winter, investment bankers."

Geldorf shook Michael's hand but seemed very reserved.

"And this is Mr. Thomas Provensano, an associate of Mr. Geldorf."

Tommy Pro stuck out his hand. "I'm very glad to meet you, Mr. Vincent; I've heard a great deal about you."

Johnson indicated a chair. "Please sit down."

When Michael had done so, he waited for Johnson to speak again.

"I've asked you to come here, Michael, to help resolve some concerns expressed by some of the board."

Michael finally spoke. "Harry, you are the only board member I see here."

"I am, Michael, but Mr. Geldorf is the chief trustee of a private trust which owns forty-five percent of Centurion stock."

Michael looked surprised. "I was not aware that anyone but board members owned any Centurion stock."

"That is probably what Leo Goldman wished you to think," Johnson said.

"I was under the impression that Leo owned a controlling interest."

"Not exactly. Leo *votes* a controlling interest, but, you see, he currently votes the trust-owned shares, in addition to his own."

"I see," Michael said, taking care to look surprised.

"This meeting was called so that I could present Mr. Geldorf and Mr. Provensano with an up-to-date account of the present condition of Centurion."

"I see. Is Mr. Yamamoto to be given this information, as well?"

"Now, Michael, Mr. Geldorf and I represent between us voting control of Centurion, and we felt it altogether proper for Mr. Yamamoto and his associates to share this information."

"Does Leo know about this?" Michael asked.

"He does not; Leo is in New York today. Mr. Geldorf and I thought it best to consult with Mr. Yamamoto in Leo's absence."

"Well, I suppose you have that right," Michael said.

Geldorf spoke for the first time. "Mr. Vincent, on behalf of the trust I administer, I would like to know your opinion of the current production schedule of Centurion. Excepting your own productions, of course. I have been very glad to hear of their contribution to the studio's profits."

"My opinion?" Michael asked.

"Please. You are the only active production

executive on the board besides Mr. Goldman, and we would like to have your views."

Michael hesitated artfully.

"Michael," Harry Johnson said, "I know very well the loyalty you must feel to Leo, but surely you feel a loyalty to the studio as a whole."

"Of course," Michael said. "Centurion has made it possible for me to do successful work."

"Then please believe me when I tell you that it is entirely in the studio's best interest that you be as frank as possible in your opinions of the production schedule."

Michael looked at Johnson and Geldorf. "Do I have your absolute assurance that what I say will be held in the strictest confidence?"

"You do," Geldorf and Johnson said together.

Michael looked at his reflection in the polished table. "I . . . have some concerns about the direction the studio is taking," he said.

"What concerns?" Geldorf asked.

Michael looked directly at him. "From what I know of Centurion's history, its reputation and its success have been built on reasonably priced but high-quality motion pictures, pictures that have earned more than their share of Academy Award nominations and an excellent profit for the studio."

"That is correct," Johnson said.

"I'm afraid that seems to be changing," Michael said.

"How so?" Geldorf asked.

"The current production schedule contains two projects that are very high-budget, indeed, and not, I'm afraid, what I'd consider high-quality."

"Which are those?" Geldorf asked.

"Two untitled projects—a science fiction film and one about the Vietnam War."

"Have you read the scripts of these productions?" Johnson asked.

"I have."

"And have you seen the budgets and production schedules?"

"I have."

"And what is your opinion of the chances for success of these productions?"

"Well, of course, both pictures could conceivably make a lot of money . . ."

"In your considered opinion, will they?"

"I think that both these projects are highly risky at best—more than the risk that usually runs with making motion pictures."

"Why?" Geldorf asked.

"The science fiction film has a derivative script, and the opportunities for budget overruns are prodigious. Mr. Goldman expects to make this film for, I think, around eighty million dollars . . ."

"Which is twice the budget of Centurion's most expensive productions, is it not?" Johnson asked.

"Yes, it is."

"And do you think the film has a chance of coming in on budget?"

"A chance, perhaps; no more."

"If you were producing this film, Michael,

what budget would you realistically expect to need?"

"I don't believe I could shoot it for less than a hundred and twenty-five million," Michael replied.

"And what sort of domestic gross would you anticipate?" Johnson asked.

"Well, of course, it could go through the roof, but I think it would be unwise to count on more than a hundred and fifty million."

"And would that figure cover production, prints, and advertising?"

"Not much chance of that."

"So Centurion might be facing a loss on the film?"

"It very well could."

"Michael, what do you think the chances are of the film doing as much as a hundred and fifty million?"

"Not good," Michael replied.

"So Centurion could be facing a very great loss indeed on the film?"

"Quite possibly."

"What about the Vietnam film? What do you think of that?"

"I think it's a very serious look at the political consequences of that war."

"Is there a demand for such a serious film at this time?"

"Possibly; I'm not at all sure."

"Are there any other risks associated with this film?"

"It is to be shot in the Philippines, and although

there has been an election recently, the communist insurgents are still very active, and there are many other difficulties associated with shooting that far from the studio."

"I see. Have any other major productions been filmed in the Philippines?"

"Francis Ford Coppola's film *Apocalypse Now* was shot there."

"And what happened to the budget on that film?"

"It went completely out of control. There was a hurricane, illness, every sort of disaster."

"Has that film ever made money?"

"I don't know; I doubt it."

"Michael, have you recently attended a screening of a new production called *Drive Time*?"

"Yes."

"What did you think of it?"

"I don't think it will be a great success."

"Why not?"

"I think they began shooting with less than a good script."

"This was Leo Goldman's personal production, was it not?"

"Yes."

"Mr. Vincent," Geldorf asked, "what sorts of films do you believe Centurion should be making at this moment in time?"

"I'm personally making the kind of movies that I think we should concentrate on," Michael said. "Very tight budgets, no highly paid stars, high-quality writing. Films with low risk and high profitability."

Geldorf continued. "Do you have an opinion as to whether Centurion could continue to make such films if under new ownership?"

Michael looked at Yamamoto, who smiled slightly.

"If good management were allowed to make good films without hindrance, yes."

Harry Johnson stood up. "Michael, we are all grateful to you for your candor. Please be assured that your remarks will be held in the strictest confidence." He shook Michael's hand. Everyone stood.

Michael understood that he was dismissed.

An hour later, Michael was parked on a side street off Sunset when a limousine pulled up next to his car and the rear window slid silently down. Tommy Pro beamed at him from the rear seat of the big car.

"Aces, *paisan*," he said. "Now Norman Geldorf will go and see Amanda Goldman."

"Good," Michael said.

"When does Goldman get back from New York?"

"Tomorrow afternoon."

"Schedule a meeting in his office, okay?"

"All right," Michael said.

The window slid up and the limousine moved away.

Michael drove back to Centurion and parked in front of the Executive Building. He ran up the stairs to Leo's office. Leo's secretary was sitting at her desk.

"Hi," he said. "What time should Leo be back in the office tomorrow afternoon?"

"He always comes straight from the airport," the woman said. "He should be here by four."

"Good. Would you schedule a meeting for me at that time? It's important that I see him the moment he gets back. Tell him I won't take no for an answer."

She flipped open a diary. "Four it is."

Michael put a hand on the doorknob of Leo's office. "Oh, there's something I left in here yesterday; it's on Leo's desk."

"Sure, go ahead," she said.

Michael stepped into Leo Goldman's office and closed the door behind him.

53

Michael looked up into the glazed eyes of Margot Gladstone and gave a little thrust. Margot's eyes closed, and she whimpered.

"Again," she said.

Michael complied.

Margot dissolved into a series of whimpers, climaxing quietly, as she always did. She collapsed onto Michael.

He held her against him, rubbing her back and shoulders while she continued her orgasm. It occurred to Michael that perhaps his secret in bed was that he derived his greatest pleasure from making women come, then come again and again. He rolled onto his side but remained inside her.

"That was a wonderful bit of weekend recreation," Margot said, sighing. "I lost count of how many times I came."

"Six or seven," Michael said.

"Stop bragging," she laughed.

"I'm hungry."

"All right, all right, I'll finish dinner."

He had interrupted her in the kitchen and had taken her on a double lounge at poolside. Margot rose, pushed back her hair, and dove into the pool. She swam gracefully to the end, picked up a terrycloth robe, and strode toward the kitchen, dripping as she went.

He watched through the glass wall between the kitchen and the pool as she went about preparing their dinner.

When they had finished dining, Michael leaned back in his poolside chair and gazed at the stars. "That was wonderful," he said. "What was it?"

"It was a caesar salad, Chateaubriand with béarnaise sauce, *pommes soufflé, haricots verts*, and Stock Exchange Pudding."

"It was the last one I meant. What was it again?"

"Stock Exchange Pudding. When I was but a slip of a girl I had a job conducting guided tours of the London Stock Exchange. There was a corps of us girls, and we cooked lunches for ourselves—quite elaborate ones, sometimes. That's where I got the recipe for the pudding."

"It was superb."

"So were you."

"What would I do without you?" he asked.

"Funny you should mention that."

"What?"

"Michael, you must remember that when I came to you I said I was serving out my time until my pension matured. You do remember."

"Vaguely," he replied.

"Well, next month I'm off."

Michael was alarmed. "You can't do that," he said. "I can't do this without you."

She shrugged. "I was thinking of Mexico. I might buy a little place somewhere around Puerto Vallarta."

"I won't let you go. I can't."

"Michael, it's been fun, but I can't go on doing that job the rest of my life. I'll be sixty in fewer years than I care to think about."

Michael was genuinely panicked at the thought of losing Margot. She made his life work; she was the closest thing to a confidant he had ever had. "Suppose you were doing a different job," he said.

"What do you mean?"

"I mean something better."

She shook her head. "I wouldn't derive the pleasure from producing that you do. Really, I wouldn't."

"Something bigger."

She looked at him closely. "Why don't you tell me what's going on? I know something is; I can always tell."

Michael sat back and sipped his wine. He was a little tipsy—rare for him—and he was enjoying her company greatly. He was not enjoying the idea of having to replace her. He made a decision.

"All right, I'll tell you."

She curled up in her chair and waited.

"In a day or two, Leo will be out."

Her eyes widened.

"And I'll be running the studio."

"Michael, you shouldn't underestimate Leo's influence with the board."

"The board came to me. They're worried about Leo—especially that he won't consider an offer from the Japanese."

"That I had heard about," she said, "but do you know that Amanda's trust has the biggest chunk of stock?"

"I do. The head trustee, Norman Geldorf, is in town right now. I met with him and Harry Johnson and . . . some other people this afternoon."

"The Japanese?"

Michael nodded. "And a friend of mine."

"Tommy?"

"You do keep up, don't you?"

"I read the papers, and I hear more than you think at the office."

"What do you hear?" he asked, a little worried.

"Oh, come on, Michael; you don't have any secrets from me. We're too close for that."

"I have some secrets from everybody," he said.

"Not from me."

"Just which of my secrets do you know?"

"All of them," she said. "I know how much money you have, where it is, and how you made it."

"Where is it?"

"Well, you've moved it out of the Kensington

Trust, but I know how it was invested there. What was it, three percent a week?"

Michael was taken aback. "What else do you know?"

"Oh, I've put the pieces together. I know about Callabrese and Moriarty. I'm damned sure you got rid of Rick Rivera, but I'm not quite sure how."

Michael was flabbergasted, but he kept his composure.

"Oh, come on, Michael; that poker face won't work with me. You know I know."

"Well, this is an unexpected turn of events," he said.

She held up her hands. "Now, Michael, you have nothing to fear from me, so don't start thinking about somehow getting rid of me. I've watched you operate with total admiration. I mean, I've seen some operators in this town, but you are truly something special. You have the single most important quality that a successful producer can possess in this town: you are a complete sociopath."

Michael stared at her silently.

She held up a hand again. "Please don't take that as a criticism. I simply mean that you have no conscience whatever and that you will do anything necessary to get what you want." She smiled at him. "Am I wrong?"

He smiled back. "You know me better than I thought."

"It has been thrilling to watch," she said. "If I

had met you when I was twenty-five, you and I could have ruled this town together."

"We still might," Michael said. "How would you like to be chief operating officer of Centurion?"

Her eyebrows went up. "That's a big leap from executive assistant," she said.

"Honestly, Margot, do you think there is anyone in administration at the studio whose job you couldn't do better?"

She laughed. "Michael, *you* know *me* better than I thought."

"I do."

"But there's a problem here."

"Nothing we can't overcome."

"So you get your way; you get Leo's job, and you're running the studio. Then Geldorf and Johnson sell out to the Japanese, and suddenly you're not in charge anymore. You'd be working for them, just as you're working for Leo now. And I don't think you'd like that."

"You're right, I wouldn't. I understand what Leo loves so much about running the studio. As he put it himself, he has the ability to make any movie he wants, without asking anybody."

"The Japanese wouldn't let you do that; not for long."

"You're right."

"So what are you going to do?"

Michael smiled. It was wonderful telling somebody this. "I'm going to take Leo's job, and then I'm going to fuck the Japanese."

"And Tommy?"

"Tommy is my closest friend. He and I can work something out."

"If you can do that, I'm with you," Margot said.

"Then you're with me."

54

Michael waited impatiently for the call from Leo's secretary, and when it came, he made his own call. "Leo's ready," he said.

"We're right behind you," Johnson replied from his car phone. "We're already inside the gates."

Michael left his office and walked toward the Executive Building, taking his time, waiting for Johnson. As he mounted the steps to the building, the limousine hove into view. He continued through the lobby and up the stairs to Leo's office.

"Hi," he said to Leo's secretary.

"He's expecting you," she said.

Michael knocked, then opened the door. Leo was sitting at his desk shuffling through some papers. He looked up. "Hiya, kiddo."

"How was your trip?"

"Pretty damn good. I got some new distribution—sixty screens for first releases."

"Congratulations."

"What did you want to see me about?"

Before Michael could speak, Leo's phone buzzed and at the same time, the door to his office opened. Harry Johnson entered, followed closely by Norman Geldorf.

Leo looked at them, puzzled. "I didn't know you guys were in town," he said. "Why didn't you call?"

"There was no time, Leo," Johnson said. "We have to talk."

"Sure." Leo waved them to chairs in front of his desk, and Michael sat down near Leo's right hand.

"I'll come right to the point," Johnson said.

"Good," Leo replied. He seemed unconcerned.

"Leo, the board is unhappy. We've met in your absence, and we've decided that it's time for you to step down."

Leo stared at Johnson. "*What*?" he demanded.

"Board members with a large majority of shares concurred in this decision."

Leo looked at Geldorf. "Did you buy into this?"

"I did," Geldorf said.

"What about Amanda? What did she have to say about it?"

Geldorf looked away. "It is not her decision. As head trustee, it is mine alone."

"You're out of your fucking minds, all of you." He turned to Michael. "You hear this? I've made these bastards richer and richer by the way I've run this studio, and now they're stabbing me in the goddamned back."

Michael looked down.

"Not a moviemaker among them," Leo said, and his face was becoming very red. "How do they expect to run this place without me?" He looked at Johnson. "Or do you just expect to sell the joint to the Japs?"

"Maybe," Johnson said. "They've made us another offer."

"So why didn't you consult me about it?"

"Because you've made it plain that you wouldn't accept under any circumstances."

Leo stared at him for a moment, then reached into his top right desk drawer and took out his gold-plated revolver. He put the gun to his head. "You know something? If I thought I couldn't run this place better than the bunch of you and the Japanese put together, I'd blow my brains out right here and now."

"Oh, come on, Leo," Johnson said, exasperated, "don't start with that old routine; I've seen it half a dozen times."

Leo took the gun away from his head and pointed it at Johnson. "Okay, instead of me, I'll do you."

Johnson shook his head. "Leo, stop behaving like a child."

Leo pulled the trigger. The gun went off, and Johnson spun sideways out of his chair.

"Jesus Christ!" Geldorf shouted. He pushed his chair aside and knelt beside Johnson.

Leo was standing, looking first at Johnson, then at the gun, a look of amazement on his face.

Michael saw his chance. He stood up, grabbed Leo by the wrist with one hand, then closed his other hand over Leo's, running his finger inside the trigger guard. "Don't do it, Leo!" Michael shouted. Then he jerked Leo's hand around toward his head and pressed Leo's trigger finger.

The gun roared again. The bullet entered Leo's head just under the temple and exited above his right eye, knocking Leo back into his chair and spattering Michael with gore.

Geldorf looked up from attending to Johnson. "Michael, are you shot?" he yelled.

Leo's secretary burst into the office, and, seeing Johnson lying facedown on the floor and her boss in his chair with part of his head missing, fainted.

Michael hesitated only a moment, then picked up Leo's phone, got an outside line, and dialed 911. "An ambulance," he said to the operator, giving her the address. "There's been a shooting." He hung up and dialed the Legal Department. "This is Michael Vincent," he said. "Leo Goldman has just shot another man and himself. Get the best lawyer you can find up to Leo's office at once."

Michael and Geldorf sat on facing sofas before the fireplace in Leo's office. The swarm of ambulance men, policemen and crime technicians was thinning out; only two detectives, Michael and Geldorf, and the Centurion lawyer remained.

"All right, let's go through it once more," a detective said.

"No," Michael replied. "You've heard it again and again. Do you have any doubt what happened?"

"We've told you the truth," Geldorf said. "Surely you don't think that Mr. Vincent and I murdered two men in this office."

The other detective put down the phone. "There hasn't been a murder," he said. "They're both still alive."

Michael looked at the man. "That's wonderful," he managed to say. "How are they?"

"Johnson wasn't hurt bad. The bullet missed the lung and exited the shoulder; broke his collarbone. He'll be out of the hospital in a couple of days."

"What about Mr. Goldman?" Geldorf asked.

"He's alive; that's about it. You can talk to his doctor when we're through here."

"We're through here," Michael said, rising. "I'm going to the hospital." He stopped. "Jesus Christ, has anybody called Amanda?"

"Mrs. Goldman?" the detective asked. "His secretary called her; she's at the hospital."

"Are you coming, Norman?" Michael asked.

"Yes, of course. Amanda will need us."

The group started to shuffle out of the office, but one detective pulled Michael back.

"Do you remember me, Mr. Vincent?"

"I'm sorry, I don't."

"My name is Hall; I was Rick Rivera's partner. We met when Rick and I came to see you about the Moriarty murder."

"Oh, yes, I remember."

"People around you keep dying or getting hurt," Hall said.

"I beg your pardon?"

"Moriarty dies right after you see him; Rick dies after he comes to work for you—and Rick was never a junkie. And now these two."

"What are you getting at, Detective?"

"The shame of it is I'm not getting anywhere," Hall said. "But I want you to know that I'm not through rooting around in your life. Rick was my friend, and . . ."

"That's about enough out of you," Michael interrupted. "You're implying that I had something to do with all these things, and you're wrong. You just do your job, and you'll find out that I'm nothing more than an innocent bystander. Go too far, and you'll find that this studio has more than a little influence with the government of this city." Michael turned and stalked out of the room.

Michael and Amanda sat in a corner of the large, sunny hospital room occupied by Leo Goldman. Geldorf waited outside. Leo lay on his back, his head swathed in bandages, his left eye open and staring.

"I can't believe any of this," Amanda was saying. She was composed now, and coming to terms with what had happened. "What happened in that office?"

"Leo was arguing with Johnson. He pulled a gun out of his desk and pointed it at his head. Johnson seemed to have seen the gun before; he told Leo to put it down and stop acting like a child. Leo shot Johnson and then put the gun to his own head. I tried to stop him, grabbed at his arm, but it went off."

"Had Johnson and Geldorf told Leo that he was finished at the studio?"

"Yes."

"Did you know this was coming?"

"I was called to a meeting with them yesterday. I defended Leo as best I could. I scheduled a meeting with him as soon as he returned to warn him of what was happening, then Johnson and Geldorf showed up."

"The worst part of it is, he's going to live and be a vegetable," Amanda said. "He'd rather be dead, believe me."

"Amanda, you aren't obliged to keep him alive artificially under these circumstances."

"Don't worry, I won't." She began to cry.

"There, there," he said. "Don't cry; Leo isn't in pain."

"That's not why I'm crying," Amanda sobbed. "I'm crying because right now, all I can think about is wanting you."

55

Michael looked around the hospital room. The entire Centurion board of directors was gathered around Harry Johnson's bed, and Harry, his arm and shoulder in a cast, was speaking.

"All right," he said, grimacing with pain. "You've all heard from Norman, Michael, and me what happened in Leo's office yesterday. Now we've got some business to conduct, and I want to get on with it so that I can have a painkiller. Norman, do you have a motion?"

Geldorf nodded. "I move that the board appoint Michael Vincent as president and chief executive officer of Centurion Pictures, with full operating authority, at a salary and with benefits to be negotiated between representatives of the board and Mr. Vincent."

"Do I hear a second?"

"Second," another board member said.

"All in favor?"

"Aye," rumbled from the group.

"Opposed?"

Silence.

"Congratulations, Michael," Johnson said. "Now, if there is no further business to conduct at this time, this board is adjourned. *Nurse!*"

A uniformed nurse entered the room with a hypodermic needle on a tray, and the board members filed out.

Outside in the hall, Michael accepted the congratulations of his fellow board members, then, when they had drifted out, he walked down the hall toward Leo Goldman's room.

Michael entered and approached the bed. Leo seemed unchanged from the day before, but his exposed left eye was closed. He opened it.

"Hi, Leo," Michael said softly.

Leo blinked rapidly.

"There was a board meeting. They chose me to succeed you."

Leo blinked rapidly again.

Michael leaned over and looked into Leo's good eye. There was intelligence there. "Leo," he said, "if you can understand me, blink once."

Leo blinked once. Leo was alive in there.

"I want to ask you some questions. Blink once for yes, twice for no."

Leo blinked once.

"Are you in pain?"

Leo blinked once.

"Do you want me to call the nurse?"

Leo blinked twice.

"Can you move?"

Leo blinked twice.

"Can you speak?"

Leo blinked twice.

"Do you want to see Amanda?"

Leo blinked twice.

"Do you want me to leave you alone?"

Leo blinked twice.

"I wish I could just ask you what you want," Michael said. "Don't worry, you'll get better in time."

Leo blinked twice.

Michael stared at the eye. "Don't you think you'll get better?"

Leo blinked twice.

"Leo, do you want to go on living like this?"

Leo blinked twice.

"Do you want me to do something about it?"

Leo blinked once.

Michael walked to the door and looked up and down the hallway. No one was in sight. He went back to Leo's bedside and looked around. Leo had an oxygen tube up his nose and an IV was running. If he tampered with those, somebody would notice. Gently, he lifted Leo's head and removed the pillow. He leaned over Leo.

"Is this what you want, Leo?"

Leo blinked once.

"Leo, I want to thank you for everything you've done for me."

Leo blinked once.

"I want you to know I'll see that Amanda is all right."

Leo blinked once.

"Good-bye, old friend."

Leo blinked once, and the eye filled. A tear trickled toward his ear.

Michael placed the pillow over Leo's face and pressed gently. He waited for three minutes by his watch, then he removed the pillow. He felt at Leo's neck, but couldn't find a pulse. He lifted Leo's head and placed the pillow under it, then he left the room. No one saw him leave.

For the first time since he was a little boy, Michael was fighting back tears.

56

Michael stood at the podium and addressed the memorial service audience. The auditorium was packed.

"I had not known Leo Goldman as long as many of you, but I counted him as my closest friend. I have been asked to address you about Leo's professional side—Leo as filmmaker.

"Leo Goldman personified what was best in the title 'producer.' He had taste, judgment, style, an appreciation of talent of all sorts, and a keen business sense. The films Leo made as a producer were always among Centurion's best.

"But Leo was more than a producer: he was a studio head, and he operated in a manner not often seen today. He was the kind of studio head that L. B. Mayer and Jack Warner were. *He was responsible.* Leo personally analyzed and approved every project that came out of Centurion, and every movie that Centurion made reflected his taste and judgment. I think that it is possible to view every film that Centurion ever made under Leo, as I have done, and conclude that Leo Goldman never made a bad movie. Not one. And that is something that neither L. B. Mayer nor Jack Warner could have justifiably said.

"What Leo Goldman did make was hundreds of good movies, and I know that Leo would be happy to be judged by nothing other than that output. *He was responsible.*

"I have been chosen to replace Leo, but we all know that such a thing is not possible. When I was offered his place at Centurion, my first emotion was awe, followed closely by humility, when I realized what I was being asked to do. Perhaps it would be better to follow a bad studio head, because it would be easier to look better; following Leo would be very hard, because he was so good at what he did.

"But on reflection, I see that my job will be made easier because Leo did his job so well; because he made decisions, knocked heads, and, no doubt over opposition, established a standard of filmmaking that is the envy of the industry. *He was responsible.*

"My gratitude to Leo is complete. He made it possible, first, for me to do what I do, and then for me to do what he did. If I don't do it as well, it won't be Leo's fault.

"I tell you now that I would rather work for Leo than run the studio. I would rather stand in his shadow than face the glare of solitary scrutiny, as he did.

"And if, in my examination of my own life

and work, I find that I had the slightest part in driving Leo to what he finally did, I will ask God to punish me.

"I loved Leo Goldman, and I miss him. In the coming days, if I find myself in a quandary, at loggerheads with my peers, in trouble with my studio, I will ask myself, 'What would Leo Goldman have done?' And I will know what to do."

Amanda Goldman received her husband's friends and admirers at her home on Stone Canyon. Some four hundred people ate, drank, and talked of Leo Goldman and The Business.

Michael found himself besieged by new admirers congratulating him on his eulogy.

Margot Gladstone was nearby. "These people are eating out of your hand," she whispered to him when she had the opportunity. "Let's try and keep it that way."

When the crowd began to drift away, Michael cornered Norman Geldorf and Harry Johnson, whose arm was still in its cast.

"I wanted to say this as soon as possible," he said. "I don't think we should sell to the Japanese. Not yet, anyway."

"I'm inclined to agree," Geldorf said. "With Leo gone, they'll try to knock down the price."

"Give me a chance to get established, to get some movies into production," Michael said. "Then, if selling is the right thing to do, you'll get a lot more money for the studio."

Both men nodded.

"That was a wonderful eulogy, Michael," Johnson said. "Just the right touch."

Michael was the last to leave.

"Don't go," Amanda said, clinging to him. "Stay the night."

"It's better that I go," he said. "We'll talk in a few days. See your friends, ignore me; that's the best way for a while."

"In a week I'll be on fire," she said.

"In a week you can set me afire," he replied.

Michael cloistered himself in the Malibu house for the weekend with Margot. He strode back and forth beside the pool, dictating notes for running Centurion, and Margot took them down. She cooked; they made love. There was little love in it, they both knew. They used each other to the fullest.

But in their developing relationship, Michael had found what he had never had—a confidant.

57

Near the end of his first week as head of Centurion Pictures, Michael was working at his desk in what had once been Leo Goldman's office, preparing for a board meeting, when Margot Gladstone entered through the door between their adjoining offices.

"Have you heard the news this morning, or seen the papers?" she asked.

"No, neither. I haven't had time for anything but this board meeting."

She placed the *New York Times* on his desk. In the lower right-hand corner of the front page, Michael found the story:

MAFIA CHIEFTAIN DEAD AT 72

Benito Carlucci, for many years head of New York's largest Mafia family, died yesterday at the age of seventy-two, at Columbia Presbyterian Hospital, of complications of liver disease. . . .

Carlucci was convicted of a crime only once, as

a young man, when he served two years in Sing Sing prison for heading a car theft ring. From the time of his release, he rose rapidly in the ranks of his criminal organization, always protected from arrest by layers of command, and at the age of only forty, he succeeded to the leadership of his Mafia family. Under his management the family took the first tentative steps toward legitimate investment, and, at the time of his death, FBI sources said that more than half the family's income derived from legitimate business, although these businesses were often operated in a fashion that flirted with illegality. . . .

Often the death of the head of a Mafia family results in a struggle for succession that is bloody, but it appears to knowledgeable observers that Carlucci, anticipating his death, mediated the succession, and arranged that the family would be run by a council, the members of which are capos of units of the family. None of the four members seems, at this time, to have the upper hand.

Services will be held tomorrow at St. Patrick's Cathedral, with the Archbishop of New York officiating.

Michael put down the paper and picked up the phone, dialing the number of a cellular phone.

"Yes?" Tommy's voice was tense.

"It's Vinnie; I just heard."

"Hold."

Michael listened as muffled orders were barked, then Tommy came back on the line.

"Sorry, Vinnie. It's been hectic around here, as you can imagine."

"I'm very sorry, Tommy; I know you loved the old man."

"I did, but he's gone, and now we've got stuff to do."

"Is everything all right?"

"Don't believe everything you read in the papers."

"When can we get together?"

"I'll try and come out there next month."

"Good. Convey my sympathy to his family."

"Of course."

Michael hung up.

"Well?" Margot asked. "What's going on?"

"He couldn't really talk," Michael said. "He'll come out here when he can, and then we'll know."

Michael called the board meeting to order. "Good afternoon, gentlemen; this will be a brief meeting. I want to bring you up to date on business, then there are two matters before the board for approval.

"Since taking charge of the studio, I have canceled the science fiction and Vietnam War projects and have written off the expenses."

There was a murmur of approval around the table.

"I have also put three pictures into production, the largest budget of which is fourteen million dollars. I expect all of them to be highly profitable.

"Naturally, there will be some personnel changes at the studio. Some of the department heads under Leo will, of course, be unhappy with working for me, and there may be some that I will be unhappy with."

Harry Johnson spoke up. "You will, of course, seek board approval of any major changes."

Michael looked at Johnson. "That concludes my update. Now I wish to bring to a vote the employment contracts for myself and Margot Gladstone. To answer your question, Harry, my proposed contract gives me full authority to hire and fire as I see fit. Do I hear a motion?"

"Move that the contracts be approved," a board member said.

"Second," said another.

"Any discussion?" Michael asked. "Harry?"

Johnson stood up. "Michael, first I want to say how pleased I am—and I'm sure I speak for all the board—at the way you've taken charge of the studio. Your actions on the production side are both prudent and creative, and we are all grateful." He cleared his throat. "However, there are potential problems on the business side of the studio. Some of the department heads have been in their jobs for many years and have proven their worth under Leo. All of these people have had vastly more experience than you in this business, and I, for one, am reluctant to give you the power to terminate and replace them at will."

"Thank you, Harry," Michael said. "What you say is, of course, true; some of these people have been here for a long time, and all of them are competent. All of them, however, are not happy about working for me, and unless that unhappiness can be modified in short order, I will regard such an attitude as disqualifying where these positions are concerned."

"Another thing," Johnson said. "Putting in Margot Gladstone as chief operating officer might be considered a rash act. Ms. Gladstone has been secretary to a number of high executives here, but that experience hardly qualifies her to administrate the business side of this studio."

"I understand your concern, Harry," Michael said, "but Margot knows more about how this studio works than anybody here, including me. She is highly intelligent, and I have always found her judgment to be faultless. She will, of course, report to me, and I can always overrule her actions if I disagree with them."

"A salary of a million dollars a year, plus benefits, for a woman who was recently a secretary?" Johnson asked.

"If she is qualified to be COO," Michael replied, "and I have already said I believe her to be, then her compensation package is a moderate one by industry standards."

Johnson began to speak again, but Michael held up a hand.

"Harry, I don't mean to squelch debate, but the decision before this board is a simple one: will I run this studio, or will I not? Let me be quite clear: I will accept this job only if I have the same authority that Leo had. My contract is before you; it gives me full authority. I have presented Margot

Gladstone's contract to you only as a courtesy. If this board approves my contract, then my first act as CEO will be to sign Margot's contract. If this board chooses not to do so, then I can have my desk cleared out in half an hour. I think it best if I leave the meeting while you discuss this. Gentlemen, the decision is yours." Michael turned to leave.

"Michael," Johnson said.

Michael turned. "Yes?"

"I don't think it will be necessary for you to leave. I move the question."

Michael looked around the table. "All in favor?"

"Aye," the men said as one.

"Opposed?"

Silence.

"The motion is carried unanimously," Michael said. "Gentlemen, without further business, this meeting is adjourned until the next regular monthly meeting."

Michael stepped back into his office, where Margot waited for him. He walked to his desk, signed four copies of her contract, and handed her one. "You are now the chief operating officer of Centurion Pictures," he said.

Margot beamed and kissed him.

"Now," Michael said, "go fire the chief financial officer."

"Yessir," Margot replied.

58

Michael sat in the chauffeur-driven stretch Mercedes that he had inherited from Leo Goldman and watched the Gulfstream IV jet land at Santa Monica Airport. It seemed an impossibly short runway for such a big airplane, but shortly the jet was taxiing toward where Michael waited.

Michael greeted Tommy Pro with a hug and a kiss at the bottom of the airstairs, then hustled him into the Mercedes while the chauffeur dealt with the luggage.

"That's a very nice mode of transportation," Michael said. "You can't be in too much trouble."

"Trouble?" Tommy laughed. "I should always be in this much trouble." He found the proper switch and raised the glass partition between them and the driver, who now pointed the car toward Malibu. "Can he hear us at all?" Tommy asked.

"Not at all. Leo bought a standard 600 sedan, the one with the twelve-cylinder engine, and had it stretched. He also had this compartment completely soundproofed."

Tommy fiddled with the TV. "Does this thing get CNN?"

"No, Tommy. You need cable or a satellite for CNN."

"Does it get any news at all?"

Michael leaned forward and changed the channel. "We get the network news at five o'clock out here." Tom Brokaw's image appeared on the screen.

"Good evening," the newscaster said. "Tonight, there's a new showdown with Saddam Hussein over inspections of his military installations, the president is in deep political trouble over the Iran-Contra scandal and—" the picture changed to one of a dead man lying on a New York street "—a generational change in a Mafia family."

Tommy heaved a deep sigh.

"What's going on?" Michael asked. "I'm not learning a hell of a lot from the newspapers."

"With any luck at all," Tommy said, "that guy lying in the street was Benny the Nose."

"Benny? Who would have the guts to whack Benny Nose?"

"You're looking at him."

"Well, I'll be damned. Tommy, bring me up to date here."

"Shhh," Tommy said, pointing at the TV.

Brokaw was back. "Early this afternoon in New York City, two Mafia capos were gunned down in the street as they left a Manhattan restaurant. These murders laid to rest the FBI theory that after the death of Benito Carlucci, power had passed to a committee of his subordinates without a struggle. Police theorize that two of the committee members had the other two rubbed out in order to consolidate their power."

"This is why I'm visiting you," Tommy said. "It's a good time to be away."

"So who's left?" Michael asked. "Who's running things?"

"Eddie and Joe Funaro are left," Tommy said, "and *I'm* running things."

"Jesus, Tommy! How'd you pull that off?"

"The old man pulled it off—him and me together. He called the four of them in and told them there was a new setup, then he told Eddie and Joe to take orders from me. Now they're running the street businesses, and I'm running everything else. They funnel the proceeds to me, and I invest legitimately."

"You're running *everything*?"

"Everything." Tommy looked very smug.

Michael leaned back in the seat. "So you're the Don."

Tommy grinned. "I'm the Don."

At sunset, Michael and Tommy strolled along the beach at Malibu Colony, Michael in casual California clothes and Tommy in the rolled-up trousers of his sharkskin suit and silk shirt, his necktie hanging loose. They had had dinner, talking of Tommy's new responsibilities, his new power.

"You're a very lucky man, Vinnie," Tommy said.

"Don't I know it."

"Luckier than you know."

"How do you mean?"

"If the Don had lived another twenty-four hours you'd be dead."

Michael stopped in his tracks. "*What*?"

"I held him off as long as I could, and he died."

"The old man wanted me dead?"

"You double-crossed him, Vinnie."

"Now, wait a minute, Tommy."

"Some people would say that you double-crossed me."

"Tommy . . ."

"You talked Geldorf and Johnson out of selling the studio to the Japs, which means *us* and the Japs."

"It wasn't the right thing to do, Tommy. Not then."

"Why not then? I had it all set up: Geldorf and Johnson were in the bag, Goldman was dead, you were—you are—in charge."

"Tommy, listen to me. I've got a movie studio in the palm of my hand; Centurion Pictures! Do you know what that means?"

"It means one hell of a lot of money to play with," Tommy said.

"It's more than that, Tommy; I can make any movie, and I mean *any* movie, I want. I can hire any star, any director, any writer; I've got the button to the green light in my hand. I *own* the button."

"You don't own shit. You're working for a salary."

"My contract gives me the right to buy two percent of the equity a year, as long as we're profitable."

"*Two percent a year*? You're telling me that you stiffed the Don, the family, and me for *two percent a year*?"

"Tommy, I didn't stiff anybody. You're not out anything."

"The old man didn't see it that way, Vinnie, and if it hadn't been for me, you'd be feeding the fishes in the Pacific Ocean right now." For emphasis, Tommy pointed out at the water.

"Tommy, I appreciate . . ."

"You don't appreciate nothing, Vinnie. Do you know that he actually gave me the order? He *ordered* me to whack you, and I didn't do it. The first time in my whole life I ignored an order from my Don. You don't appreciate, Vinnie; you suck at the tit, and you kick everybody else in the teeth."

"Tommy, this was my chance, don't you understand?"

"Your chance to stiff your friends?"

"My chance to run my own operation, my own life, and not be under anybody's thumb."

"That's not how you were raised, Vinnie. Shit, we're all under each other's thumbs; that's why what we have works—we all owe each other. And you thought that you could just step into Leo Goldman's shoes and not owe anybody?"

"Tommy, I owe you, I know that. I'll do anything I can to make it up to you. Just say the word; you can have whatever you want."

"You think this movie studio is some kind of toy, don't you? It's like some giant Erector Set that you get to play with and nobody else can touch, you know that? You don't recognize it for what it is, which is a machine for printing money."

"Tommy, just tell me what you want."

"I want sixty percent of the stock of Centurion Pictures. That's Harry Johnson's stock and Amanda Goldman's—her trust that Norman Geldorf runs. I'll get the rest myself."

"Tommy, if I talk them into that, I cut my own throat. I won't be in charge anymore; I'll be working for somebody else again, don't you see?"

"Vinnie, let me tell you a story. You remember Shorty?"

"Shorty? With the gimpy legs that ran errands for the Don?"

"That's the one. His legs were useless, so he sat on that little plank with the rollerskate wheels, and he pushed himself around the neighborhood, doing for the Don."

Vinnie laughed. "He could go like hell on that skateboard thing, couldn't he?"

"Sure, he could, and you know what? The Don trusted him."

"The Don trusted Shorty? I didn't know he trusted anybody."

"Very few people, but he trusted Shorty. You know why?"

"Why?"

"Did you know that once—this was before you and me were born—Shorty had the richest funeral parlor in Little Italy?"

"No, I didn't know that. How'd he end up on the skateboard."

"The Don gave it to him, practically; loaned him the money, no interest, sent him business—a *lot* of business, if you know what I mean, and all the Don ever asked of him was that, once in a while, he would bury somebody for the Don. The Don would send him a stiff, and he would bury, it, two for one, with another, legit stiff that Shorty happened to be burying anyway."

"So what happened?"

"Shorty got scared of the cops and the feds. They were sniffing around, and he got scared, and the Don sent him a stiff, and he wouldn't bury it, said he couldn't afford to take the chance, what with the cops sniffing around." Tommy stopped walking and turned to Michael. "Then one night the funeral parlor burned down. And a few days after that, two men came and broke the undertaker's legs. And that's how Eduardo Minnelli, the wealthy and highly respected undertaker, got to be Shorty, the gofer."

Michael looked into Tommy's eyes, and he didn't like what he saw.

"But after that," Tommy continued, "the Don always trusted Shorty. He trusted him with important stuff, stuff that could have sent the Don himself up. Because he knew Shorty would never betray him again." Tommy looked at Michael. "That's a story you ought to remember, Vinnie."

Then Tommy turned and walked back toward the house, wading in the surf. Michael followed behind, like a puppy.

59

Michael and Amanda Goldman both reeked of cocoa butter as they stood under a hot shower, soaping each other. Amanda knelt and took him into her mouth, but he pulled her to her feet.

"Not again, no, no; I'm raw as it is."

"I can't get enough of you," she said, reaching around him and rubbing the soap into his back. They stood, kissing, until the soap had washed away, then Michael turned the shower off. He stepped out and held a terrycloth robe for her, then found one for himself.

"I feel like some eggs," he said. "Can I make you some?"

"Love some. You do that while I dry my hair."

Michael went down to the kitchen and began to work. He put some bacon on, slipped a pair of English muffins into the toaster, and whipped half a dozen eggs with a little cream while waiting for half a stick of butter to dissolve in a saucepan. He added some salt, then scrambled the eggs slowly, on the lowest possible heat, until they were fluffy and still moist, and, as Amanda came into the kitchen, he served the bacon, eggs, and muffins on large white plates.

"It smells wonderful," she said. "I didn't know you could cook."

"Almost my only dish," he said, opening a bottle of Schramsberg blanc de noirs.

"My favorite champagne," she said, sipping it. "How'd you know?"

"I've had it at your table often enough; that's where I discovered it."

She shook her hair and it fell, golden, around her shoulders. "You know something?" she asked, eating her eggs.

"What?"

"I thought I would be in some kind of shock for a while, but it's only been two weeks since Leo died, and I feel . . . liberated."

"I think a lot of people must feel that way when their other half dies. It's just that nobody wants to admit it."

"I mean, I loved Leo in my way, but I'm also glad to be free."

"Not completely free," he warned. "Remember how small a town this is. You've got to be a widow for a while."

"I don't mind that, as long as I can see you," she said.

"You can see me whenever you want," he promised. "But we have to wait a year or so before we turn up at dinner parties together."

"I can stand it if you make love to me often enough."

"How often is enough?"

She laughed. "You don't want to know."

"Let's wait until I recover before we do it again."

She placed a hand on his cheek. "I'm sorry, sweetie. I didn't mean to wear you out."

Michael took a deep breath. "Listen, we've got some business to talk."

"Okay, shoot."

"I want you to tell Geldorf that you want him to sell all the Centurion stock in the trust account."

She gaped at him. "Are you mad? I thought you wanted my backing so you could run the studio."

"Believe me, it's just the right time to sell. The Japanese are knocking on our door again, and we're in good enough shape to demand a big price."

"What about Leo's stock?"

"Tell Geldorf to sell that for you, too."

"What about the other directors?"

"When they see a majority get sold they'll get on the bandwagon fast."

She looked down at her plate for a moment. "Michael, do you remember once I told you what Leo did for me in our marriage?"

"I think so."

"I said that I could have anybody I wanted at my dinner table, remember?"

"Yes, I remember."

"Well, the reason I could do that was because my husband ran a major movie studio."

"Yes, I remember, but Leo is dead."

"But when you and I are married I want you still to run the studio."

This was the first time marriage had been mentioned, and Michael tried not to look flustered. "Don't worry, I'll still be running the studio, just under different ownership."

"But the only way I can be sure of that is by hanging on to my stock."

"But . . . at one time, before Leo died, you said you'd sell." He reached over and took her face in his hands. "Amanda, I want you to trust me on this. It's the right thing to do, believe me. The Japanese have offered me an ironclad contract."

"But they can always buy out your contract; it happens all the time in this town. They get tired of you, they want a change, they just write you a nice check and ship you out. Leo always told me that."

He was becoming irritable now. "Goddamnit, Amanda, just do as I say."

She stood up. "I think you're forgetting who you're talking to," she said, then stalked out of the house.

Michael, wearing only a robe, couldn't chase her.

Later in the afternoon, Margot came into his office.

"Michael," she said, sitting down, "I've been rereading my contract, and I find that I can be fired at any time for any reason on ninety days' notice."

Michael looked up from the script he was reading. "Margot, I've made you chief operating officer of this studio. Why would I want to fire you?"

"I know you wouldn't," she said, "because I know too much about you, but suppose something happened to you? The board could throw me right out on my arse, and I'd only have ninety days' pay to keep me."

"Margot," he said, irritated, "you've already got your pension nailed down; in such an unlikely event, you'd have what you would have had if I hadn't promoted you. That should be enough."

"It isn't enough," she said. "I'm in a whole new financial ball game, and I like it. I don't want to be in a position where I can get thrown out on my ear; can't you understand that?"

"You mean you don't want to have to rely on my word."

"If you want to put it that way, yes," Margot said.

Michael was near to losing his temper now; he was getting too much flak from women today, and he didn't like it. "Your contract remains as it is," he said. "If you don't trust me, then go fuck yourself."

Margot turned white, then she stood up. "I'm glad to know where I stand," she said coldly. Then she walked out of the room, slamming the door behind her.

Michael went back to his script, but he had

trouble concentrating. Finally, he got up and opened the door that joined their offices. "Margot," he said, "I'm sorry, I . . ." He looked around the room. She was gone.

60

Michael stood at the mirror and expertly tied his black silk evening tie. The phone rang, the private number that only a few people had.

"Hello?"

"It's Tommy."

He sounded unhappy, Michael thought. "Hey, Tommy, how are you?"

"Not so good. I just had a drink with Norman Geldorf."

"And?"

"He won't sell the trust's stock."

"Wait a minute, I told Amanda Goldman to tell him to sell everything, including Leo's stock."

"She didn't get the message."

"Look, Tommy, I can fix this."

"I don't think you're getting the message either, Vinnie."

"Look, she'll do whatever I tell her to; I've got her wrapped around my little finger; she thinks we're going to get married."

"Geldorf told me it was her express wish that she hang on to the stock, just so she can keep you in power at the studio."

"Tommy . . ."

"In fact, Geldorf had the distinct impression that you were playing her along, just to get her to do that."

"Tommy, that's not so; I . . ."

"Good-bye, Vinnie," Tommy said. "Or maybe I should say good-bye, Michael. That's who you are these days, isn't it?" He hung up.

"Tommy . . ." Michael crashed the phone down on the receiver. "Goddamnit!" he screamed at nobody in particular. He grabbed his dinner jacket; he was already late for an industry dinner at the Beverly Hills Hotel.

He ran down the stairs to the garage, to find the chauffeur working under the hood of the car. "What the hell?" he said.

"I'm sorry, Mr. Vincent. The starter's not getting any juice from the battery; I think there's a broken wire."

"Never mind, I'll drive myself," Michael said, getting into the Porsche.

He roared out of the garage, flashing his lights at the security guard, who got the gate up just in time, then drove down the Pacific Coast Highway, forcing himself to keep it at eighty, lest he be arrested. He was receiving an award tonight for his support of the campaign against AIDS in the Hollywood community, and he didn't want to be late for his own party.

* * *

At the predinner cocktail party he stood in line for a gin and tonic, chatting with whoever came up to him. Everybody was there this evening, the big-time players—the studio heads, talent agency heads, top actors, agents, producers. There were no more than fifty women in an audience of five hundred, he reckoned.

Margot Gladstone was one of them. She came up as he was talking with an agent and waited discreetly nearby until she could catch his eye.

"How are you, Margot? I wanted to talk to you . . ."

"That's over," she said.

He looked around and managed a smile, not wanting anyone to catch the hostility in their exchange. He took her arm. "Listen, let's talk after this; come out to the house, and . . ."

"*It's over*," she said sharply. "The only reason I'm here is to tell you that face to face. My resignation is on your desk." She pulled her arm away from his grasp. "*All bets are off*," she said, then she smiled. "Good-bye, Michael." She turned and made her way through the crowd.

Michael was about to go after her when an amplified voice said, "Ladies and gentlemen, please take your seats for dinner." A studio head he knew took his arm and guided him toward the head table.

Late that night, after the speeches and his acceptance of the award, Michael finally was able to disengage himself from the congratulators and get out of the ballroom. He walked out of the hotel and waited for five minutes while the Porsche was retrieved from its parking place, then, tipping the valet parker twenty dollars, he got into the car and started down the drive toward Sunset Boulevard.

He was a little drunk, he knew. It had been hot in the dining room, and a waiter had kept bringing him fresh gin and tonics. He took a few deep breaths and tried to clear his head.

Driving carefully and not too fast, Michael turned onto Sunset and headed toward the freeway that would take him to Malibu. He released the levers that held the top down and pressed the button that retracted it. The cool night air made him feel better, and the perfume from the lush gardens along Sunset made him feel happy to be in Beverly Hills.

He was right where he wanted to be, he thought. He held the reins of a great studio in his hands, and he could make any movie he wanted to. He would get square with Tommy tomorrow; this was only a little tiff between lifelong friends, and he would make it right. He would talk to Margot, too; she'd come around. He'd even give her the contract she wanted—anything to keep her happy. He needed her, after all.

A red Corvette was overtaking him on the left and, it seemed to him, crowding him a bit. Not in an aggressive mood, he gave way a little to let the sports car pass. Then, suddenly, inexplicably, the corvette veered sharply to the right, as if to ram him.

Michael yanked hard on the wheel; he would run onto the sidewalk, if necessary, to avoid this maniac. Fortunately, there was a street to his right, and, shifting down, he turned the corner, swearing loudly. But he was still not all right. Directly in his path, two cars were stopped, side by side, taking up the whole dark street. He stood on the brake, ready to scream at these people, and, suddenly, the Corvette was beside him. Two men got out of the car and walked to either side of the open Porsche. Panicky now, Michael slammed the car into reverse, but a glance in the rearview mirror showed him another car stopped directly behind him.

"Put your hands on your head," a young voice said. An automatic pistol appeared near his head, and it was wearing a silencer.

Michael obeyed, then looked up into a face that might have been his own a few years before. He looked to his right: another such face—young, hard, free of any conscience. How could this happen to him?

"This is a robbery," the young voice said. "Let's have your wallet."

Michael slumped with relief. This was no hit; he'd already be dead if this were a contract job. He fished his wallet from his inside pocket and handed it to the young man.

"Very nice," the gunman said. "Thank you, Vinnie."

Startled, Michael looked up into the young face. "How do you . . ."

Then the young man moved the barrel of the gun from Michael's head, pointed it instead at his lap, and fired twice.

Michael screamed. His lower belly was on fire. He grabbed at his crotch, then jerked his hands back. They came away crimson with his own blood.

Michael screamed again and again. He was only vaguely aware of the cars around him roaring away, even less aware of reaching for the car phone, dialing 911.

61

Michael sat at his desk, going over the budget for a film he would soon put into production. He ran through the figures, using his life-long faculty for numbers, mentally comparing them with the figures for other, past productions, making a note here and there, indicating that the number should be discussed later with the production manager.

There was a soft knock, and Margot came through the door from her office.

"Time for the screening," she said. "Everybody's waiting for you."

Michael looked up at Margot, cool, elegant as ever. She dressed better these days on her new salary. She moved behind him.

"Shall I . . ."

He raised a hand. "No!" he barked. "I'd rather do it myself." He was more and more irritable these days, especially since there was no longer any sex to relax him, to take his mind off work. He grabbed the joystick and reversed. The chair rolled back from the desk. He moved the stick forward, and the chair rolled toward the door. Margot was there to open it for him, and he guided the chair expertly down the little ramp that had been built for him, right into the screening room.

Tommy Pro and Mr. Yamamoto turned to watch him enter.

"Hiya, Vinnie," Tommy said as Michael rolled into the place where a chair had been removed to accommodate him.

"Good morning, Tommy, Mr. Yamamoto." He made a little bow from the neck in Yamamoto's direction. How he hated the smooth little man.

"Ready?" Tommy asked.

Michael picked up the phone. "Roll it, Max."

He sat and numbly watched the film, a sorry, violent mess, riddled with car chases and shootouts, starring a kung fu expert who, until recently, had been Tommy Pro's personal trainer. Tommy was looking very trim and fit since he'd moved his operations to L.A.

The film ended and the lights went up. Yamamoto was the first to speak.

"Veddy goood, veddy goood," he said in his Oxford-accented English.

"I'm glad you liked it, Mr. Yamamoto," Michael said.

Tommy leaned over. "Vinnie, there was a car crash I saw in the dailies—the one where the guy hits the school bus?"

"I didn't think we needed it," Michael said. "It seemed a little too much."

"I liked it," Tommy said. "Put it in."

Michael died a little more. "Of course, Tommy," he said.

62

Michael straightened his desk, squared away the legal pads, scooped up the pens, and placed them in the small Acoma pot he used for a pencil holder. Satisfied that all was neat, he pushed back from the desk and lifted the heavy briefcase onto his lap, then wheeled himself across his office toward the door to the conference room for what would be his last board meeting at Centurion.

As he took his place at the center of the long table (he no longer sat at the head of the table—Tommy Provensano now occupied that seat) he felt a certain peace in knowing that his work at Centurion was nearly completed.

Certainly he felt no joy in the fact that he had publicly presided over the studio's rapid decline in the quality of its productions and the growth of its debt; he did not take it kindly that his own name was now synonymous with schlock; he felt no affection for the men—and one woman—who had sucked the very viscera from the studio that had been the preeminent maker of quality Hollywood films and turned it into an industry joke. Still, he felt a certain peace, knowing that it was nearly all over. He placed his briefcase on the conference table.

"Gentlemen," Tommy said, "please be seated."

The dozen men and one woman took their places at the table—Tommy Pro at the head, and Margot Gladstone to his right.

"This regular monthly meeting of the board of directors of Centurion Pictures will come to order," Tommy said. "The vice-chairman of the corporation, Ms. Gladstone, will act as recorder for this meeting."

Margot gave first Tommy, then the others at the table, her warmest smile.

"This meeting," Tommy continued, "will be brief, since there is little business to conduct. We . . ."

"Mr. Chairman?" Michael said.

Tommy looked irritably in Michael's direction. "If we could just stick to the agenda," he said, and his tone brooked no argument.

"Mr. Chairman," Michael continued, despite Tommy's warning. "If I may interrupt for just a moment. The board is aware that today is our chairman's birthday, and I have been asked to say a few words and present a small gift."

Tommy looked startled, then smiled. "That is very kind of you, Michael. And may I thank all of you?"

"I will not dwell on the chairman's years," Michael said, to light laughter, "but it is well known to all of us that he has a keen interest in the weapons used in Centurion's films, so I have asked our special effects department to supply something which will be used in our forthcoming production, *Armed Force*, one that our chairman is taking a particular interest in."

Tommy leaned back in his chair and smiled broadly. "What do you have for me, Michael?"

Michael released the locks on his briefcase and opened it. Inside lay two gleaming automatic weapons and a number of accessories. Michael picked up one of the guns and began screwing a suppressor onto its barrel. "This, Tommy, is a prototype of the production model of a new automatic weapon developed by the CIA, in conjunction with the Drug Enforcement Agency. I was able to persuade the Director of Intelligence to allow us to use it in *Armed Force*." He passed the weapon down the table to Tommy, who received it gingerly.

"Is it loaded?" Tommy asked.

Michael began screwing a suppressor onto the second weapon. "Of course, Tommy—but only with ammunition formulated by Special Effects. I assure you, it would be quite safe if you raked the conference table with automatic fire." He slid back the bolt on his weapon and released it. "It cocks like so."

Tommy stood up and cocked the weapon. "I hope you don't mind, Michael, if, in light of previous events at this studio, I don't point it at anyone."

"Of course, Tommy," Michael replied. "Try that beautifully panelled wall. I assure you, it will come to no harm."

Everyone stood and backed away from the table as Tommy raised the weapon. "All right; let's pretend that all of the New York film critics are lined up against that wall." He pointed the machine gun at the wall and pressed the trigger.

The weapon exploded in Tommy's face. Pandemonium broke out in the boardroom. Some board members dived under the table, others rushed to Tommy's aid. Margot Gladstone dragged him away from the table and propped him up against a wall.

"Tommy!" she was crying, "Are you alive?"

Tommy was, indeed, alive, though his face was ruined, and he seemed able to make only croaking sounds.

"Thank you for your tender efforts on Tommy's behalf, Margot," Michael said, then he fired a short burst in her direction. Margot spun around, bounced off a wall, and fell in a heap before Tommy, who was still trying to speak.

Michael swung his weapon toward a group of directors who were now huddled in a corner of the room. "Now, Mr. Yamamoto," he said. "You may join your ancestors." He fired a long burst at the group, sweeping back and forth across the corner. The gun stopped firing, and the bolt locked. Michael reached into the briefcase for another clip, then reloaded and cocked the weapon. He swung his wheelchair back toward Tommy. "I don't want you to think that the exploding weapon was designed to kill you, Tommy," he said.

There was a hammering on the door leading into the hallway, which, as Michael knew, was always locked.

"I have kept that particular pleasure for myself."

Tommy roared something, but his words were unintelligible. One or more persons was now attempting to break down the stout mahogany door.

Michael pointed the weapon at Tommy. "On behalf of movie lovers everywhere, I give you this," he said. He fired, and Tommy's body did a little dance under the withering rain of large-caliber slugs. After a few seconds, the weapon was again out of ammunition.

Michael was reloading for the final coup when efforts to break down the door succeeded. Michael hurried, but he was not fast enough. Two uniformed security guards were emptying their weapons in his direction.

Michael felt himself fly sideways out of his wheelchair.

Epilogue

Michael slowly opened his eyes. He had been aware, over the past days, that heroic efforts had been made to save his life. He had been in some sort of intensive care room that was noisy and busy at all times, but now he was in a quiet place. He tried to lift his head, but the muscles would not work. He tried gripping the sides of the bed with his hands, but that didn't work either. He tried moving his toes, to no effect. In his rising panic, he tried to scream, but couldn't.

Michael spent some moments calming himself; then he swiveled his eyes around to take in as much as he could. There was a stand next to his bed that held a plastic bag of some sort of fluid; apart from that, he could only see the ceiling. He closed his eyes, and a few minutes later he dozed.

A noise awakened him; a door had opened, and now it closed. Footsteps approached his bed. Michael swiveled his eyes to try and see who it was. Amanda Goldman's face moved into his vision.

"Oh, my darling," she said, "you're awake." She moved a finger back and forth across his field of vision.

Michael's eyes followed the finger.

"You really are awake, aren't you? I've been visiting you for weeks, and they've always told me not to expect any response. Something about brain damage."

Michael's eyes widened.

"Can you hear me?" she asked. "If you can, blink once for yes and twice for no."

Michael blinked once. He could communicate! If he could communicate, then there was some way out of this!

"Can you move?" she asked.

Michael blinked twice.

"My God, you *know* me, don't you?"

Michael blinked once.

"I want you to know what's been happening," she said. "A lot of Japanese turned up at the studio, and they've been running things."

Michael closed his eyes.

"I've been taking care of your personal affairs," she said.

Michael opened his eyes again.

"My lawyers got a trust established to run your affairs, and I'm the trustee. Somebody found the will you left, naming me as beneficiary, so the court appointed me."

Michael stared at her.

Amanda sat on the bed and positioned herself so that he could see her easily. "I'm all right, I guess. Michael, there's something I want to tell you. I feel that I can confide in you more than anyone else."

Michael blinked once. He was impatient with all this talk. He had to find a way to let her know what he wanted to do.

"I've met somebody, and I've been seeing a lot of him. He's younger than I am, but that never made any difference with you and me, did it?"

Michael blinked twice. Better to humor her until he could figure out something.

"He's somebody you know, somebody you worked with," she said. "His name is Chuck Parish."

Michael's eyes opened wide again.

"You remember; you made a couple of films together. This is all real incestuous, you know, because until recently, he was living with Vanessa, your old flame. *She*, my darling, is living with Bob Hart! Can you believe it? She must be some smart cookie to have been able to winkle him out of Susan's clutches, but she did it. The divorce is the talk of the town!"

Michael blinked rapidly. This was insane.

"Chuck is sweet," she said. "Not as good as you in bed, of course, but quite all right. He doesn't seem to like to talk about you, but I knew you'd be glad I was with a friend of yours. I've taken the money in my trust that I got for my Centurion stock and formed a new production company to produce Chuck's work. He's a wonderful director and writer, as you well know, having discovered him!"

Michael closed his eyes tightly. How could he get her to shut up?

Amanda was quiet for a moment, then she wiped a tear from the corner of an eye. "You know why I'm here, don't you?"

Michael stared at her.

"I remember our conversation when Leo was in the hospital. You were right then, and I want you to know that I understand what you must be feeling about your condition. I've had a second and a third opinion, but no one gives you any hope of any sort of a recovery. I'm afraid the best you could hope for would be to be propped up in bed and pointed at a television for the rest of your life."

Michael blinked rapidly. He had to think of some way to communicate what he wanted.

"I know what you want, my darling, because you as much as told me when Leo was ill."

Michael saw her hand go past the corner of his eye, and his head tilted up for a moment, so that he could see more of the room; then it was tilted back again.

"You changed my life," she said, and she was weeping now. "I owe you everything, but now there is only one thing I can do for you."

Michael saw something move into his field of vision, and it was white.

"Good-bye, my darling," Amanda said. "I love you."

The pillow filled his vision, and then it was dark.

Michael couldn't even blink. He fought the pillow with his mind, but it didn't work.

Suddenly it wasn't dark anymore. There was light coming from somewhere, and, miracle of miracles, he could move! He held up a hand to shield his eyes, but then it wasn't necessary. The light was kind, and it seemed to originate down a hallway or tunnel. Michael walked toward it.

Then there was a dark shape in the light—another person, and somehow he felt he knew who it was! He walked faster. It was a man, and he was walking toward Michael, his hands reaching out for him. Behind the man were other people.

Michael reached out for the man, and then he knew who he was. Onofrio Callabrese took his son's hands and held them tightly. His smile was ghastly.

Michael struggled to free himself, and then other people were around him, pulling him forward into the light. They were glad to see him, in some odd way, and he knew them all. There was a woman, and it was Carol Geraldi. She held onto him particularly. Rick Rivera was there, and—my God! It was Leo! Leo put an arm around his shoulders and hurried him forward. Benedetto and Cheech walked alongside him, and there, coming out of the light, was the lawyer, Moriarty!

Michael felt a terrible fear, and he tried to dig

his heels in, but nothing could stop his progress toward the light. Inexorably they drew him into it.

Michael suddenly found that he could do more than walk. He could scream.

THE END
Santa Fe, New Mexico, September 9, 1992

Acknowledgments

I am grateful to my former editor, Ed Breslin, who is now writing his own novel, for his fine work in editing this book; to Gladys Justin Carr, my new editor, for working so hard for the book's success; to all the other people at HarperCollins for their help; to my agent, Mort Janklow, his principal associate, Anne Sibbald, and their colleagues at Janklow & Nesbit, who have been so important to my career over the past dozen years; and to Chris Connor, for helping me to understand Hollywood.

Author's Note

I am happy to hear from readers, but you should know that if you write to me in care of my publisher, three to six months will pass before I receive your letter, and when it finally arrives it will be one among many, and I will not be able to reply.

However, if you have access to the Internet, you may visit my website at *www.stuartwoods.com*, where there is a button for sending me e-mail. So far, I have been able to reply to all of my e-mail, and I will continue to try to do so.

If you send me an e-mail and do not receive a reply, it is because you are among an alarming number of people who have entered their e-mail address incorrectly in their mail software. I have many of my replies returned as undeliverable.

Remember: e-mail, reply; snail mail, no reply.

When you e-mail, please do not send attachments, as I *never* open these. They can take twenty minutes to download, and they often contain viruses.

Please do not place me on your mailing lists for funny stories, prayers, political causes, charitable fund-raising, petitions, or sentimental claptrap. I get enough of that from people I already know. Generally speaking, when I get e-mail addressed to a large number of people, I immediately delete it without reading it.

Please do not send me your ideas for a book, as I have a policy of writing only what I myself invent. If you send me story ideas, I will immediately delete them without reading them. If you have a good idea for a book, write it yourself, but I will not be able to advise you on how to get it published. Buy a copy of *Writer's Market* at any bookstore; that will tell you how.

Anyone with a request concerning events or appearances may e-mail it to me or send it to: Publicity Department, Penguin Group (USA) Inc., 375 Hudson Street, New York, NY 10014.

Those ambitious folk who wish to buy film, dramatic, or television rights to my books should contact Matthew Snyder, Creative Artists Agency, 2000 Avenue of the Stars, Los Angeles, CA 90067.

Those who wish to make offers for rights of a literary nature should contact Anne Sibbald, Janklow & Nesbit, 445 Park Avenue, New York, NY 10022. (Note: This is not an invitation for you to send her your manuscript or to solicit her to be your agent.)

If you want to know if I will be signing books in your city, please visit my website, *www.stuart woods.com*, where the tour schedule will be published a month or so in advance. If you wish me to do a book signing in your locality, ask your favorite bookseller to contact his Penguin representative or the Penguin publicity department with the request.

If you find typographical or editorial errors in my book and feel an irresistible urge to tell someone, please write to David Highfill at HarperCollins Publishers, 10 East 53rd Street, New York, NY 10022. Do not e-mail your discoveries to me, as I will already have learned about them from others.

A list of my published works appears in the front of this book and on my website. All the novels are still in print in paperback and can be found at or ordered from any bookstore. If you wish to obtain hardcover copies of earlier novels or of the two nonfiction books, a good used-book store or one of the online bookstores can help you find them. Otherwise, you will have to go to a great many garage sales.

STUART WOODS

Novels Featuring Stone Barrington

NEW YORK DEAD
978-0-06-171186-2

Suddenly New York City cop Stone Barrington is on the front page of every local newspaper, and his life is hopelessly entwined in the shocking life (and perhaps death) of Sasha Nijinsky, the country's hottest and most beautiful television anchorwoman.

DIRT
978-0-06-171192-3

Desperate to save her reputation from an anonymous gossipmonger, Amanda Dart enlists the help of New York lawyer and private investigator Stone Barrington to learn the identity of who's faxing info about Amanda's personal peccadilloes to anyone who can read.

DEAD IN THE WATER
978-0-06-171191-6

On a Caribbean vacation to St. Mark's, attorney and ex-cop Stone Barrington finds himself defending a beautiful young woman accused of killing her rich husband on board their luxurious yacht and then burying him at sea.

SWIMMING TO CATALINA
978-0-06-171193-0

Stone thought he'd heard the last of former girlfriend Arrington after she left him to marry Vance Calder, Hollywood's hottest star. But now Arrington has vanished and her new fiancé wants Stone to come to L.A. and find her.

WORST FEARS REALIZED
978-0-06-171190-9

Not a man to dwell on the past, Stone Barrington has no choice but to rattle old skeletons when the people closest to him start dying, and he suspects the killer may be someone he once knew.